THE PRIC

or

REVENGE IS A DANGEROUS ROAD

by

Ian Taylor and Rosi Taylor

Some horses might cost you your life

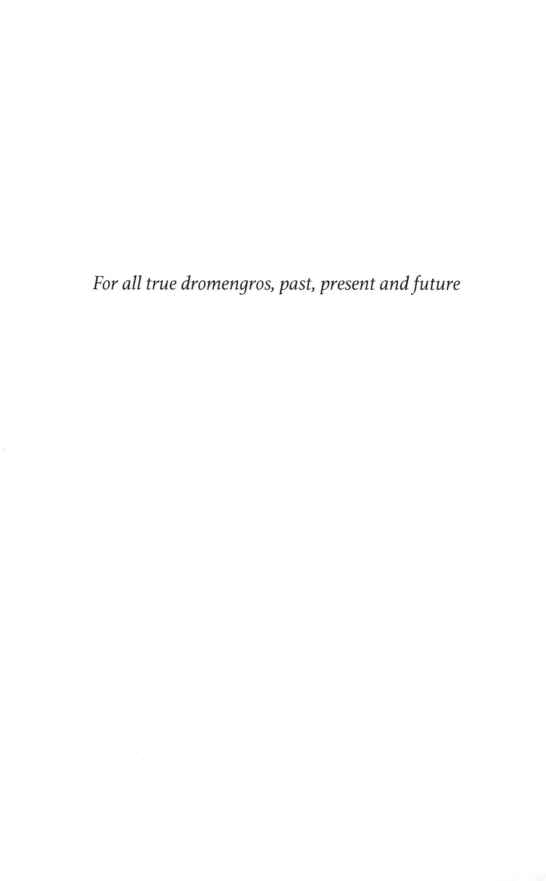

For all true dromengros, past, present and future

1

The country lane lay quiet in the lingering evening light of early summer. The leaves of the oaks and hawthorns in the field hedgerows on each side hissed softly in the gentlest of breezes. The sun was slowly sinking below the horizon, leaving mottled bands of alto-cumulus to the north-west glowing violent orange-red, like the reflection of some far-off conflagration. With barely audible flutterings, nesting birds settled down into ex-hausted sleep, the long day feeding hungry fledg-lings over for a few brief hours.

A Romany travellers' trailer with ornamented chrome work and steel trims stood on the grass verge. Voices and laughter drifted from the open door. A small truck was pulled up nearby. Between the truck and the trailer, an open fire burned brightly. Above the fire a blackened kettle hung from a kettle iron. A smooth-haired brown lurcher, tethered by the trailer, watched everything that moved.

Further down the lane, a dozen piebald gypsy vanners, tied to their plug chains, grazed the coarse grasses on the verge. The munch and stamp of the horses and the rattle of their chains as they grazed was at first all that could be heard. Then voices arose, strangely disembodied among the dense screen of hawthorns.

Luke Smith, a fifteen-year-old Romany youth, and Riley, his elder brother, worked among the bushes, grooming the family's prize chestnut mare. Riley brushed the mane, Luke the tail. Seniority in such tasks was strictly observed.

"You done good mushgaying, brother?" Riley asked. "There's no posh rawni's gryes in the field? No bokros and gurnis?"

"I've dikkered every inch of it!" Luke replied hotly. "No sheep. No cows. There's only drummers as round and fat as firkins! And a couple o' snoring elephants."

Riley was used to his brother's strange mixtures of fact and fantasy. "We'll put Nip in later to get us a drummer."

Rabbit stew for supper! We'll be living free as princes!" Luke exclaimed.

By the trees across the lane, Old Musker, a tramp with a bushy grey beard, erected a small, hooped bender tent. He kept up a muttered commentary in traveller cant as he worked. No one knew Old Musker's age; he had been announcing that he was "nearer seventy than sixty" for as long as anyone could remember. He had attached himself to the Smith family for the past year, and in spite of him not being of their blood, they had kept him fed and watered. But he always set up his bender at a distance, as privacy mattered, too, on both sides.

Ambrose Smith, the youths' father, a dark wiry man, stepped out of the trailer, followed by his wife, Mireli, and Athalia, his thirteen-year-old daughter. Both mother and daughter wore brightly patterned dresses, with headscarves over their long glossy black hair. Ambrose was in his weather-worn work jacket and heavy boots, his flat cap, shiny with time, set at a jaunty angle.

He glanced at the sky. "Be a dark moon tonight. Reckon we'll get ourselves some free grazing." He gave a short whistle as a signal to his sons and waited until they emerged from the trees. "It's a beautiful evening, with only us here to please our-

3

selves. Unplug the gryes, boys. We'll be putting 'em in that empty meadow yonder."

Mireli cautioned them. "Riley. Luke. Look after the gryes. And your dadu. They's all we got!"

"Let me come with you!" Athalia pleaded.

"Your job's to take care o' your dai, my girl," Ambrose admonished her with a kindly smile. "She's all *we* got!"

Luke, handsome and easygoing, laughed at her. "We're only gonna nick a little gorgios' grass, a bit o' chaw ta pani. It's no big deal."

Riley, habitually scowling, took exception as usual. "Big deal? This Romanichal's a yank now!"

Ambrose waved to the women, who watched their menfolk leave. Mireli glanced at the lurcher. "If anyone comes prowling, Nip will tell us."

The lurcher looked up at them at the mention of his name.

Mireli waved to Old Musker. "Drop o' tea when you want."

"Two minutes!"

Mireli knew that clock time to Old Musker meant nothing. Two minutes could become as many hours.

But she topped up the kettle from the water jack, placed more wood on the fire and got the drinking mugs ready.

"You think Musker will live another year?" Athalia asked her mother as they went back into the trailer. "What if he dies? Where will we bury him?"

"He said he wants to be laid in the churchyard in his village, or his mullo, his ghost, won't let him find peace. He told me he'd paid for his grave years back. Next to the birch tree he said, so he could be a part of its roots and travel in the underworld. But I don't know if he was just telling a mumpers' tale. Anyhow, who says he'll be dying? We're looking after him now."

* * *

Riley and Luke released the horses from their plug chains and walked them for a quarter mile to where Ambrose had opened a field gate to let the horses enter the wildflower meadow that bordered the lane.

"Be some sweet grazing for 'em tonight," Ambrose remarked. "It'll help get 'em in shape for Appleby Fair. We've to meet Taiso there next week."

Luke looked at their prize mare with pride. "I ride her over the field?" he asked eagerly.

Riley frowned. "What makes you think you can?"

Luke grinned. "I can ride anything! I could ride a wild boar if we'd any left in England. Or even one o' them African osteriches!"

"You be riding for a fall!" Riley seemed about to punch his younger brother. Luke stepped back, laughing. He enjoyed annoying Riley, but the fun was beginning to sour, as increasingly he was growing to think of him as weak—and only a bully makes sport of a coward.

"Freedom's wasted on you, brother. You gotta live it or lose it! One o' these days you'll wake up and wonder where it's gone!"

Before Riley could reply, Ambrose stepped between them. "Wait till we get to Appleby. You can ride her there, both o' you. It'll help us sell her. Too risky to ride her down here in the dark. She might get a hoof in a drummer's hole and go down. Then where'd we be?"

Ambrose, a man of practical good sense, was right, of course. His mind was filled with nuggets of wisdom, the fruits of forty years on the road. Luke stored his father's observations away like a secret coin hoard, but he also picked up something else: a sense of sadness that hung around the man like an invisible aura with no obvious cause. While Luke chased the impression away like an irritating bug, Riley seemed to have no power to banish it. Sometimes it seemed he was sucked into their father's sadness, as if the two of them were privy to some disturbing secret.

But Luke's enthusiasm remained undiminished. "Can I swim her in the Eden at Appleby, Dadu?"

"We'll see," Ambrose said thoughtfully. "We'll mebbe race her in Flashing Lane. If she wins, we'll get a good price for her."

They stood a while, watching the vanners gallop around the field, enjoying their freedom. As the light faded, the horses settled down to graze and drink at the field trough. Then, at last, the chestnut mare was put into the field.

"Beat you at Appleby this year, brother," Luke taunted Riley good-naturedly. "You'll be a loser!"

"Loser?" Riley scowled. "Another word for gorgio, ain't it?"

They all laughed. The sound of two gunshots, followed by a sudden explosion, took them by surprise. Flames leaped into the sky in the direction of the trailer.

"Dordi! Dordi!" Ambrose exclaimed. "Run, boys! Run!"

They closed the field gate and sprinted towards the fire. Luke raced ahead, Riley and Ambrose a stride behind. Gradually becoming visible through the lane-side trees were flames engulfing their campsite.

The trailer was a fireball. Old Musker and Nip were nowhere to be seen. Luke, Riley and Ambrose tried to get close, but the heat beat them back.

"Mother! Athalia!" Luke yelled. He leaped forward, as if about to hurl himself into the flames.

Ambrose grabbed him and held him back. "It's too late, son. We're too late. We've lost our dearest treasures."

They stared helplessly at the inferno that had once been their home, tears streaming down their faces.

Luke released a terrible yell of despair. "Who's done this to us? Who's done this to us, Dadu?"

His father and brother stared in despair at the flames. They shook their heads but made no reply.

"Who's done this?" Luke persisted. "Who hates us so much?"

"No one," Ambrose managed to reply through his tears. "No one's done it." He looked at Riley for confirmation.

"An accident," Riley said, his voice choked with emotion. "Just an accident. Those gas bottles are dangerous things."

Luke didn't believe them. He couldn't explain how he knew, but their words were hollow.

"Who's done this?" he yelled again.

"No one, Luke. Believe me."

"An accident, brother!"

But Luke's mind was screaming NO! NO! NO! "Who hates us so much, Dadu? I swear by my blood I will find them and kill them!"

2

A derelict four-storey Victorian building stood close to the centre of a city in the English Midlands. Brick-built but crumbling a little, it was screened off from the surrounding streets by a solid eight-foot fence topped with razor wire. A few broken windows could be seen on the building's upper floors, and a long row of pigeons perched on the roof ridge like architectural adornments. Across the front of the building were the faded words *RAD-FORD BUILDING SUPPLIES*.

An area of cracked concrete surrounded the building inside the fence with, to one side, a range of repair shops for the firm's vehicles, which were now long gone. The yard, which had once held breeze blocks and soft sand, was empty, as was the cement and plaster store. In front of the repair shops stood two travellers' trailers occupied by the current minders, who were there to prevent raiding or squatting by the city's opportunist elements. Everything of value, which was mostly copper wire and items of metalwork, had already been stripped by the minders.

The site's owners, who themselves had gypsy traveller connections, had no wish to see their property overrun by gorgios. They were waiting for the outcome of a planning application to turn the site into a creative centre, which included a cinema and live performance space. If that was refused, plan B was to transform the building into flats, with retail units on the ground floor. Much less imaginative.

The families in the trailers were Boswells, who had been pleased to let one of their extended clan occupy part of an upper floor as an added deterrent to intruders. The single male occupant kept himself to himself, rarely intruding on the families in the trailers, nor they on him.

There was little evidence that anyone lived on the fourth floor. One end of the floor had been tidied up. A set of wooden shelves that had once held rainwater fittings was now a store for cat burglars' equipment: screwdrivers, lock pickers, knives, torches, ropes and straw packaging. A frameless rucksack and a neat pile of clothes lay at one end, and a simple pallet bed was spread on the floor.

Luke Smith, now thirty, had grown into a tall, athletic, muscular man, with black shoulder-length hair. Dressed in joggers and T-shirt, he lay asleep on the pallet bed one mid-afternoon in early summer, having driven up from the Wickham horse fair that had been held the previous day. He had bought two dull-spirited cobs at Wickham, groomed and ridden them, using his natural talent to coax them back to energetic life. Then he had sold the transformed animals for twice what he had paid for them. It had been a good day.

He was something of an outsider in the gypsy travelling community, an enigma around which dark rumours circulated. How did he make his vongar, his money, travelling folk asked? Why was he so secretive? Where had he learned his undoubted skills with animals? Luke did nothing to dispel the mysteries; rather he encouraged them by his sudden appearances at travellers' fairs and by his equally abrupt vanishings.

He had a reputation at the fairs for a certain degree of honesty, which, broadly speaking, was rare. Anyone who bought a horse, a dog or a hawk from him more often than not got good value for their investment. He had plenty of travellers' tricks when it came to enhancing the appearance or disposition of an animal, but he also had something else, which the rumours described as a gift, some going so far as to say he had a magical touch.

This particular rumour started years earlier at Stow fair, where he had come across an acquaintance in a state of despair and on the brink of furious tears. It turned out that a horse the man had bought earlier in the day had collapsed an hour later and seemed at the point of death. Luke had offered to buy the horse for half what the man had paid for it. The traveller eagerly accepted the deal, thinking the young man must be a bit simple in the head. An hour later, the same horse was sold for more than twice what the man had paid.

"How did you do it, mush?" the traveller asked resentfully when he came across Luke later in the day, having heard the price the animal had been sold for.

"I talked to him," Luke replied, looking serious. "I told him it was no way to behave, and he was letting his bloodline down getting sick for no reason. He decided to get up to prove me wrong!"

The traveller shook his head, not knowing what to believe.

Luke didn't mention that the animal had been drugged by his good friend Sy, who just happened to meet its unhappy buyer when the horse was sinking to its lowest ebb. Luke had bought the vanner and immediately administered the herbal antidote, plus a secret remedy he had gotten from an old horseman whose ancestors had been members of the East Anglian guild. Half an hour later, the animal was as lively as a horse of his mature years could be.

"It was magic, I tell you!" the gullible traveller insisted that evening in the pub. "I've never seed a grye changed like that!" The rest, as they say, is history.

The police had Luke's mugshot on file, as he had been brought in for questioning a dozen or more times in connection with daring burglaries that involved "unprecedented" climbing feats and "inconceivable" escapes if the alarm had chanced to be triggered. He had never been convicted, and, by rights, his photograph should not have neen retained. But he was the source of much official frustration and the desire—perhaps even an obsession—in several constabularies to put him behind bars.

His reputation as a cat burglar extraordinaire was based on one brief frame of surveillance footage where he emerged from a property in West London's stockbroker belt in the act of pulling his balaclava over his face. It wasn't enough to put him in court, but the rumours spread like a virus from one constabulary to another until burglaries involving difficult climbs were rated as *a Luke Smith five* or *a Smith eight.*

The world beyond Radford's was full of him, but no one knew very much about him, at least nothing that was certain, including where he lived. The minders in the trailers, when they heard the latest "factual" rumour, thought it was all hilarious. Luke himself characteristically said nothing...

His mobile rang. He was awake and on his feet in one bound, snatching the phone from a shelf.

"Tam! How you doing, mush?"

As he talked, he moved to a grimy window and looked out. It was his favourite pastime. From his vantage point, views extended from the railway station and bus terminus to the inner ringroad and, beyond that, to the distant suburbs. On the skyline to the north, about ten miles distant, he could see the vague outline of woodland, almost obscured from view by the intervening smog of exhaust fumes.

What held his attention was movement: the main-line trains entering and leaving the station, express coaches to distant cities making their way from the bus terminus, threading their route out of town to the motorways. Movement was something he understood. It was in his blood, going back more than a thousand years to the time when his people roamed the desert and hills of Rajasthan.

Hidden in his secret eyrie, he spent hours watching movement. He had observed the flights of geese and wild duck through the winter months, carving their passage between the city's waterways and their feeding grounds in the surrounding countryside. Whenever he saw the birds, his own wild spirit leaped to greet them, as if he was about to join them on their timeless journeying.

Closer to his base were the flights of the resident urban birds: the jackdaws that roosted in the parkland trees, the starlings that slept in the old warehouses by the river and the pigeons that lived in his block and in the tower of All Saints church half a mile away.

The arrival in the city centre of a pair of peregrine falcons had caused some excitement. They had made their home on the sheltered southern side of the roof of a redundant church that stood between his block and All Saints. The parent birds were raising offspring, and he had watched as the male picked off pigeons in mid-air on their perilous journey from All Saints' tower to the railway station roof.

He felt a keen affinity with the peregrines, while in his imagination the hapless pigeons were the members of the settled world, the gorgios, slow-moving and sluggish-witted.

Members of the settled world surrounded folk like him with as many laws and petty regulations as they could. They tried to shackle the gypsy traveller because they couldn't tame him. So the traveller had no choice but to seize his chances or succumb to the pressure to conform. He had decided long ago that he was never going to give in.

Luke listened to the Scotsman's voice on the other end of the phone telling him how hard life was these days and how resourceful a dealer in "quality merchandise" had to be merely to stay alive. There was nothing in Tam's spiel he hadn't heard before. It was Tam's long-winded way of softening him up for some favour or risky project from which they would both make enough money to put their feet up for six months "in Scarborough or Skegness."

As far as Luke knew, the antiques dealer had never been to either town. But Tam, like every born hustler, could never stop working, not for six months or even six hours. Luke imagined the man even dreamed of cutting deals in his sleep.

It was true he had made a lot of money with Tam, most of which he had used to buy pasture land that he rented out to other gypsy travellers for rough grazing. He had even bought a small hill farm in the Welsh Marches, where his own horses were cared for by an extended family of traveller craftsmen who had rent-free use of the buildings.

But he had no interest in money for its own sake, and to cap it all, he had developed a growing dislike for the Scotsman. He had come to the conclusion that it was impossible to believe a word the dealer said, even to someone like himself, who had known him for over a decade. When Tam got around to asking about his state of health, he was ready with his own stock reply.

"Me? Not good, mush. This kind o' work's getting too dodgy. Last time, if you care to recall, I almost got nicked... I know there'll be a moon, but I ain't up for it tonight... You want to find a younger guy to do this sort o' work."

While Tam continued persuading, Luke reached on to a shelf for a can of beer. He put the phone on the window ledge and took a long swig. He almost choked.

"How much?... You're taking the piss, mush—there ain't such a figure! We gonna be nicking an old master? You know some Chinese billionaire buyers now, right?"

He took another swig of beer as Tam continued his sales talk. Eventually, as usual, Luke's curiosity got the better of him.

"Okay, I'll come down. But no promises! I don't care if it's an easy climb or not. You give me something tonight, mush, if it's gonna pay so much... 20K in advance, right? Make damn sure you've got it! You will? Okay, see you later."

He rang off, drank his beer and stared from the window. He shouldn't have agreed. Tam McBride was trouble. He was taking bigger and bigger risks—or, truth be told, the cunning dealer was expecting that he would take the risks for him. And Tam knew too many dangerous people who could brush a poor burglar aside like a flea on a fox's ear if things went wrong. But where the dealer was concerned, there was always a challenge to be faced and a stack of money to be made. Maybe he'd be able to sign off on that derelict North Pennine hill farm only forty miles from Appleby...

3

An hour later, after he had been out to his favourite diner for a big fry-up and a mug of tea, Luke began to organize himself for the night to come. He took items from the shelves and laid them out on his bed in reverse order of requirement: packing straw, soft cloths, lock pickers, a small torch, flat-bladed knives, a small screwdriver, a coiled nylon rope, a balaclava and a pair of supple leather gloves. He checked the items thoroughly, almost reverentially. His life might depend on some of them.

He put on a light showerproof zip-up jacket with elasticated cuffs, then rehearsed swinging his frameless rucksack on to his back with a ten-kilo weight inside and snapping the waistband strap closed. The movement required perfect balance. He couldn't risk damage to items in the rucksack, but he might have to leave in a hurry.

With great care, he placed his gear in the rucksack, the small items in the side pockets and the rest in the body of the bag. Finally he took a pair of surgical gloves, folded one inside the other, then put them in his inside jacket pocket. He checked to make sure he had not forgotten anything—then, clad in the perfect disguise of hard hat and overalls, left by the rusting fire escape. A workman checking the state of the building was not likely to arouse much curiosity.

By six o'clock he was driving his old Renault Estate through an area of darkened yards and warehouses in a rundown industrial sector by a disused railway siding. He could hear the constant wail of police sirens through his open driver's window. They filled him, as always, with a toxic mix of dread and detestation.

Most of the businesses on the industrial estate had either moved or gone bust in the recession, giving the area the appearance of an abandoned wasteland. He pulled up outside Tam's yard and stared at the fancy carved sign above the double gates:

T McBRIDE

ANTIQUES DEALER & FURNITURE RESTORER

The sign was no more than a front. Very little dealing and no restoration work at all had ever occurred in the place. It was like the whole of Tam's life—a facade, behind which lay a world of trickery and deception. He wondered what would be left in the dealer's character when all the subterfuge had been removed. Nothing perhaps. Silence. A black hole.

Luke sat a moment, beset by fresh doubts. He had the disconcerting feeling that it would be a very long time before he came that way again, if ever. Would he be caught tonight for the first time and get five years in jail? Would he be killed? But his curiosity got the better of him again. He took out his mobile and stared at it as if it was an unexploded bomb, then he tapped in Tam's number and announced his presence.

The gates opened remotely, and Luke drove into the yard. He pulled past a range of disused outbuildings and stopped by a shabby door marked *OFFICE*. The place looked even more derelict than the last time he visited, designed to support Tam's claim, should the Revenue guys start pressuring him, that he had given up the antiques trade and was getting used to retirement.

Nothing much had changed in Tam's office, either. There was a scattering of the usual antiques dotted about—odd items of porcelain, glassware, bronzes and silver—that gave the impression of a film set that could be packed up and disappeared in minutes. Anything of real value was kept elsewhere, in a location known only to the cunning dealer himself.

Tam, at fifty-five, was a thickset, tough-looking Scot with a mass of greying curly hair and florid features. He sat at his desk, a stack of out-of-date invoices at his elbow, held down by a damaged pseudo-Greek bust.

"Spring Heeled Luke," Tam grinned, "my lucky charm! Glad ye could find time to drop by."

Something wasn't right, Luke could sense it. He was picking up a bad vibe. "Ain't gonna be lucky tonight, Tam. Bad omens—gavvers everywhere."

"The *po*-liss, eh?" Tam emphasised the first syllable. His grin slipped slyly sideways. "And who, I'm wondering, would they be after?" He fixed Luke with a questioning glance.

Luke was used to the Scotsman's attempts at unsettling humour. But he was not going to be fazed. "Dunno, Tam. Some tricky dealer like you mebbe."

The Scotsman laughed. "That's more like it. If ye canna conjure a joke, ye's unfit for purpose." He watched Luke pacing restlessly around the room. "It's the past that's vexing ye still, is it, laddie?" The Scotsman fashioned a look of feigned sympathy.

Luke shrugged. "What if it is?" But it wasn't the past that was unsettling him. It was more like a premonition. Was he losing his nerve, or was he developing second sight? But now Tam had mentioned it, images of the lying police officer Nigel Hirst rushed into his mind. Hirst with his sneers and his talk of "filthy gyppos."

Tam poured his companion a mug of coffee. "Whisht. Clear your head. Ye canna live wi' ghaists at your elbow."

For a moment Tam seemed to be genuinely sympathetic. How much did he know of the past, Luke wondered? Did he know who had started the trailer fire? Did he know *why*? But he was aware if he asked him the slippery Scot would insult him with denials.

He sat on the only other chair in the room and drank the offered coffee. He disliked the stuff, preferring tea like most gypsy travellers, but decided to avoid further friction. He needed to relax, or the task ahead of him might prove to be his last.

* * *

Tam's Volvo Estate moved slowly through the quiet suburban streets of a small county town forty miles to the north of London. Could be anywhere, Luke thought. Anonymous dormitory England.

His restlessness and anxiety had left him at last. He could no longer hear police sirens, which always reminded him of the tragedy in his life and its unsatisfactory conclusion. He felt calm, his innate curiosity beginning to stir as he wondered about the shape of the night that lay ahead of him.

"What's so special about this job?" He didn't expect an entirely honest reply.

Tam smiled. "I was hoping ye'd get round to showing an interest. We're paying a call on a rich ex-con. He's a top guy. Speciality's antique smuggling. Likes to get hold o' stuff that's still rare. Guess it makes him feel special. Some call him eccentric. Others just say he's a twisted sense o' humour. By common consent he's a bit of a psycho. Lives on his own. Hates people."

"Sounds like you."

The Scotsman laughed. "That's the spirit, laddie! Takes one to know one!"

"What's he got?"

Tam was grinning widely now. "Treasures, my friend! Vases. Seal stones. Bronzes. Jewellery. Stuff from Egypt. A load o' loot from museums in Iraq." He paused for dramatic effect. "But they're *not* what we're after now."

Luke was intrigued. He realized Tam had him well and truly hooked. "What then? I can't get a Turner landscape into my backpack!"

"Whisht! We're after Ming ch'i, laddie. Spirit objects —*embodiments* o' spirit."

"You sound like a goddamn sales catalogue!"

Tam elaborated. "T'ang tomb figures to me and ye. He's a cabinet full. But we just want the horses."

"Why the horses?" Luke asked in puzzlement.

"My client believes in 'em. He's a horsey guy. He thinks they'll bring him good luck."

"He's a superstitious fella."

"Guess he is."

"He got a name?"

Tam shook his head. "Just ye bother about the horses, laddie!"

That subject was evidently closed. "So what's the deal?"

"C.O.D. And that's up to ye."

"I need an advance. And *that's* down to you!"

Tam feigned exasperation. "Whisht, laddie! Ye'll be paid."

"Ten percent tonight, Tam. We agreed. How do I know I'll see another penny? I'm taking the risk here, y'know!"

"Dinna fret. Ye'll be able to retire to Skeggy on this. Trust me."

"Stuff Skeggy! You should've got a career as a stand-up!"

They drove on in silence for five minutes. Luke's mind was focused, and he needed answers.

"What's the get-in?"

Tam turned the Volvo on to a leafy minor road. "Gable end wall. On'y bit that isna watched. Ye've done harder."

"One guy? Only one? You sure?"

Tam showed signs of impatience. Luke was unable to tell if they were genuine or for effect.

"Give me some credit, laddie! The guy sleeps alone in the first floor back. Not even a paid-for escort. He has his London associates round but only at weekends. Most rooms are unused."

Luke's mind flooded with doubt. "How d'you know all this?"

"I ken the body who installed the security."

"How come? A long way out o' your field, ain't it?"

"I bought his gambling debts. Small stuff really. But now, unofficially, he works for me."

That was as much as Luke could get out of the Scotsman. He would have to be content or call it off.

The Volvo entered a village main street. Expensive properties, a few newly built but most older, lined both sides of the road. All were in darkness. The car clock showed 1.45 a.m. Tam drove more slowly, checking his mirrors, glancing keenly out of the windows. Luke leaned forward, attentive.

"I've changed my mind, Tam. There'll be cameras everywhere round here. Every brick's a gold bar! It's too much risk."

"Risk?" Tam exclaimed. "What about me? I'm a businessman!" His tone softened. "Don't ye worry, laddie, our guy has no cameras on the end wall, on'y front and back."

The Volvo pulled into a field lane and stopped in the cover of trees. Its headlights were doused. As if synchronized, the full moon slid free from a bank of cumulus.

Tam pointed to a large detached property that stood at the far side of a small paddock. "That's the one."

A minute later, Luke's shadowy figure left the car.

4

Luke crossed the paddock, vaulted a post-and-rail fence, then found himself in the large back garden of the old three-storey brick-built manor house. From experience he guessed the building's date at around 1700-1710. He could see in the moonlight that the property stood in extensive grounds, with lawns, ranges of outbuildings and borders filled with low-maintenance shrubs. Wide gravel paths led around to the front of the house. As he drew closer, he could see that the place had a double-pitched roof.

Following Tam's advice, he moved away from the back of the house where there were supposed to be surveillance cameras, although he was unable for the life of him to spot any. He supposed he must be too far back to see them, but he began to wonder if the Scotsman had been economical with the truth. Looking at the layout of the property, the logical place for cameras was on the northwest and southwest corners of the house, covering the back, front and western gable end wall. The eastern end of the house was attached to a range of outbuildings and was too exposed to be approached. He was wary of cameras. They were the one and only cause of his unfortunate police reputation.

He came closer, crouching among the bushes and studying the gable end wall in the moonlight. The wall itself was in shadow, a problem only for gorgios with no night vision. But it was obvious now that there were no motion-sensitive lights and no cameras fixed to the house walls. How the hell was the property protected? He cursed Tam under his breath. What else had the slippery Scot lied about? He began to have serious misgivings about the entire business, but the lure of large profit kept him focused. When he was paid for the heist, he would spend a few days exploring the potential of that hill farm.

First he had to decide if the climb was possible. After five minutes' examination, he decided there was only one route, and even that might prove too difficult. Damn that greedy oat-brained Scot! He had every right to back out, telling Tam the wall was unclimbable.

But, as so often before, a part of him refused to give in. It wasn't that he had a reputation to uphold, because very few people actually knew he was involved in this line of work—it was all supposition—and the few who did know kept the knowledge to themselves, not wanting to lose a man with such skills to punters with deeper pockets.

It was a personal thing. He was proud that he could achieve climbs that had defeated the best cat burglars. Occasionally he'd had to resort to rock-climbers' gear, but mostly his free-climbing skills relied solely on speed, strength and agility.

This was going to be one of those climbs. Tightening the rucksack waistband, he began to work his way up the wall via drainpipes and window architecture. He found a few good finger holds where loose mortar had come adrift and scratched out a couple more with the small screwdriver hooked to his jacket collar. He could have saved himself the forty-foot climb by breaking what he assumed was a small bathroom window on the first floor, but he resisted the temptation. The window would almost certainly be wired.

He could have used a grappling hook. But he had learned from past experience that the higher you climbed the more unreliable the brickwork became on a property of this age. If it gave way, all you could do was go down. He had only fallen three times in the last ten years, but each time he had managed, parkour-style, to roll through the fall upon landing, saving himself broken limbs and a terminated career.

As he reached the gully between the double-pitches of the roof, he lost his grip on a loose, unmortared coping stone and had to hang by one hand for a half minute while he shifted his weight so he could grab a rainwater hopper to save himself. He'd had these moments before, and his pulse hardly registered the danger. Then he was into the gully, getting his breath back and refocusing.

His distrust of grappling hooks was confirmed. The brickwork at the western end of the gully was seriously frost-damaged and would have given way under his weight. He opened his rucksack, removed the rope and left it neatly coiled in the gully, ready for his escape. He would loop it behind the bracket that secured the hopper and pull it through when he reached the ground.

He knew there would be some means of access from the house to the gully, and sure enough, there was a wood-and-felt dormer-type trapdoor at the far end. He inserted a flat-bladed knife between the door and its surrounding framework, relieved to find there were no locks. With firm downward movements, he freed the two wooden catches that held the woodwork in place, and the trapdoor swung inwards on its hinges with no more than a brief squeak. He put on his leather gloves and bala-clava, then vanished through the door into the house.

He was in a large attic, set out like a workshop for repairing damaged furniture. The room reeked of lacquers, varnishes and glue. Obviously the rich ex-con liked to indulge in practical activities. He crossed to the next attic room and peered out of a window. The front garden lay below: a wide moonlit terrace with urns leading to a lawn and a shrubbery. He left the room and descended a flight of stairs to the first-floor landing. Moonlight streamed in through a large uncurtained window. The doors from the landing were all open except one. He listened at the closed door... Silence.

A ground-floor rear reception room was his target. He found the room shuttered, the air stale and life-less. It was merely a place for the owner to gloat over his illegally acquired possessions. He located two large cabinets: one contained figurines and seal stones from Iraqi museums; the other held the T'ang figurines.

With his torch between his teeth and wearing the surgical gloves, he quickly picked the cabinet's lock. He removed soft cloths from his rucksack, took the four horse figurines Tam had described to him, wrapped them in the cloths and packed them carefully in the straw inside the rucksack.

As he moved to the door, he spotted an infrared security light winking in a recess. He froze, shocked.

"Damn you, Tam, you lying Scots fishbrain!" he cursed the dealer under his breath.

Then he tightened the waistband on his rucksack and hurried from the room.

He stepped warily into the moonlit hallway. Before he could reach the stairs to the first floor, he felt the cold steel of a double-barrelled shotgun pressed to the back of his neck.

The infrared had done for him. He stood absolutely still, every faculty stretched to its limit. He heard the distinctive rhyming slang of an East End voice behind him. The voice seemed filled with amusement.

"A greasy little tea leaf! D'you think you can take my bread and honey? Help yourself, just like that, to my stuff? Your kind don't deserve quality goods. You're too stupid to appreciate them. But you're in my world now. I'm the only law that exists here. I can tell you I'm a believer in capital punishment. And I've a special hell for lawbreakers like you." The voice grew harsher, more authoritative. "Put down the bag, tea leaf. Put it down and take two steps away from it."

Luke obeyed. There was nothing to be gained from heroics. "You can have it, mate. I'm on my way. Don't want no trouble."

"But I do! I enjoy a bit of Barney Rubble. Especially other people's. It's punishment time, tea leaf. Hands on your head! Do it now!"

Luke obeyed. He caught a glimpse of a figure behind him dressed in a burgundy satin robe and fancy leather moccasins. The figure prodded him with the shotgun.

"See that door, tea leaf? Go through it and keep walking."

All Luke could do was play for time and watch for any lapse of attention on the part of whom he assumed must be the rich ex-con.

"Look, mate, just forget it, okay?"

"Too late, me old China plate! Too late! Through the fucking door! Now!"

Luke obeyed. He found himself in a corridor. More prodding from the shotgun propelled him to the far end.

"Turn the key, open the door and go outside. Hands back on your crust of bread! Do it now!"

Luke found himself in a rear courtyard. In the moonlight he could make out stables and other out-buildings surrounding a central paved area. Now he was outside he felt his chances of escape might increase.

"I made a mistake, mate, okay? You got your stuff back. Why can't you leave it at that and let me go?"

But his captor was not going to succumb to the distraction of dialogue, continuing to drive him forward with savage stabs of the shotgun barrels and rasping commands: "Move! Move!"

Luke realized the man was doing something with a mobile phone. He heard the lock click open in the door of an outbuilding ahead of him. His captor's voice came again:

"Open the door in front of you." He laughed. "We're off for some tea and cakes!"

Obediently Luke opened the door of the out-building.

"Light switch on the left at shoulder height. Switch it on."

Luke entered the building and put on the light. He found himself in a large vivarium occupied by at least a dozen sleeping snakes that were coiled on the sinewy branches of what looked like real trees and on the sand of the floor. The temperature had risen by at least twenty degrees Celsius.

His captor laughed again. "This is the punishment block, tea leaf!"

"Jesus!" Luke exclaimed involuntarily.

"Welcome to hell!" His captor cackled in huge amusement. "In ten minutes' time you'll be brown bread, me old China!"

Luke recalled Tam's words: *By common consent he's a bit of a psycho.* How did Tam know? Did he have insider contacts in the London mob?

Disturbed by the light, the snakes began to uncurl and writhe towards Luke.

"It's a long time since I took their venom," his captor commented airily. "Any one of them could kill you in a most unpleasant way." He prodded Luke in the back with the shotgun. "I'll leave you to savour your last moments in this life and contemplate your complete stupidity!"

Luke had to make a move before he found himself locked in. He bent down suddenly and blew on the head of the nearest snake. It was an introductory technique hc used when approaching a horse for the first time, his breath conveying the mystery of his life energy—but he had no idea if it would work with snakes! Then he reached fast and picked the creature up. He turned to face his captor, a lean, balding fellow of fifty with grey designer stubble, saw his look of astonishment and fear as he flung the animal at his head.

"The last moments are all yours *me old China*!" Luke yelled.

The rich ex-con fell backwards with a startled cry. The shotgun went off, blowing a hole in the roof. The shock of the deafening report sent the snakes crazy; they began writhing purposefully towards the two men. Luke ran, slamming the outbuilding door as he reached the paved yard. He heard his ex-captor's cries of terror coming from within the vivarium...

He ran back into the house, grabbed his rucksack, swung it onto his back and snapped the waistband firmly closed. He unbolted the front door and sprinted from the building as an alarm bleeped somewhere in the house. He was out, but where the hell was Tam?

He reached the field lane and was just in time to see the Volvo pulling out slowly from the trees. He caught up with the vehicle and hammered on the roof, forcing Tam to brake to a halt. Then he whipped off his rucksack and pushed it ahead of him onto the back seat. He ducked down as the Scotsman drove away fast.

"What went wrong back there?" Tam asked as he headed for the M1.

"You're a liar!" Luke roared from the darkness at the back of the Volvo. "That's what went wrong! I'm never gonna work with you again. And to prove it, I'm gonna kill you!"

5

Back in Tam's office the Scotsman repacked the T'ang figurines in four small wooden crates marked *SCOTTISH RASPBERRIES*.

Luke paced around the room. "You were gonna damn well leave me!" he yelled, "You heap o' Scotch shite!"

Tam fussed with the repackaging. He was unable to meet his accuser's eyes. "I wasna, Luke," he blustered. "Believe me. On my mother's life."

Luke, incensed, continued pacing. "That guy had infrared! He'd have known I was there as soon as I crossed his goddamn garden!"

Tam flung out his arms in a gesture of helplessness. "I didna ken it. Must be new."

Luke swept the papers from Tam's desk. "You're a bloody liar! You said you knew the security guy!"

"He must've brought in some other body. How was I supposed to ken that?" Tam countered. "The bastard misled me! He set us up for his ain fun and games!"

Tam's reply checked Luke's outrage. The Scotsman was tricky, but he was no fool. He would never have risked sending him into the place if he had known about the infrared security. But Luke's anger quickly welled up again at the thought of his narrow escape. "I could've been killed in there! What would you have done then? If I'd been caught, you'd have had the whole of my clan out to lynch you! You'd be finished!"

This wasn't strictly true. Luke's extended Romany family knew little of substance about his secret nocturnal life—and anyway, Tam would deny the association. There was also the chilling possibility, if the rich ex-con had got his way, that his remains would never have been found. Killings at the upper levels of the criminal underworld rarely left bodies behind.

"But you're alive, Luke," Tam replied. "You're alive— and we've got the booty!"

"So what's my escape worth to you?" Luke asked, expecting an evasive reply.

Tam shrugged. "As a private sale? I'd say we'd get around 80K."

"Bollocks!" Luke exploded. "You promised me fifty before we even set off!"

Tam pursed his lips, feigning a difficult mental calculation. "Well...a hundred then, mebbe. But I'd ha'e to go to auction to get that much. And obviously I canna do that."

Luke's fury erupted again. "You're full of lying tinker shite!" He grabbed an antique vase and smashed it on the floor.

The Scotsman threw up his hands in alarm. "Okay, laddie—enough! 160K. But it's hot. My man will only gi'e me half the value."

"Know what I think?" Luke replied coldly. "I think 600K. Your guy gets them cheap at three hundred. I want half for risking my neck. 150K. Now!"

"Ye's a crazy man! I don't ha'e that kind o' lucre here! I'll ha'e to wait till my man pays me—and ye'll ha'e to wait too!" Tam closed the last of the four crates.

Luke grabbed the Scotsman by his coat collar and slammed him against the wall. "You don't tell me what I'm gonna do! Not anymore! I risked my life for this deal! You're gonna pay me!"

Tam reached for a hammer, which he had used to pin the crates closed. Before his fingers could close on the handle, Luke struck him half a dozen hard blows about the face and body, and the winded Scotsman fell to the floor. Luke leaped on top of him, his knife to Tam's throat.

"For the love of Jesus!" Tam exclaimed.

"Going religious now are you, you Scotch bastard?" Luke roared. "Well, this is the gospel according to Luke: Pay me—or I'll cut your goddamn throat!"

Tam appeared to resign himself. "You know where the safe is, laddie."

Luke ripped Tam's keys off his belt and unlocked a false cupboard which concealed the wall safe. He tossed the contents of the safe on to Tam's desk. There were only a few small bundles of notes. He riffled through them, thrust them into his inside pockets, then turned angrily to Tam, who was still on the floor and in pain.

"There's no more than 5K here. What the hell d'you take me for? I thought we could trust each other enough at least to get the job done! After all these years, you were gonna rip me off with a few quid when those antiques are worth at least half a million! You dirty lying Scottish scum! One day you'll meet the wrong fella who'll blow you away like the nasty little louse that you are!" He hit Tam again. "Who is this guy I've risked my life for?"

Tam shook his head. "I canna say. I gave my word."

"Your word?" Luke exploded again. "It's worth sod all!"

Luke cracked Tam again, then snatched up the antique bust and raised it over the Scotsman's head. "Who is he? I want paying!"

Tam appeared to give in. "Folk ca' him...Lucky." His voice was barely a whisper.

Luke lowered the bust. "Is he a dog? Lucky *what*?"

But Tam had passed out. Luke shook him.

"WHO'S THE MUSH CALLED LUCKY?"

Tam was unconscious, a bloody mess.

Luke drove his Renault Estate through a ramshackle assemblage of semi-permanent traveller sites that had been allowed to straggle for miles between the motorway and a marshy loop of the river. The area was constantly threatened with enforcement notices, that immediately became bogged down in legal disputes. The local council was wary of pouring taxpayers' money into the pockets of lawyers, and little official action had been taken to remove anyone. The travellers were also fortunate that only the northern limits of the area were overlooked by houses, and these were mostly rented, or more commonly sub-let, by other travellers to a range of kindred groups from poshrats to pikies.

He pulled up by a pair of galvanized iron gates, which bore the hand-painted information *SMITH. MOTORS*.

An integral door opened and Samson, a gypsy traveller youth of seventeen, stuck his head out, then grinned and disappeared. The gates creaked slowly open, and Luke drove into the yard.

He was met by a chaos of second-hand vehicles: cars, vans, pickups and small trucks. Workshops, hidden behind walls of galvanized iron, stood to one side of the yard. Two smart but unostentatious travellers' trailers occupied the opposite side. Luke got out of the Renault and studied the scene. He could hear diesel generators throbbing in the background. Samson hung around watchfully.

Riley, now a lean and swarthy Rom, appeared in a trailer doorway. The brothers stared at each other in silence. Ambrose, still sprightly, though the passing years had lined his face, appeared from the other trailer. He smiled with pleasure when he saw Luke.

Father and son embraced warmly.

"Been a good while, son." Ambrose pulled a reproachful face. "I thought I'd lost you to the gorgios!"

Luke laughed. "You think I'd settle for a dull life like that?"

Riley stepped down from his trailer. "Only time we see him it's trouble."

"Mornin' to you, brother," Luke replied with a mocking grin. "Happy in the motor trade, are you?"

"Let him alone, Riley." Ambrose gave his eldest son a warning look.

"Any chance of a better motor?" Luke asked.

Riley sneered. "Didn't I know it? Gavvers looking for the Renault, eh?"

"Wrong, brother. I fancy a spot o' man hunting. That's a bit out o' your league though, ain't it?" Luke smiled at his scowling brother. "I need a better class o' motor."

Ambrose turned to the watching youth. "Sam, bring out the BMW. Come in, Luke. Have a bite o' breakfast. Rose is making it for us now."

Ambrose and Luke followed Riley into his trailer, where they drank tea while they waited for Rose, Riley's wife, a very dark oriental-looking Romany, to prepare the usual fry-up.

"Still at Radford's?" Ambrose asked. He didn't want to probe too much and risk arousing his son's quick temper.

"I like it there," Luke replied. He grinned. "See all, unseen."

"Ain't you nothing better to do than watch gorgios all day?" Riley scoffed.

Luke smiled. "Peregrine falcons. Heard of 'em have you? The world's best hunters. They teach me something every day."

Before Riley could reply, Rose came in from the kitchen with their breakfast. She averted her gaze when Luke looked at her. Two young children appeared behind her.

"Take the chavvies to the other van, Rose," Riley ordered. "We got business talk here."

Rose ushered the children out. The three men ate in silence until the meal was almost finished. Riley suddenly thumped his fist on the table.

"What I got for a brother, eh? We're honest travellers here! Should be working with me, not for rogues like Tam McBride!"

"You should be setting yourself up on my land, not hiding away down here with this riff-raff," Luke retorted angrily. "Anyway, who says I'm working with Tam?"

"You were dikkered driving up there last night. We got more spies than the gavvers! You gonna ruin the fam'ly with a crook like that—that's the truth!"

"Our fam'ly was ruined fifteen years ago, brother— and *that's* the truth!"

"What happened back then ain't no excuse for thieving!" Riley replied accusingly.

"Who's thieving?" Luke's face was an image of guileless innocence.

"You telling me Tam McBride's an honest trader?" Riley replied scornfully.

"Know what I think, brother? I think that fire back then took your spirit. I think you've been like a beaten man since. Been trying hard as you can to be a gorgio!"

"Gorgio? Me?" Riley stood up and aimed a blow at Luke, but he brushed it aside and caught his brother in an arm lock.

"You ain't no traveller, hiding in here! I'm more traveller'n you! I live by my wits and care naught for tomorrow!"

"Enough!" Ambrose shouted. "Ain't getting us nowhere fighting. Sit. Make an end o' these insults."

Riley and Luke backed off and resumed their seats at the table.

"Like the gavvers said, that fire were an accident. Accept it, Luke," Ambrose almost begged his younger son.

"You know a mush called Lucky?" Luke asked. He noticed the warning glances, quickly hidden, that passed between his father and brother.

"Hell d'you want with him?" Riley demanded.

"You know him then?" Luke tried not to sound too eager.

"Might do," Riley replied. "Why?"

"Ain't none o' your business why. He owes me is all. Who is he?"

"No one." Riley wafted a hand dismissively. "A jumped-up piece of English shite."

"Give me his name," Luke demanded. "He owes me."

"You keep away from him," Riley replied savagely. "You'll come off worse if you don't! I'm telling you for your own good!"

Luke got to his feet threateningly, outraged by his brother's attitude. "You don't tell me what to do! I can look out for myself! Just give me his goddamn name!"

Riley didn't want to risk more blows with a man he knew could easily beat him, but he didn't want to lose face, either. Anyway, he reasoned, his brother would find out from someone else. "Phil Yates. You any wiser for knowing that?"

Luke had heard the name mentioned often in the world of gypsy travellers, and every time it had been accompanied by disparaging remarks and muttered insults.

"Racehorse owner, ain't he?" Luke asked. "From what I've heard among our folk he ain't a well-liked man."

Ambrose took up the story. "Travelling farrier, Phil Yates was once, like his father afore him. He calls hisself a poshrat, a half-blood, but I doubt he's more'n a diddekai, even with the name Yates. He'd go out of his way to con us Roms if he could, Boswells, Woods, all of us. Did some shady big-money racecourse deals. Got rich and bought hisself a big old country place."

"Why don't you like him?" Luke persisted.

"He's evil!" Riley growled. "No true Roms will deal with him."

"Phil Yates was our enemy once." Ambrose cast a warning glance at Riley. "But we don't talk of him no more. You watch out, son, when you find him. He's trickier to deal with than a nest o' hornets!"

* * *

An hour later Luke sat in the BMW, waiting for Samson to open the yard gates. Ambrose leaned in at the driver's window. "I'd be happy to see you with a woman. Be a good influence on you."

Luke laughed. "Ain't I too big a risk for a Romany juval? The way Riley goes on, you'd think I was carrying the Mark of Cain!"

"Don't you bother your head about Riley. He worries too much. Get yourself to your uncle Taiso's," Ambrose advised. "Do some strong rockering and make peace with him. Give yourself a new start."

Luke objected. "Taiso could banish me. I'd be worse'n a beggar. I'd end up tarmacing with pikies. And they'd despise me, 'cos they'd know I was no one."

His father disagreed. "Taiso's the best judge of a man I know. If he judges you to be true in your heart, you've nothing to fear from him."

Luke laughed. "He thinks I'm like the priest with a fox's face! Last time I saw Taiso he hardly spoke to me."

"Give yourself a chance, son. I'll speak up for you with Taiso. Tell him you want to make a good life and you need to be wed. Don't be too proud to ask for help from your people. Remember that."

Luke nodded. His father meant well, but he held out no hope of reconciliation with Taiso. The patriarch of their clan was a hard man whose word was law. He was nowhere near ready to speak with him yet.

Samson opened the gates.

"Jal! Jal!" Ambrose cried.

As Luke drove from the yard, Riley joined his father.

"Mebbe we should've told him what really happened back then," Riley suggested.

Ambrose shook his head. "We do that now, he'll be as lost to us as your dai and Athalia."

"He's gonna find out," Riley said gloomily, "but from the wrong folk. Then there'll be no end to the trouble til he's truly mullo. Dead as a dead mush can be. And his ghost tied to this world forever."

6

After four hours' sleep and a change of clothes, Luke left Radford's in mid-afternoon and drove north up the motorway for ninety minutes. He turned off, passing through a succession of yuppified villages, until he located the minor road that led to the ancient green lane he remembered from the happy days of his childhood.

His dadu had told him that the lane was a surviving fragment of a complex of drove roads, when Galloway horses and cattle had been brought south to sell to the English. Luke hung on his words, imagining the whole of England crisscrossed by these ancient ways, where drover and gypsy were free and at peace, one with the land.

They lived in a workaday Open-lot back then, trading in horses and lurchers. Ambrose occasionally got him to climb an oak tree or an elm to take a fledgling hawk from its nest; then he showed his eager son how to rear it until it was ready for sale. They were mostly kestrels and sparrowhawks, with an occasional merlin or hobby. But what Luke wanted was a goshawk or a peregrine. He still hoped that one day he would have the chance to rear one.

Two hundred yards down the lane, traveller families were camped on the verge. Three trucks and three fancy trailers were pulled on close to an open fire.

Luke stopped at a respectful distance and approached the camp on foot. He was pleased to see that the trailer windows were dark and there were no chuntering generators, no flickering TV screens. Everyone seemed to be outside, and that very fact separated the gypsy travellers' world from that of the gorgio. It was a sad day when the traveller was forced to shut himself away and a thousand years of campfires and conviviality were abandoned.

The tranquillity of the evening reminded him of similar scenes from his childhood, the long-lingering light of early summer evenings giving the scene a magical timelessness. At a short stretch of the imagination, the figures around the fire seemed as if they might belong to ancient times and a world of untamed places, where the invading presence of settlers had never occurred.

A burly Rom in his mid-forties got up from the fire and came to greet him.

"I know you. You're Boswell kin. We met at Stow fair last year." He offered his hand. "Davey Wood."

Luke introduced himself and the two men shook hands warmly. Davey gestured for Luke to join them at the fire, where he shook the hands of Davey's kin. Twenty travellers, from grandparents to toddlers, enjoyed a supper of rabbit stew, sitting around the fire at peace with themselves and the world.

As Davey put more wood on the fire and his daughter served mugs of hot sweet tea, Davey's father got out his fiddle and played a haunting lament.

"My Dadu's still a great boshomengro, ain't he?" Davey remarked. "I don't have half his skill."

Amos Wood interrupted his own playing to make a comment addressed primarily, it seemed, to Luke. "This is music from the sadness of our present times," he explained. "I'd be pleased if a singer could put the right words to it one day. I mean a proper singer, not a gypsy pop star!"

Everyone laughed, which saved Luke the embarrassment of having to respond. He knew no gypsy singers. Maybe he should try to find one, someone with the power of the Gitano singers of Spain, who could melt your heart in a minute—if such a singer existed in England.

He felt the company was sufficiently at ease with his presence for him to introduce the subject of his mission. He moved closer to Davey.

"I'm after a mush who used to be a putcherlengro, a travelling farrier, but now he's got to be a big shot in the horse-racing world. Know anyone like that?"

Davey pulled a sour face. "Sounds like you're wanting that nasty little runt they call Lucky Phil Yates." He paused, pursing his lips in thought. "I can mebbe get a message to him if you want."

"I'm in no great rush," Luke cautioned. "I'm just starting a rumour. I know all about his T'ang horses."

Davey raised his eyebrows in polite surprise. "You do?"

"Yeah. It's a real small world, ain't it? But I don't wanna meet him till I'm ready. Know where I can dikker him?"

Davey thought a moment, then nodded. "He'll most likely be up on the gallops first thing, but you'll need field glasses. Got a new chestnut stallion. Calls it Good Times. 'Bout sums the mush up. Why don't you meet with my good friend Sol Boswell's palesko, his brother's boy Sy, tomorrow up on the hill? You've had a few adventures together, you and him, so I hear!" Davey pointed in the general direction. "Say I sent you. You might have to help him break a spotted'n he's got up there. He tells me the grye can't be tamed."

Luke thanked Davey for his help. Night encircled them as they sat around the fire. They drank more tea, and the conversation turned to general traveller topics.

"This still a good atchin tan for travellers?" Luke asked. "I recall it was a stopping place for my fam'ly twenty years or so back."

"We'd have lost it," Davey replied. "But my dadu bought the grazing land both sides, so they can't really stop us living here—though they try—as we have to see to the gryes. And we let other kin pull on, too, so it's grown into a good meeting place. We even applied to build a bungalow here, but the council turned us down." He shook his head sadly. "I think they'd rather we all died out than tried to make a life for ourselves."

"I've a little spot you can pull on if you need to. But it's only for folk I know." Luke told Davey the location. "And I'm after another place soon as I've done with this Lucky mush." He smiled. "Mebbe he won't be so lucky time I've finished!"

Davey grinned. "You know where you can find us then."

"Is it okay if I kip in my motor tonight?" Luke asked. "I'll find Sy in the morning."

"You're very welcome. We'll be eating at first light."

Luke got to his feet. "Kushti rardi."

"Kushti bokt."

Luke came on the vehicles first: two big pickups, one hitched to a horse trailer, the other to a modest living van. He parked the BMW next to the pickups to avoid driving too close and spooking the horse. A couple of hundred yards further on, he found his friend Sy (short for Sylvano) Boswell, a very dark Rom of thirty, with two younger male helpers, breaking a handsome spotted stallion on the grassy hilltop.

They held the horse on two ropes while the frisky animal circled them. Luke had prepared himself for the encounter by rubbing a few drops of a herbal decoction on his forehead and hands, the recipe for which he had learned from his East Anglian contact. Then he approached the three men on foot.

"How much d'you want for him, mush?" Luke asked. It was the gypsy travellers' regular opening gambit.

Sy laughed and gave the customary reply. "He ain't for sale." They embraced warmly. "Good to see you, Luke."

"I've been down at Davey's."

"I know. I've been expecting you."

Luke was impressed by the reliability of clan communication. Mobile phones had evidently replaced telepathy, at least that was what some of the old folk told the few credulous gorgios who cared to listen.

He had no wish to intervene, but after a few minutes watching Sy's unrewarded efforts with the grye he suggested as tactfully as he could that maybe he might have a go.

"I bought him a week back, but he don't seem to like me," Sy admitted. "All he does, as you can see, is try to break from the circle and lame me. I should've known better. It should've been obvious to a dinilo, a complete idiot, that mush I paid had made naught of him. But I fell for the grye's looks. I've rarely seen a spotted'n so strongly marked."

Luke agreed with his friend's observation. The stallion's markings were bold and striking. He had a sense that the animal was aware he was unique and would only allow himself to be ridden by a man who thought of him as at least an equal.

"However good you are, you always meet someone smarter when it comes to gryes," Luke said. "I lost a bit o' vongar on a grye trade last year at Stow fair. He was an older mush—one o' the Herons—and I should've guessed he'd know more'n me."

Luke took one of the ropes and walked slowly towards the stallion, talking quietly all the time, while Sy and his helpers disappeared among nearby trees. As he expected, the horse showed an immediate interest in him because he could smell the herbal mixture on his skin. Luke took the ropes off the horse and rubbed his hands over the animal's nose and mouth, whispering to him all the while and blowing on his nostrils. The animal nuzzled up to him, and he rubbed his hands over its chin.

Luke's next move was to walk around the hoof-worn circle and to wait while the stallion followed. Then he ran across the hilltop and the stallion tried to get in front of him to cut him off. But he changed direction each time, and the horse found he was chasing a shadow. Luke laughed; the stallion neighed in reply. It was huge fun.

After a while Luke allowed himself to be caught. He rubbed his hands on the horse's nose, then vaulted effortlessly on to its back. The stallion stood still, rigid as an effigy, as if it had been poleaxed and would collapse to the ground any second. Then it sprang into the air, twisting and bucking like a maddened bull at a rodeo. But Luke hung on.

All at once the stallion quieted and stood still. Luke walked it around the circle, then galloped it across the hilltop. When he trotted it calmly back to the circle, Sy was waiting.

"Never seen a grye with a strong spirit charmed so fast," Sy remarked with undisguised awe.

"Takes one to recognize another," Luke replied with a laugh. He took a bundle of notes from his inside jacket pocket. "Name your price." He was pleased he had taken all the cash he possessed from Radford's when he left.

Luke tied his newly acquired spotted stallion to the smooth trunk of a young sycamore. He felt the horse was a kindred spirit—one of those rare animals that truly knows what you're thinking, that knows your every mood as clearly as it senses changes in the weather.

Sy echoed his thoughts. "He's been waiting for you. No one else was going to ride that grye."

Luke talked quietly to the stallion, knowing it needed the reassurance of his presence. After a while he turned to Sy. "I didn't aim on buying a grye this morning! I wanted to ask if you could show me the gallops?"

Sy laughed. "Gonna ride your new grye against Phil Yates?"

Luke smiled. "Who knows? One day I might."

"You got a name for him yet?"

"Thought I'd call him Prince of Thieves."

"Mush—that's a winner!"

* * *

After a fifteen-minute walk, Luke and Sy stood among trees at the edge of a belt of hilltop woodland, watching four riders exercise their mounts on the smooth grasses of the gallops below them. Four men observed the riders through field glasses from a dirt car park, where an E Class Mercedes, a Range Rover and a Ford Focus were parked up.

"Recognise Phil Yates?" Luke asked.

"Like a bug in a blanket," Sy replied sourly.

Sy pointed out a man of around forty, turned out like a country gent but a little too loudly. He wore a check-patterned jacket and cap with knee breeches and knee-length hosiery.

Luke observed him in his binoculars, shielding the lenses with his free hand so they didn't catch the sun. "So he's the little guy in the snazzy jacket?" he remarked.

"That's him. Anyone would think he'd dressed for the winners' enclosure," Sy commented with undisguised contempt. "He's like his clothes, a show-off and a loudmouth. The big guy next to him is Harry Rooke, Phil Yates' personal minder and brother-in-law. He's another cruel bastard like his little buddy, but mebbe not so tricky."

Luke studied the big man. Dressed in smart casuals, he looked to be about the same age as Phil Yates but a giant in comparison. Luke estimated the man must be six-foot-five and weigh at least three hundred pounds. "Who is this Harry Rooke? I've heard the name, but it was a while back and I can't recall much else."

"He used to travel round the fairs, not just horse fairs but traction-engine rallies and the like. He'd set up a boxing ring and challenge anyone to bare-knuckle him for a tenner. If they were still on their feet after three minutes, they'd get fifty back. He had a big clock on a stand that everyone could see. No one managed it for years til a young Irish traveller took him on."

Luke's interest was aroused. "I heard about that fight, but it didn't mean much to me at the time. I recall my dadu years back talking to a mush from County Down at Wickham. Didn't the Irish lad get hurt?"

Sy continued his narrative. "Be ten or twelve years ago now when Harry Rooke and that Irish mush fought. By all accounts at the end of two minutes Harry was getting beat. He couldn't lay a fist on the Mick, who was giving away five inches and as many stones, but he was picking Harry off as he pleased. Now Phil Yates was courting Harry's sister Dorothy —she'd have made a great stand-up when she was sober, she's got a rare wit—and he'd taken over the refereeing from a retired pro called Jimmy Hobbs. They say Jimmy would've stopped the fight, but Phil had other ideas."

Sy paused to light a roll-up. "My nano, who was there, said Phil shouted, *'Come on, Harry, use your head,'* and Harry must've thought he meant for him to head butt the Mick, not smarten up his fighting. So, my uncle said, that's what Harry did, and he sent the Mick down with a broken nose. The crowd was shouting *foul!*, but Phil raised Harry's arm as the winner. Harry only did a few more fairs before he retired, so my nano told me. Some folk said he didn't fancy meeting the Mick again, who was after getting his revenge."

So that's the team, Luke thought. Phil the schemer and Harry the muscle. "Who are those other two?" he asked.

The figure next to Harry Rooke seemed about ten years older, a man who looked very much at home in cords and waxed jacket.

"That's Clive Fawcett, the trainer," Sy commented. "He's by far the best o' the lot."

"Who's the mush at the end who seems to keep muttering into Phil Yates' ear?" Luke asked.

"That's Detective Inspector Nigel Hirst, meanest gavver that ever was born." Sy spat to emphasize his contempt. "Word is he's on the Yates payroll. Watches his back."

Sy's revelation hit Luke like a blow. So this was the man his father had denounced as a criminal in uniform. This was the police sergeant who had dismissed the incident of the trailer fire, brushing it aside as an unfortunate domestic accident.

Luke studied the man in his binoculars: a lean reptilian figure in his mid-forties, dressed in a charcoal grey suit like a bank manager, except Hirst's suit was ill-fitting and crumpled.

Nigel Hirst. A name to conjure with. Now a detective inspector. Hirst, a cop who no doubt thought he was untouchable.

"A bunch o' rogues if ever I dikkered the like!" Sy gave voice to his companion's thoughts.

They continued watching the horses, taking turns with Luke's binoculars.

"Davey said Phil Yates has a horse called Good Times. I've a mind that's the chestnut out in front, am I right?" Luke asked.

Sy confirmed Luke's observation. "That's the one. Fine looking animal. That little shit Yates don't deserve him!"

"Mebbe I'll race that grye one day on Prince of Thieves," Luke commented thoughtfully.

"That's not a good idea," Sy cautioned. "He's a dodgy fella, Phil Yates. My advice to you would be to keep away from that mush." He showed Luke an ugly raised scar on the back of his arm. "Horse deal years back that didn't go his way. He accused me of cheating him, said I'd given the grye a stimulant to make him seem more lively."

"And had you?" Luke asked.

Sy laughed. "Never dream of such a thing! But out comes his blade." He gave Luke a warning frown. "Phil Yates don't like losing! Whatcha want with him anyway?"

"I know all about his T'ang horses." Luke tapped the side of his nose and smiled mysteriously.

"That so?"

"Some mush wants to get that across to him."

7

Phil Yates and his companions watched the horses flowing gracefully around the fenced-off circuit on the gallops.

Phil turned to Harry. "What a sight, Harry, eh! If there's a god he's a horse, you know that?"

The four horses picked up to a full gallop. A glossy chestnut stallion with a distinctive white blaze moved a length clear of the rest.

Phil beamed with admiration. "Good Times is looking sharp, Harry."

Harry nodded. "Sure, Phil. You could put your life savings on him."

"But you're not, are you, Harry?" Phil looked up at the big man reproachfully.

"He ain't a gambling man!" Hirst smiled sardonically.

Harry, impassive, soaked up their laughter. "Mebbe, if I was, I'd stake my life on him."

"Your life did you say, or your wife?" Hirst grinned.

Harry joined reluctantly in the fresh round of laughter. Did Hirst know he was having problems with Maureen, the bonny lass from Kilkenny he'd met in Liverpool and who he'd left his family and his circus strongman act to marry? She had abandoned her tinker past and had urged him to settle down. But he couldn't.

He had met Phil Yates at a horse fair, and they'd gotten on well. He missed the circus and the travelling life, but Phil offered the next best thing: the horse fairs and the professional racing circuit. His boxing venture provided an introduction to an alternative society. They made a healthy living buying and selling gypsy vanners. Then Phil entered the shady world of race fixing. He began to make big money and to buy racehorses. They bet heavily but discreetly on guaranteed winners, and Phil's own horses, with Clive Fawcett's involvement, soon became winners themselves. He would never have made this kind of money if he had stayed in the circus.

While Phil stuck mostly to the world of racing, he discovered a hidden talent for buying up failing businesses and ruthlessly turning them around. They bought into each other's financial activities, and their accountants disappeared the profits offshore.

But the more money he made, the unhappier Maureen became. He couldn't understand it. Over the past decade, he had watched her slipping slowly away from him, as if she was floating steadily out to sea until he lost sight of her. She accused him of becoming a stranger, but the fault was hers. How could they be a unified couple if she had no interest in his new business life?

What he did know for certain was that he was impotent. Ever since his fight with the Irish lad his sex life had started to go wrong. Was it simply his humiliation, or something deeper, some kind of punishment? Did the cause of it go back even further? He was baffled. But, as always, he kept his feelings hidden, even from Phil. He had good reason to distrust the man.

Ten minutes later Harry and Phil left the car park, Harry at the wheel of Phil's Mercedes. Phil had never been happy behind the wheel of a motor, preferring to travel on foot or on horseback. It was one of the many old-fashioned quirks in the man's nature.

"Found us a stud yet, Harry?" Phil's manner towards the big man was, as usual, slightly patronising.

"I might have."

"Come on Harry," Phil said, exasperated by his companion's reticence. "Loosen up. It ain't gonna kill you to tell me!" What was happening to him, Phil wondered. Why had their one-time lively relationship become so cool? Had Harry started to suspect him of betrayal?

Harry enjoyed annoying Phil these days. It gave him pleasure to watch the little guy squirm. He had enough business interests of his own not to need him any more and Phil knew it. But they were co-owners of a portfolio of property that would be a hellish task to sort out. One day soon, though, he would have to face it and get a life back he could call his own. Perhaps, too, he could revive his sex life, but not with Maureen...

He waited another minute while the tension between them rose, then he relented. "It's a small farm called Cuckoo Nest. I've got the paperwork on me, as a matter of fact. Drew it up last night."

"Nice one, Harry! You've been keeping me in the dark."

So I have, Harry thought. And it serves you right, you two-faced twat. "Early days, Phil. I wouldn't put any money on this one, either. At least not yet."

"Who's the owner?"

"Catherine Scaife. Husband's deceased."

Phil reflected. "I know the name, but I can't put a face to it. Any debts? Any dependants?"

"200K to the bank. One sixteen-year-old daughter."

"Profit?"

Harry smiled. He took pleasure too in showing off his thorough due diligence, courtesy of his resourceful accountant. "Hardly covers the loan interest. In my opinion they're too diverse. Should put the whole place down to cash crops. But I'm not going to tell 'em!"

"You've done a good job, Harry," Phil replied with apparent sincerity. "Means we've got some leverage. Why don't we take a look?"

"I've looked. It's promising."

"But *I* haven't seen it, Harry, have I?" A hint of menace crept into Phil's tone. "It's *my* money that'll buy it."

"It's you who wants a stud, not me."

"Okay. You've made your point. Let's just take a quick look."

The balance of power between the two men was entirely in Harry's favour. He relented.

"Fair enough. I've a spare couple of hours."

Harry swung the Mercedes around and drove back the opposite way. Half an hour later, the car was pulled up on the road bridge that spanned the intercity railway lines that ran beneath. A long goods train rumbled slowly past on one of the down lines. The road over the bridge was never busy. It was little more than a lane that connected the nearby farms, a recent descendant of the original bridge that had been built when the lines were first laid.

Phil and Harry leaned on the stone parapet, scanning the farm buildings and the land surrounding them in their field glasses. Harry guessed his companion was interested from the length of time he was taking looking at the place.

"Good brick ranges. Paddocks and a big barn. Harry —I like it!" Phil exclaimed. "How many acres?"

"One-ninety. Bit on the small side for these days, unless you've a contract for broiler birds or with a distillery. Crop fields are let out to neighbours who grow taties and carrots to secure their supermarket contracts, but they don't bring in enough rent to produce a surplus when you take in the bank debt. Place is getting rundown. There's nothing spare to keep up with repairs and renewals."

Phil didn't ask how Harry had found all this out. His colleague's contacts in the world of local finance were obviously happy to accept his backhanders, or one of the East European escort girls he had started running as a sideline. "Let's take a closer look."

They drove across the bridge and down the rough track that led to the farm, parking the Mercedes in the stackyard. They approached the farmhouse, a rambling brick-built place that dated from the time of the parliamentary enclosures. It was obvious at a glance that the building had seen better days. Tufts of couch grass sprouted from the guttering, and the windows on the first and second floors were in urgent need of repair. The brick ranges were no better, with broken gutters and missing roof tiles.

"Looks like they're on the way down," Phil remarked with undisguised optimism.

Harry studied the house and buildings. "Nothing a bit of routine maintenance won't sort. The structures seem basically sound. They're obviously short of cash."

Before they could knock on the door, it was flung wide open and two angry females burst out into the yard.

Phil studied them: the older woman in her thirties, attractive, with short dark hair; the younger version, which must be the daughter, with her long brown hair in a pony tail. Both of them dressed in work clothes. The women stared at their visitors in hostile surprise.

"Who the hell are you?" the older one asked. "Can't you read the sign by the drive? *NO HAWKERS. NO SCRAP LADS.*"

Phil smiled coldly. "We're not hawking or looking for scrap, and we're *not* people to be shouted at. I'm Phil Yates. This is Harry Rooke, my business associate. I assume I'm addressing Catherine Scaife?"

Cath tried to suppress the sudden fear that swept through her as she recognised the man in the check jacket. "What d'you want with me? There's another sign out there that says *CALLERS BY APPOINTMENT ONLY*. It gives a phone number if you want to speak with me."

Phil ignored her frosty tone. His mind was focused on one purpose only. "Nice paddocks you've got here, Mrs Scaife. Bit on the rank side mebbe. They need sweetening up. I see they're empty now, but I'd like to put a few of my horses in. I'll pay you well, of course."

Cath recovered her self-possession. "I'm not interested, Mr Yates. Why don't you advertise for grazing in the local paper? Or ask Charlie Gibb at the sawmill yonder? He knows all the landowners hereabouts."

"You haven't seen our offer yet, Mrs Scaife." Phil glanced at Harry.

The big man handed Cath a folder of papers. "It's all in there. You'll find we're making an offer it would be in your best interests to accept. Read it through. Check it out with your legal people. They'll see it's a very generous proposition. Sign it and send it back to Birch Hall in the reply-paid envelope."

Harry's manner was detached, as impersonal as a debt collector. But his tone, coupled with his size, made his presence very intimidating.

"You'll benefit as much as we will. It's a win-win for us all, Mrs Scaife," Phil stated confidently. "We look forward to hearing from you. Have a good day now."

Without another word, the two men returned to the Mercedes and drove out of the yard.

The women returned to the kitchen where they had been packing eggs for the local village shop, a well-stocked store that was still managing to survive because it was also the only post office for miles around.

Cath felt cold. It was an inner chill and numbness that began in her feet and rose until it filled her entire body, as if she had suddenly been told she had only months left to live.

Her daughter, Angelica, known to everyone as Angie, divined her mother's mood. "What's up, Mam? What is it with this Yates guy?"

The shock of the unexpected visit had left Cath speechless. She struggled to find her voice. "I'm not exaggerating if I said this is the third worst day of my life," she managed at last. "The first was when Matt died."

"Sure," Angie agreed. "And the second?"

"You don't want to know," was the enigmatic but firm reply.

Angie had never seen her mother like this. When Matt's tragic sudden death had happened it was a shock and subsequent grief that the two of them had shared. This was different. Her mother was suffering a personal crisis that appeared to have no explanation. "So what's the problem with this Phil Yates?"

Cath took a deep breath. "He's one of those poisonous guys who preys on the weak. He wants what he sees and usually gets what he wants. He never gives up. Folks who've had him on their backs say it's like they've been singled out for torment by a demon. He bought Birch Hall for half its real value because its owner had been driven to despair by lawsuits. Phil Yates had him in a corner, and, so I was reliably told, he gave the man a financial thrashing."

Angie was stunned by her mother's words. Her dominant emotion of outrage came to her rescue. "To hell with 'em, Mam! They're a pair of bloody jumped-up nowts! They've absolutely no business coming down here waving their bits o' paper!"

Cath had great respect for her daughter's fighting spirit. It had been largely Angie's bloody-mindedness that had kept them on their land after her husband's death. The last thing she wanted was to undermine her daughter's efforts, but there was no obvious cure for their financial situation. She sighed. "We've no business down here either if we can't pay the bank."

Angie tried to reassure her. "We'll find a way. We're farmers. Farmers are used to dealing with problems. Our accountant might come up with some ideas."

He might, if he wasn't already in Harry Rooke's pay, Cath thought. But she kept her gloomy ideas to herself. "Let's finish the eggs. That's cash and *not* declarable! We don't want the Revenue men getting fat at our expense now, do we?"

Hooray for the Cragg Vale coiners, Angie thought. "No, we definitely do not!"

* * *

Five hundred yards away, high up in the loft of his sawmill, wall-eyed Charlie Gibb had been watching the two women with his telescope clapped to his good eye. He spoke to himself, as was usual in his solitary life.

"Ah, Cath Scaife, the vultures are circling. There's only one way you'll get free of 'em now, and that's to do business with Charlie!" He swung his lean six-foot-three-inch frame through the web of roof timbers in the top of the mill, emitting his eerie high-pitched laugh as he went. "You'll have to learn a hard lesson, oh yes! You'll have to get down on your knees before Charlie Gibb!"

He swung himself down to the first floor and descended the stairs to his office, talking to himself as he went. "When I do a deal with Cath Scaife I'll be a farmer. I'll own land and I'll have respect!" It wasn't his fault that he was an albino. It wasn't his fault that folk thought he was weird. He cursed his father for not leaving him a farm and only a sawmill.

But he'd be changing that and soon. He'd be a farmer. He'd own a piece of the planet! Then when Phil Yates came a-calling it would be him, Charlie Gibb, who'd be saying what was what.

* * *

Twenty miles southeast from Cuckoo Nest, Harry's Mercedes was approaching the imposing stone gateposts of a small country estate close to the motorway. As the Mercedes turned on to the long private drive the name Birch Hall could be clearly seen, carved on the gateposts and picked out in black paint against the pale local sandstone.

The main building was Jacobean, with smaller eighteenth-century extensions on each side. The entire place was the same colour as the gateposts, except for the stonework surrounding the main entrance, which was a tasteful contrast of much harder old red sandstone, carted in at considerable cost by the hall's original owner, a friend and supporter of King Charles the Second.

Phil loved the place. One of his deepest pleasures was to stand on his front lawn, stare at the imposing southern elevation of the house...and gloat. He, Phil Yates, was the owner of this eight-bedroom country house, which he liked to think of—not strictly accurately—as a mansion. He, Phil Yates, born the son of an itinerant farrier, who had spent the first twenty years of his life in a horse-drawn Open-lot! No wonder they had nicknamed him Lucky on the horse-racing circuit.

But it wasn't just luck. It was having a good team. Harry had arrived with his shrewd business brain and a killer instinct equal to his own. Over the years, sometimes separately, sometimes together, they had bought cheap and sold high: asset-stripping failing businesses, buying properties and horses. And DI Nigel Hirst had stood guard over many of their more slippery deals. Occasionally together, sometimes apart, they had pressured, bribed and blackmailed their way to the top, not to mention a bit of race fixing on the way. Between them they owned houses, including several HMOs, and an expanding stock of fine racehorses, with Good Times the pinnacle of their achievement.

What was actually his and what was Harry's was a moot point. But what did that matter? Truth be told, he owned Harry as well; the man rarely made moves on his own without approaching him for co-investment. He even owned twenty-five percent of Harry's escort girls, though Harry liked to think of them as all his own. Ah, well, he had to humour the man. When it came to physical intimidation, Harry was the best and indispensable.

But Phil was troubled. He was the poor boy made good. Envied by those with less nous and ambition, despised by the old-money horsey aristocracy, he occupied an uncomfortable middle ground: affluent but with no landed pedigree. And his money was undoubtedly dirtier than most. The irony of his rags-to-riches journey was that it had left him beset by a chronic anxiety he could never shake off. Any day, any one of his questionable deals could come back to threaten his precarious security. And there were other deeds too dark to countenance that had to be buried in the deepest abyss of his memory...

Brian and Steve, two muscular minders, exercised a pair of Dobermans on the wide front lawn. They waved to Phil and Harry as their bosses got out of the Mercedes to ascend the long flight of steps to the front entrance. Only Harry condescended to wave back.

When Phil and Harry stepped into the panelled dining room, they found Dot, Phil's wife and Harry's younger sister, sitting with Maureen eating a late breakfast the non-resident cook had prepared. Dot had secretly poured brandy into her glass of orange juice. She raised the glass as the two men walked in.

"Here's to husbands. May they remember who we are!"

Phil and Harry ignored her, both of them hoping she wasn't about to create a scene. They helped themselves from the hostess trolley.

"I've got a good feeling about Cuckoo Nest," Harry remarked as he spooned large quantities of mushrooms and tomatoes onto his plate.

"So have I," Phil replied. "You know, I've always wanted a stud. It's been a dream of mine since I was a boy." He didn't know if his claim was strictly true, but he liked to pretend that it was.

Dot stared sourly at Phil over her orange juice. "What am I then—the rude awakening?"

Phil gave his wife a withering look. She was in one of her moods, and the less he said to antagonise her the better.

Harry kissed Maureen on the cheek. "Okay, love?"

"Well, no arms or legs fell off as I was coming down the stairs, so I guess I must be," she replied with a matter-of-fact shrug.

Maureen glanced at Phil as he took his place at the table. The look conveyed the faintest hint of some ongoing secrecy between them. Phil avoided her gaze and focused on his sausage and hash browns. Harry, as usual, absorbed the situation.

"Will we have another winner on Saturday, Phil?" Maureen asked with an ingenuous smile.

"It's a cert. Good Times is ready." Phil laughed. "Even Harry's getting excited!"

Harry weathered their laughter. He cast a glance around the table as he ate his gammon and eggs and wondered how long it would be before their relationships became unendurable. Perhaps he should remind them how much better off they were compared with their humble beginnings. But it was always the same with people: they had short memories when it suited them—and short memories were often the prelude to a demise.

It was only money, after all, that held them together —and the complex ties that money brings. If they severed their connections with Birch Hall, the winds of life would scatter them across the earth like so many strangers.

8

Luke drove fast on a long empty stretch of minor road. He was furious with himself for getting involved in a heist with so many unanswered questions attached. He should have pressed Tam for more information and pulled out when the Scot refused to give it. Instead he had rushed headlong into almost suicidal danger, blinded by the goal he had set himself of buying land in order to help his people.

He cursed the gorgio society that had caused gypsy travellers so many problems. He railed at travellers for accepting the unacceptable and shackling themselves to fixed sites. His task to free them was impossible. The only people he could work with were dodgy characters like Tam McBride who had no other aim than making money for themselves. The plight of gypsies didn't touch them.

He should have realized that Tam would not have been able to pay him the full amount up front for a major heist. He regretted his savage attack on the Scotsman, which would not encourage the dealer to pay him any time soon. But it was violence borne of desperation.

His only consolation was that Sy had given him Phil Yates's address. But the more he had learned about this Yates mush, the less likely it seemed that he would be willing to pay 300K for the T'ang horses. He was in a hurry and needed the money because he wanted to look at the small hill farm that was for sale an hour's drive northwest. He was hoping, if the place was any good, that he might persuade some of his clan to go shares with him, if he was unable to find the full purchase price himself. This depended, of course, on whether he could find anyone who trusted him. His ingrained secrecy and his dark reputation had done him few favours.

Too late he noticed the patrol car parked in the side road. His heart sank when he glanced in his mirror and saw it pull out and pursue, blue light flashing. Then he heard the hated wail of the siren.

He had no choice but to try to outrun it. The BMW had a good turn of speed, but it wouldn't have been his first choice as an escape vehicle. He floored the accelerator, but the patrol car clung to his tail. The chase went on for five miles, Luke expecting that any moment a second police vehicle would appear up ahead, blocking the road. His attention divided by glances in his rear-view mirror, he failed to register the roadworks and set of temporary traffic lights on the bend ahead of him until it was too late.

A county highways maintenance crew was spreading tarmac. A tipper truck was shooting a load of stone chippings on to the newly laid road surface. Luke braked, but he might as well not have bothered. He shot past the red light and came to a sudden stop, the tyres of the BMW plastered with chippings and wet tarmac. He had spent his adult life trying to maintain invisibility, but now, in his imagination, he was as naked as a plucked chicken in a butcher's shop window.

The familiar figure of PC Noel Bailey, flaccid and pale, tapped on his window. Luke opened it an inch.

Bailey could hardly speak for laughing. "Well, now, my old pal Lulu! I think it's time we took you in and asked you a few hard questions."

Luke shut his eyes, resigned. Five minutes later he found himself handcuffed to Bailey on the back seat of the patrol car. PC Alan Pearson, compact and muscular, was behind the wheel. Luke's last glimpse of the BMW was of it being towed on to the grass verge by a county highways truck.

"Only guilty men run, right, Al?" Bailey remarked with a smirk.

Pearson agreed. "He's guilty all right. You can smell it on him." He opened his window, wafting the air with his hand.

"You've no right to handcuff me," Luke protested. "I ain't under arrest. I'm not a danger to anyone."

"We don't want to lose you now we've got you." Pearson chuckled. "I don't see there's much you can do about it. And we can soon arrange to arrest you anytime we like."

"Slipped up this time, Lulu." Bailey smirked. "Dropped right into our arms like a baby."

Luke feigned bewilderment. "What's going on? I was just running late for an appointment."

"An *appointment*?" Bailey echoed. "You're a big-time businessman now, eh?"

"None of your concern, Bailey," Luke snapped.

Bailey shook his head. "Bad news for you, Lulu. Whoever you're meeting's gonna be waiting a very long time. And I've got even worse news." He sniggered. "We've got a dead 'un this time."

"Snake charmer now, eh?" Pearson commented. "Learn it in the jungle where you came from, did ya?"

Luke's heart sank. This was serious. But he had to keep playing the innocent.

"What the hell are you two on about?" he asked in a show of exasperation. "Just 'cos you spotted me in a motor don't mean you can pin every crime in the country on me! And that motor's legit, by the way. Belongs my brother. He'll be suing you for wrongful impounding."

The cops laughed uproariously, as if he had told them the joke of the century. Bailey leaned forward and whispered into his fellow officer's ear. Pearson nodded, saying nothing.

"Who's moving the loot, Lulu?" Bailey asked. "Tam O'Shanter, is it? See—*we know*. You'd never believe how smart we are these days."

Luke was furious. Someone had been talking—but who? Not Tam and not the Boswells. And surely not the Woods. Maybe the incident had been on the local TV news? And these two cops, just for the hell of it, had thought they might try and stick it on him —for one simple reason: He was a gypsy. It was just a lucky guess, but there was no way they could prove it. At least he'd learned that the rich ex-con had died. Serve him goddamn right, the bloody psycho.

But there was more to it than that. Or was there? Was it just the abandoned rope on the roof that had led the cops to think of him? A *Luke Smith nine*, case closed. He had left no fingerprints, wearing the surgical gloves until he had burned them in Tam's old Potbelly stove. He had worn his balaclava until he had flung himself on the back seat of the Volvo. Had the car been picked up on a local camera? Surely not. Surely Tam had chosen a camera-free route, taking care of himself, as usual, letting the cat burglar take all the risks. If he had been taken in for questioning, he would have invoked his legal guys and walked. It had happened many times before when valuable antiques had gone missing.

It had to have been a TV news item. And the rest was simply guesswork—plus, of course, his reputation. He had nothing to fear. Pearson had let his HQ know they had picked him up, but he had still not been arrested. He would be free by tomorrow morning. He just had to stay cool.

A sudden storm burst over them, with thunder, lightning and heavy rain. The car windows streamed. Pearson's wipers could barely cope.

"Hell did this come from?" Bailey exclaimed.

"I did it!" Luke laughed. "I put a curse on you! I can change the weather whenever I want. That's another thing you gorgios didn't know!"

"Like hell you can!" Bailey replied angrily. "Where d'you keep your cloudbuster? You just stick it up your arse and blow, eh?"

But Luke could tell that for all Bailey's bravado his voice held a detectable smidgeon of unease.

Pearson seemed to be having problems with his driving. "Damn this rain. Road's slimy as shite! I can't see more'n fifty yards."

A farm loomed up ahead through the rain. A tractor in a gateway pulled out, front wheels on the road. Pearson, still struggling at the wheel, didn't seem to have registered the vehicle's presence.

"Watch that goddamn tractor!" Luke yelled.

Pearson swerved to avoid the tractor, wrestling with the wheel. "We're skidding!" he cried. "It's not responding!" He tried to steer away from the tractor, but nothing happened. He hit the brakes. "Oh God!"

The skidding car slammed into the grass verge fifty yards past the farm gateway. There was a loud report like a gunshot. The three men in the car realized it was a blowout.

"Oh Christ, Al!" Bailey wailed.

The patrol car veered across the road, collided with the right-hand verge, then rebounded back and hit the opposite verge. At this point the vehicle left the tarmac. The men in the car heard the horrible ripping and crunching sounds as the car tore through the lane-side hedge.

The patrol car bounced and rolled down a sloping field, turning over and over as it went, eventually coming to rest on its roof, its engine still running.

Luke heaved Bailey off his right leg with his left foot, then reached for the keys on the officer's belt and unlocked the handcuffs.

"Bye, gorgios."

Before the police officers could recover their wits, he climbed through the broken back window and disappeared into the encroaching dusk.

Luke leaned on a woodside gate at the end of the field and looked back towards the scene of the accident. Bailey and Pearson had emerged from the car and were stumbling groggily away from the wreck. Then the vehicle burst into flames and exploded, and the officers flung themselves to the ground.

Luke had seen enough. He vaulted the gate and vanished into the trees.

The track through the wood led to a further gate and, beyond it, to another sloping field that levelled out and ended at railway lines. The light was fading fast, and his right knee was starting to hurt. He cursed. What had seemed a stroke of good fortune was quickly becoming the opposite. He hobbled down the field and followed the railway lines, knowing only from his innate sense of direction that he was going north.

How long could he continue walking with an injured leg? An hour? Two hours? Then what? He couldn't strike out across open country with a leg that was rapidly worsening. He would have to follow the railway lines and hope they would lead to a town where he could nick a motor. Buying one was now out of the question. He needed to hang on to his remaining cash as his future became uncertain.

But his escape and a stolen motor would soon be connected. He would have to change his plan, head back to the city and lie low at Radford's. But would he even be able to drive? His right knee hurt more with each step he took. He cursed his bad luck. He had escaped the law for his own body to take him prisoner!

As the moon rose he arrived at a tunnel. He stared at the black gape of its entrance in the moonlight. He sat on a rail for a minute massaging his knee and wondering what he should do. He didn't like the idea of stepping into the tunnel, but he didn't have the luxury of choice.

He set off warily into the tunnel. It was pitch black, and his torch was lost to him in the BMW. He almost turned back. But he had an uncanny sense that it was the wrong thing to do. Whatever it was that lay in wait for him, he felt his future was beyond the far end of the tunnel.

He heard a goods train entering the tunnel behind him. He tried to run, but his knee wouldn't respond. At the last moment he flung himself into a recess in the tunnel wall and watched the monster as it thundered past. Then he dragged himself back to the lines and hobbled resolutely onwards.

* * *

Cath and Angie collected the eggs from their deep litter houses. It was a task they performed every morning after milking their goats in the milking parlour. An intercity train hurtled past on the nearby railway lines.

Cath pulled a resigned face. "That's tomorrow's orders. Might be able to pay the electric bill."

"We'd best get signed up with Phil Yates fast as we can! A fella like that could clear our debts without blinking." Angie, provocative as always, watched her mother's reaction.

"Never!"

In spite of Cath's uncompromising reply, Angie was unconvinced. The lack of eye contact and her mother's conflicted body language told a different story. Angie studied her as they collected the last of the eggs. Cath looked tired and was beginning to lose her vivacity. How long would it be before she simply gave up the struggle?

Where some daughters would have felt like weeping at this sad observation, Angie was filled with outrage. Why should they have to battle so hard just to earn enough to eat and to keep the predators at bay? There was no easy money for them, as they received no farm subsidies. Every penny they earned was the result of hard work.

She watched another intercity express flash past in the opposite direction. Her attitude towards the railway lines had changed. For the first fifteen years of her life her feelings towards them had shifted from fascination to mild irritation. Now they were taking on a more sinister aspect; they were beginning to symbolize the divided state of the nation.

The express trains symbolized the future, which would be reached by speeding indifferently through a hinterland of floundering lives. If you were making it, you were on the train, the suffering world beyond the windows no more than a meaningless blur. If you weren't on the train, you were a mere helpless spectator, sinking in your personal morass, watching the winners hurtle by. The fact that no one on the train, conditioned as they were by the notion of progress, had the remotest idea of where they were heading wouldn't occur to her for a little while longer...

On their way back to the house and the egg packing that occupied every mid-morning, Angie glanced at the two empty farm cottages that stood a mere thirty yards from the railway lines. It had been many years since they had housed farm employees. Her mother had tried to let them, but no one had stayed for long, as families these days preferred central heating, rather than crouching around open fires on winter nights. Holiday lets were out of the question, as the proximity of the railway lines, as well as the unmodernised interiors, had condemned them as a non-starter.

The cottages were beginning to deteriorate like the rest of the buildings on the farm. Angie felt like screaming in frustration. It was a criminal waste that nothing could be done with them. Had expectations changed so much that even the homeless would reject them? But then, the urban poor would never cope in such a basic environment. She and her mother were rapidly descending towards the level of Transylvanian peasants. How long would it be before they only had a horse and cart to rely on?

She pushed her negative thoughts away and began helping her mother, performing the routine tasks she could do with her eyes shut. But she knew this was only blind survival. Life lay in another direction. Not on the fantasy intercity express but in something more creative. It was their debt that was killing life off. Was the second-worst day in her mother's life the day she and Matt took out the loan?

After the egg packing was done, mother and daughter sat on the garden seat by the back door drinking tea and smoking cigarettes, their last remaining indulgence. The May morning was sunny and warm, and they shared the brief pleasure in silence. A flash of light from the top of the nearby sawmill caught their attention. Angie leaped to her feet and bared her breasts.

"Screw you, Charlie Gibb!"

"Angie!" Cath exclaimed in dismay. "Don't go giving him ideas!"

"He wouldn't know what to do with me if he had the chance!" Angie replied with furious contempt.

"Don't give him any encouragement—you never know what might happen!"

"Nothing will happen! He's afraid of females. He's only after our land."

"Are you sure of that?" Cath asked.

"Of course. He's had plenty of chances to grab me when I've been working alone round the farm. He's a voyeur." She laughed. "End of."

Charlie Gibb swung himself down from the loft to the first floor then descended the open wooden stairs to his ground-floor office. The shock of seeing the young girl like that had left him hot and confused. For a minute he didn't know what to do, as a torrent of repressed images cascaded through his mind. He was disturbed by the images, frightened by their power. There was only one safe way to quiet them, and he rushed outside into the bushes.

Returning to his office, he sat at the time-scarred desk that occupied the length of one wall, put his wide floppy hat over his shock of albino hair and adjusted the eye patch that covered his wall eye. He took a file of papers from a drawer and studied the contents, his head turned sideways like a bird. He muttered to himself as he read.

"This'll fix you, Cath Scaife. Then I'll have the pair o' you to myself. I could have been a lawyer. Ain't no one smart as Charlie Gibb!"

He returned the file to the desk then sat back in his chair, smiling to himself. He had gone through the changes he would make when he had control of Cuckoo Nest a thousand times—and what he would do with the two women a thousand times more. He just had to wait until the pressure from Phil Yates got too much for them. And it would; it would wear them down like an illncss. Then he would make his move. He would be Mister Gibb then, not just Charlie as he was now. He'd have respect.

His reverie was interrupted by the ringing of his desk phone. It was an order from a local farmer, one of his many regular customers, for field gates and fencing. "Ayup, Charlie, can thoo cum oot reet away?" Of course he could. Charlie could. But not when he was Mister Gibb. Mister Gibb would have the power to keep folk waiting. He locked the mill, swung his spare frame into his old Land Rover and drove off to the farm to measure up.

* * *

After making a start on spreading horse manure by hand around the fruit bushes in their orchard, Cath and Angie returned to the farmhouse for lunch. It was heavy work without a tractor, and theirs had been refusing to start for the last couple of months.

Angie volunteered to do the cooking, letting her mother rest on the sitting room sofa. She wanted to surprise her with something tasty. The problem was she wasn't much of a cook. Despite countless attempts to turn out something delicious, they invariably ended in disappointment. To make matters worse, her mother always pretended to enjoy them.

Today the result was no different, the best part of their meal being her mother's mug of tea, brewed in the old teapot she had brought with her to her marriage.

"Sorry," Angie said apologetically. "Seems omelettes aren't my thing."

They spent the next hour working in the orchard, then it was time to make up feed supplements for the recently born goat kids.

"These goats are bloody hard work," Angie complained as they crossed the yard. "We'd make more money if we kept cattle."

"Goats use a lot less land," Cath replied. "And the vet bills are nowhere near as high. I like goats. They're characters."

Angie gave up arguing and went into the barn. She was lifting a sack of supplement on to a sack barrow when she caught a movement in her eye corner. She grabbed a pitchfork.

"Come out of there!" she yelled. "Come out, you bloody thief! Mam—get the shotgun!"

Luke emerged from the shadows, limping heavily with a broom as a makeshift crutch. Cath appeared in the barn doorway with the shotgun. The two women advanced on him.

"You're in the wrong spot, fella!" Angie called accusingly. "We shoot chicken thieves round here!"

"What the hell are you doing on our property?" Cath demanded to know.

"I was sleeping," Luke revealed with a smile, making no attempt to advance further. "Guess I'm a late riser."

Angie probed the shadowy corner of the barn with the pitchfork. "Who's hiding back there?"

"A gang o' fat rats," Luke told her with a grin. "Eating your feed and laughing like a den o' thieves."

"What's wrong with the leg?" Cath asked, noting Luke's right foot was raised clear of the ground.

"Squashed by a two-ton cop," he replied, still smiling.

Cath stepped forward aggressively. "On the run, are you, eh? We don't want any criminals here! On your way, fella! Else I'll report you!"

"We get a reward if we turn you in?" Angie asked suddenly.

Luke laughed. "Sure. I'm Lucky Lucan."

He took a small bundle of notes from his inside pocket. He had nothing to lose, so he made his pitch. "Sy Boswell said you might help me. I can pay." He held out the money, riffling the notes.

"With stolen money?" Cath said accusingly. "That's not going to happen!"

He disagreed. "Ain't stolen. I'm owed a lot more'n this." He held out the notes. "Take what you want."

Angie looked interested. Cath, still wary, lowered the shotgun.

9

Five minutes later Luke sat on an old wooden dining chair in the farmhouse kitchen, his jeans on a coat hook and his injured right leg propped on a milking stool. Cath sat on another chair inspecting his swollen knee. Angie perched on the edge of the plain pine table with the shotgun beside her.

Cath prodded Luke's knee and frowned. "The cartilage is all over the place. It'll take a while to get it right."

He grinned. "I've got the rest of my life. Looks like I'm all yours, ladies."

Cath eyed him sternly. "We've naught worth running off with, y'know."

He shrugged. "Who's running?"

"We've a cottage to rent," Angie said suddenly, catching her mother's eye.

Cath was impressed with her daughter's opportunism. "Two hundred a week," she said. "Take it or go on your way."

He thought a moment. Was it worth haggling? Sy's name had got him this far. He decided not to push his luck. And his knee was swollen and painful. "I'll take it," he said with a sense of relief.

He produced a roll of notes, peeled off ten twenties and held them out. Angie reached for them, but Cath beat her to it.

She stood up. "I'll get a bandage for the knee."

Cath began the massage, shaking a few drops of sweet-smelling oil on the swollen area from a small brown bottle, then gently working the oil into the flesh around the knee. After a few minutes' massage she wrapped the knee tightly in the bandage, then she and Angie helped him across the stackyard and past the deep litter houses. He supported his weight on a walking stick that Matt had used when prodding tardy cattle on their way to fresh pasture. The stick was redundant now, as were the cattle, sold off soon after Matt's death.

They arrived at the cottages, but before they went any further Luke stopped them, looking puzzled.

"I dunno if this is, like, normal for you, but I saw we'd gone a very round-about way to get here from the house. Why didn't we come here directly? Why all the dodging round the sheds?"

"We kept behind the farm buildings," Cath explained. "We don't want Charlie seeing you."

Cath's response gave him cause for fresh concern. "Who the hell's Charlie? Is he your fella?"

"Charlie's got nothing to do with us. He's the weirdo in the sawmill." Cath pointed in the direction of the mill, which could not be seen from where they stood. "He spies on us with his telescope."

Angie laughed. "We're the only females in his life!"

He suffered a twinge of anxiety. He didn't want any more confrontations—and certainly not with a gammy leg. "Sawmill Charlie don't own this farm then?"

"No, thank goodness," Cath replied with undisguised relief. "He's too damn near as it is!" She gestured at the cottages. "Which one d'you want?"

He laughed. "I've a choice?"

"They're both pretty much the same, inside and out," Cath told him.

"I'll take the one by the train lines."

An intercity passenger train hurtled past as they were talking. Cath noted his reaction, the energy in his gaze focused on the train.

"I thought you'd have wanted the quieter cottage," she remarked.

"I like movement," he confessed. "Any kind o' travel. It's been in the blood since the day my people arrived in the world of time."

Angie was surprised by his strange reply. She was going to ask where his people lived before they arrived in time, but the opportunity passed as Cath unlocked the cottage door.

He hobbled ahead of them through the ground-floor rooms. He could see at a glance that the house was getting rundown; areas of plaster had become loose and chunks of it had fallen behind the sideboard and sofa, which were the only items of furniture in the sitting room, apart from a couple of scuffed dining chairs and a cheap extendable table.

The kitchen, like the sitting room, was basic, with a deep old-fashioned porcelain sink and an old free-standing Belling cooker fed by bottled gas. Although he had never been a regular house dweller, he could see they would need to spend a fair bit of vongar before they could attract a long-term tenant.

"You're the first to rent the place this year," Cath announced, trying to hide her embarrassment at the neglected state of the place.

He wasn't surprised. He smiled at his companions. "The first, am I? Let you know if the jacuzzi works."

"What d'you expect for two hundred quid—a valet?" Angie quipped.

He knew they were ripping him off, but he was in no position to argue. In spite of his dislike and deep distrust of all gorgios, he felt a rare moment of sympathy for his companions, who were obviously short of money and struggling. But the emotion passed as quickly as it had arrived. They were farmers. If they sold up tomorrow, they would be worth at least double the value of his heist of T'ang horses. Much more if they had a large acreage.

He knew his assessment was accurate because he had been looking at the prices of land for a good few years and had bought small blocks of grazing land and a remote hill farm already. The price he had paid was well below the national average—in some parts of the country the figure had climbed to more than 10K an acre. He had quickly become aware that only top businessmen, some of them billionaires from China and the Middle East, could afford it. Talk about an invasion!

He realised that if you had worked a patch of land all your life it must be hard to part with it. Your own spirit had merged with the soil that you walked on every day. But it also meant you had to care for it because it was an extension of your life. If you didn't care what did that say about yourself? It said you had no respect for life. You were simply into making money.

And what did you do with the money? You could always become a country gent and buy venomous snakes for a laugh, for a bit of Barney Rubble.

Swallowing his sudden anger, he led the way up the steep staircase, using the handrail and the stick to swing himself up three steps at a time. The women behind him shared a look of surprise at his strength and agility.

The two first-floor bedrooms were as sparsely furnished as the ground floor rooms, with inexpensive double beds, chipped wardrobes and rickety bedside tables. To the women's further surprise, he chose the bedroom that overlooked the railway lines. He lay on the bare mattress watching Angie as she knelt in the window seats hanging clean curtains at the two small windows. One of the windows faced the railway, the other the farm buildings. Cath sat on a bentwood chair that needed a coat of dark oak stain.

He frowned at his companions. "I'm trusting you if I tell you my name. I hope you don't use it against me."

"I'm Cath," Cath volunteered, "and the worker in the window is my daughter, Angie."

"I'm Luke."

"How d'you know Sy Boswell?" Cath asked.

"Same clan," he replied. "My purodad—that's my grandfather—married a Boswell. But we'd got Woods and Bucklands and Lees blood before that. How's Sy know you?"

"His sisters come here fruit picking."

"You must be one o' the last," he mused, "giving farm work to gypsies. It's mostly gone to foreign work gangs now."

"I'm old-fashioned, I suppose. I believe in loyalty. Gypsy travellers have done seasonal work at Cuckoo Nest for years." Then she added, after a pause, "I don't think we have a big enough acreage to attract foreign crews."

She stood up as Angie finished the curtains.

"Lie still," she advised. "Keep your weight off the leg."

He looked awkward suddenly. "Y'know, it ain't all that likely, but the gavvers might come looking for me."

He had to warn her, but his words left a tense silence in the room. She stared at him thoughtfully, then seemed to reach a decision.

"The police don't hassle law-abiding farmers."

The look she gave him conveyed the clear implication that she would not give him away. He was impressed. She was a very rare gorgio. A glance of mutual respect passed between them, with an added hint of curiosity on her part.

She turned to leave. "I'll bring some food and bedding later."

He smiled. "I'm your prisoner, doc."

* * *

When they had given the goat kids their extra feed and moved the nanny goats' tethers so they could reach fresh browsing, Cath and Angie returned to the farmhouse. They prepared food for themselves and their new tenant which they would cook when the farm work was done for the day.

Cath looked worried. "Maybe we shouldn't have started this."

"Why not?" Angie objected. "He's got money. We don't."

"He's trouble." Cath realised she was giving voice to feelings she didn't yet fully understand. Powerful emotions were rising up in her that she hadn't experienced for years. She was anxious but oddly elated, which left her feeling confused.

"Can you show me anyone these days who isn't trouble?" Angie replied with unassailable conviction. "The bank's onside when you're making a profit, when you're not they lean on you like you're a problem schoolkid that can be bullied into line. The neighbours are happy to help out, but only with a mind to getting hold of the land if we go under. Elephants have more compassion."

Cath was surprised to hear such cynical thoughts from her daughter. She had obviously been keeping her feelings hidden for some time.

"He's still trouble." He might force me to face myself, she thought. Will I be strong enough?

Angie smiled. "He's good-looking trouble though. Nice change from Charlie Gibb, ain't it?"

"We'd better be watchful," Cath warned. "If Charlie thinks there's something going on he doesn't know about, he's sure to come snooping."

"He's an example of what I just said. The neighbour with a mind only for his own profit. The human race sickens me."

Cath was privately appalled. Her daughter was only sixteen. What would she be like by the time she was thirty? Was there such a thing as a state of innocence these days? Was there just the despair of the wise and oblivion of the rest, with only a howling emptiness between?

"You're too young to be so gloomy, Angie. At least we have each other."

"That's true. We can give each other a big hug while we sink into the abyss."

Charlie crouched in the sawmill loft, scanning the farm through his telescope. He searched the orchard, the area around the deep litter houses, the stackyard. Nothing amiss there.

The lights in the farmhouse kitchen were on, which was normal for late afternoon. But something had changed—he could feel it in the air. The two cottages, was that it? Ah, yes, there were brown curtains in that upstairs room last time he looked—and now they were green. But he hadn't seen anyone going in to change them. He lowered the telescope.

"What are you up to, Cath Scaife?" he muttered. "Who've you got in there?"

He scanned the cottages again, but there was no sign of movement. If there were new tenants in occupation there was no evidence of a vehicle, which was a mystery in itself. No one ever came down to these parts without a vehicle. There was no public transport for five miles—and then only four buses a day. He felt annoyed and frustrated, as if they had deliberately chosen to torment him with some new secret development.

"Gonna keep my eye on you, Cath Scaife," he cried, loud enough to scare a pigeon perched on the end of the roof ridge. "You got something going on you think you can hide from me! But I'll find it out." He descended to his office, his lips drawn tight in vexation. "Ain't no one ever been born that can fool Charlie Gibb!"

* * *

Luke hobbled cautiously from the cottage with the aid of the walking stick, doing his best to keep his weight off his right leg. He had lain on the bed with the idea that he might sleep, but he was unable to relax. The thought occurred to him that he should have a key for the cottage door, and he set off towards the farmhouse to ask for one. He had never bothered about keys before, but with gorgios like Sawmill Charlie around it was best not to take any chances.

Cath and Angie appeared, going into what looked like a tractor shed. He set off to join them. At the same time Charlie approached the farm through the boggy strip of willow wood that lay between Cuckoo Nest and the sawmill. Just in time Luke spotted the tall figure in the eye patch and floppy hat and ducked into a nearby doorway to watch.

Cath and Angie were attempting to start their old Ford tractor.

Angie shook her head. "It's no good. We'll have to get someone out."

Cath sat on a toolbox and lit a cigarette. Angie helped herself from Cath's pack.

"They won't come," Cath said despairingly. "They know we can't pay 'em."

"We should buy a newer one. Why don't you talk to the bank?"

"I can't see the bank being willing to help. I can't repay the loan interest on time as it is."

Charlie appeared in the shed entrance. He paused, ogling the women with his good eye. "Machine trouble, eh?" He emitted his eerie laugh. "You'll be able to afford a new one now."

Cath was taken aback. "What the hell d'you mean, Charlie? D'you know something we don't?"

He made a wild guess, hoping that out of falsehood the truth might emerge. "Sold one o' them cottages, ain't you?"

"What makes you think that?" Angie asked. "Not that it's any of your business."

"New curtains. No vehicles. Reckon someone's paid you a big fat cheque and they'll be moving in the first o' next month."

"What kind of fantasy world do you live in?" Angie asked the albino accusingly.

"We're just decorating the place, Charlie, that's all," Cath said. "Doing a few repairs. Might have a mind to sell once we've finished. But it's not likely to happen till next spring, if ever."

He didn't believe her. No one was going to buy a house stuck between a farmyard and a railway line. She was going to try to let them again, though she wasn't prepared to admit it. Not that she could charge much rent the state they were in. Four hundred a month at most. Had she offered them to a housing association? If she had, she'd have to put central heating in. Townies couldn't cope with open fires.

He decided it was time to make his pitch and to see how she reacted. "If I was a partner here I could fix that tractor. I'd do more'n that. I'd get the bank off your back. You wouldn't need to be letting those cottages. I'd knock 'em down and build new ones away from the lines."

"That's none of your business, Charlie," Cath said firmly, trying to hide her growing anger. The idea of building new cottages had existed from her husband's time. The albino knew she couldn't afford to build them. He was rubbing her nose in her penury.

"I'd make the place pay," Charlie insisted with a crooked grin. "I'd be a good farmer." He waved a sheaf of papers at them. "You sign these and there ain't no more problems. I can service that machine and the pair o' you just as easy."

His eerie laugh seemed suddenly more menacing.

Cath was furious. "No deal, Charlie! Have you got that straight? That's my last word on the matter!"

"Get the hell out o' here!" Angie yelled.

He held on to his anger. He knew he couldn't lose. "You'll rue the day you spoke to me like that, Cath Scaife. You'll be bankrupted within the year. Then you'll come begging—pussy and all!"

He strode out of the shed.

Angie cursed under her breath. "One of these days I'll kill that Charlie Gibb!"

"Not if I kill him first!" Cath hissed through clenched teeth.

Luke watched them thoughtfully from the nearby doorway. He didn't like the look of things on this farm. He hoped his knee would have recovered by the end of the week and he could move on.

10

The Coach and Horses Inn stood to one side of the green in a village a few miles from Birch Hall. The inn dated back to the mid-eighteenth century and had been an important coaching inn on the Great North Road between London and Scotland. In recent years the A1 had been moved a few miles to the east and straightened to speed up the increasing volume of traffic and the inn had lost its primary source of custom. It was frequented now only by locals and was never busy except at weekends.

Early one weekday evening, Sy and his two assistants sat drinking beer at a corner table in the public bar. The room was otherwise empty. George, the barman, emerged from the cellar where he had been changing barrels, just as Phil Yates and Harry

Rooke entered and walked up to the bar. George wondered if they would object to him serving gypsies, an unofficial policy that had become the norm in the few surviving local pubs. But he didn't mind as long as they caused no trouble. He hoped for the best and reached for a glass.

"The usual, Phil?" he asked with a smile.

"Make it a double, George. Get one for yourself. I'm in a good mood." Then, almost as an afterthought: "Orange juice, Harry?"

"Why not?" Harry concurred.

Phil and Harry sat at a table with a view of the village green. Sy, carrying a half-full glass of beer, approached them.

"I'd like a word, Phil," he said quietly.

"I'll give you two," Phil replied with a condescending smile. "For old time's sake."

The two men held each other's gaze, the air between them becoming charged with mutual loathing.

Sy maintained his deadpan expression. "Gypsy traveller was asking 'bout you."

"Oh, yeah?" Phil's features showed complete indifference.

"Yeah," Sy echoed. "A real Rom. Black blood: the *kaulo ratti*. Best horseman I ever seen."

Phil's eyes narrowed. "Mebbe you ain't seen 'em all." He ground the words out as if each syllable was barbed.

Sy took a drink of his beer. The tension between the two men became electric. Harry shifted slightly so his seat was facing the gypsy.

Sy's gaze darkened and seemed to acquire a deeper intensity. "He said he knew all about your T'ang horses."

Phil was visibly shaken by the gypsy's words and unable to hide their impact. "What else did he say?" he managed at last.

"He sent you his regards. For old time's sake."

Phil was rattled. He struggled to regain his composure. "Did this *real Rom* give you his name?"

"He said you'd remember him. Seems he knows you real well."

Still holding Phil's eye Sy raised his glass to take another drink. There was a moment, as the gypsy's eyes hardened, when it seemed he might just as easily have smashed the glass into Phil's face. Before he could make another move, Harry stood up with surprising speed and seized the gypsy's wrist. Sy's two assistants got to their feet, their hands on the knives sheathed on their belts. Phil was on his feet too.

"Game over, sport," Harry growled.

George intervened. "No trouble in the bar! Take it outside please!"

Harry let go of Sy's wrist. Unhurriedly, without any visible sign of emotion, the gypsy took a slow drink of his beer. He still held Phil's eye, ignoring Harry completely. "You wanna cast your mind back a-ways Phil. Mebbe you'll remember him then. He told me he was gonna be looking for you.

Sy finished his drink, placed his empty glass in the middle of Phil's table, then moved to the door with his two assistants.

He turned in the doorway. "Kushti bokt."

The three gypsies left the public bar. As soon as they had gone, Phil's features creased with suppressed emotion. He tossed back his whisky, caught George's eye and raised his glass. The landlord brought him another double.

"Everything okay, Phil?" George asked with a look of concern.

"Everything's fine, George." Phil forced a smile. "It was just a guy who dislikes me. A sad case, really." He laughed to prove it was a matter of no significance. "Resentful of my success, I s'pose."

George returned to the bar, relieved Phil hadn't bawled him out for serving gypsies.

"Someone's been talking," Harry said quietly.

Phil's mobile, lying in front of him on the table, rang twice. He glanced at it. "Guess who?" he replied with undisguised venom.

* * *

Tam's Volvo Estate was parked up next to the Mercedes in the farthest corner of the inn's car park. The dealer was looking forward to getting rid of the T'ang horses and being paid. They had already cost him a beating by Luke and a visit from the police, who had turned his house inside out just for the hell of it, because they couldn't find any evidence to pin the heist on him.

Tam climbed out of the Volvo as Phil and Harry approached. His face bore the marks of Luke's assault.

Tam smiled painfully. "Phil! Harry! Good to see ye."

"Looking well these days, Tam." Harry smiled at Tam's discomfiture.

Tam shook hands with the two men. "It's dangerous times we's living in."

"Weren't they ever?" Phil replied. "Let's see 'em, Tam."

Tam raised the rear door of the Volvo, removed the heavy curtain material that was covering his cargo, and revealed the four crates marked *SCOTTISH RASPBERRIES*. He prized open a crate for Phil's inspection. "Packed with loving care by yours truly." He took the figurine from its box and handed it to Phil.

Phil stared in wonder at his new acquisition, a T'ang Sancai-Glazed terracotta sculpture of a Caparisoned Horse with the horse's head slightly turned and the mouth a little open.

Tam pointed. "See the wee turn o' the head and the open mouth? Collectors would kill for that, ye ken."

"Oh—what a beauty!" Phil exclaimed in delight. "Absolute quality, eh? And what do we get in these sorry modern times? Cheap copies—nothing to compare!" He kissed the figurine and replaced it in its box. "Be perfect in my bedroom, watching over me all night." Phil's chronic insecurity, for the briefest of moments, was banished from his mind. Tam's voice brought it back.

"That wee chappie would be on the market at 190K." Tam gestured at the boxes in the back of the Volvo. "Six-forty in total, as I said it would be. We agreed three-twenty, gents, as I recall." He smiled as ingratiatingly as he could.

His smile was not mirrored by either Phil or Harry.

"Give me your car keys, Tam." Harry demanded icily.

"Eh?" The Scotsman was dumbfounded. He swallowed his rising fear. "What seems to be the problem, gents?"

Harry pocketed Tam's offered keys. Phil pointed a handgun, fitted with a silencer, at the dealer.

"Jesus and Mary save us!" Tam exclaimed.

"They won't," Harry replied laconically.

"But we had a deal!" Tam looked at them imploringly.

Phil stared at the Scotsman in cold fury. "Sure. We *had*. Unload the boxes."

Tam, at gunpoint, took the boxes from the Volvo and put them carefully in the boot of the Mercedes.

"Phil, please..." The dealer was on the point of pleading.

"Shut up!" Phil snapped. "Get in the Merc. We're going for a ride."

* * *

Harry drove slowly through thickly-wooded lanes. Phil, as usual, occupied the passenger's seat. Tam sat apprehensively in the back.

Phil opened his window. "Listen to that birdsong. Springtime in England, or what's left of this sad old country. Magic, 'ey, Tam? I love it. When I was a boy I'd sit on the steps of the waggon and just listen."

Tam, his throat clogged with fear and his mouth dry as a vacuum cleaner's dustbag, was unable to speak. Phil rested his arm on the open window, letting his hair blow freely in the draught.

He suddenly closed the window. "Who d'you tell, Tam?"

Tam's voice was no more than a husky whisper. "No one. I swear it. On my mother's life."

"She died ten years ago, Tam," Harry said stonily.

"Someone knows more'n they should." Phil turned in his seat to glare at the Scotsman. "Someone knows about the T'ang horses, Tam. Someone fucking knows!"

Tam shook his head. "I didna breathe a word." He tried unsuccessfully to lick his dried-out lips with his bone-dry tongue. "I didna. Not even in my sleep. I'd be getting mysel arrested if I had."

The dealer had a point. Phil changed tack.

"Who did the climb, Tam?" Phil asked. "Who got it on TV and all over the goddamn papers?"

Tam tried to swallow. He choked and coughed. Phil waited, drumming his fingers impatiently on the passenger's door.

"Only guy," the dealer began, "only guy who coulda managed it. He got caught...by the fella wi' a shot-gun. But he got away—and he got the horses." He choked again. "He risked his life for 'em, Phil. And he hasna been paid a penny." The implication hung briefly in the air that neither had he.

Phil reached across and took his handgun from the glove compartment. "I asked *who did the climb*?"

"Gyppo guy I use. No one."

Phil plugged Tam in the leg. The Scotsman yelled with shock and pain.

"Name, Tam. Give me his goddamn name!"

"Luke Smith," the dealer confessed.

Phil plugged Tam in his other leg. The Scotsman screamed.

"You fucking stupid bastard!" Phil yelled. "You god-damn idiotic Scotch twat!"

"I did it for ye!" Tam exclaimed with considerable passion. "I risked my life for those horses! I've been loyal to ye all these years! I was there, in the field with ye and your dad, remember? I've been a loyal friend to ye ever since. I did it for ye, Phil! I was gonna top that smartarse gyppo. I swear it! But he jumped me."

"You're a liar," Phil said coldly. "You did the whole fucking thing for money!" He pointed his gun at Tam. "For money, Tam. Simple as that. Lucre's the only loyalty you know."

The Scotsman's face crumpled in terror. "No, Phil. No!"

"Shut up," Phil said quietly. He put his handgun back in the glove compartment. "Just shut up."

They drove on in silence. Despair took hold of Tam's features.

* * *

Ten minutes later, after passing through several miles of arable landscape, the Mercedes pulled on to a dirt track that led through a stand of tall pines. Three figures left the car, Tam climbing unaided from the vehicle and falling face down in the mud.

The figures made their way along the track through the pines, Tam dragging himself painfully forward on his forearms, while Phil and Harry, with studied indifference, ambled slowly along on each side of him.

Phil glanced down at the struggling Scotsman. "Not far now, Tam. Then you can take a long rest."

Tam had stopped pleading. He had stopped talking altogether. Exhausted, sweating with effort and pain, wheezing and gasping for breath, he struggled onwards, like a self-confessed heretic compelled to undergo an intolerable penance.

After a little under half a mile, Phil and Harry stopped at the edge of a steep-sided ravine. There was no sound among the trees except for thin scatterings of birdsong and Tam's wheezing. His efforts had generated copious volumes of mucous and saliva, that streamed from his nose and mouth and dripped from his chin. He lay in the mud and pine needles, catching his breath and blinking the sweat from his eyes. His coat was filthy, his trousers soaked with blood.

"Okay, Tam," Phil's voice cut through the hissing of the gentle breeze in the pines, "you just take it easy now. Lie here as long as you want and marvel at the wonders of nature."

Tam tried to talk. "Phil—"

"Shut up." Phil pressed the silencer of his handgun against the back of Tam's head. "D'you think today's gonna be your *Long Good Friday*? Do you, Tam?"

Tam remained silent, too terrified to say a word.

Phil continued the one-sided conversation. "You know, if I wasn't a reasonable man I'd kill you now and Harry would kick your body over the edge. You'd never be found. But I can see you're the victim of your own stupidity. So I'm prepared to let you live. But only on one condition: you tell me where I can find Luke Smith. You've got till midsummer. If you fail, or if you lie about his whereabouts, you're a dead man walking. Or, in your case, on crutches. Understand me?"

"Okay, Phil," Tam managed. "I'll find him. I promise."

"Not a day later than midsummer. I'll be waiting to hear from you."

Phil and Harry left Tam at the edge of the ravine and walked back through the pines.

"I think we should have a good look in the Volvo," Phil said thoughtfully. "It'll take Tam a while to get back to it."

"What are we looking for?" Harry asked.

"Who knows? Anything we can benefit from. And we may as well leave him his keys. He'll be phoning his lackeys now to get them to take him somewhere to have the bullets removed." Phil laughed. "We don't want him dying of an infection, do we?"

"I thought you'd just pop him and make an end of it," Harry said, sounding as much mystified as disappointed.

"This business isn't over," Phil explained. "As they said somewhere in the movies, he's more use to us alive than dead. And tell Bri and Steve to clean the Merc as soon as we're back. We don't want the blood to get too dry."

They climbed into the Mercedes and drove away through the long shadows cast by the soft May evening's sunlight.

11

Cath and Angie waited until it was too dark for Charlie to spot them in his telescope before setting off across the stackyard to the cottage. Cath had reasoned that if Charlie thought they were giving shelter to a gypsy traveller—and Luke's appearance was a long way from white Anglo-Saxon—they should try to keep his presence secret if they could. Charlie was unpredictable. Who could say what he might do? Start unfounded rumours? Phone the police? The less the albino knew the better.

They arrived at the cottage in the gathering dusk with a tray of food covered by a tea towel and a large bag containing sheets and blankets. They made up the bed while Luke tucked into the food. When they returned to the sitting room they found their tenant wiping his plate clean with a chunk of bread.

"When did you last eat?" Cath asked, amazed he had finished the homemade meat and veg pie so quickly.

He replied with his mouth full of bread. "Sunrise yesterday. But I'm used to it. My people mostly only cook twice a day. When I'm alone on the drom—that's our word for *road*—I never eat till I feel safe. You only want a full stomach when you can relax. When you're travelling you need your wits—you gotta be sharp. There's always gavvers or someone wanting to hassle you."

Cath was intrigued by his talk. "I know it's harder these days for your people to move around the country. Sy's sisters often mention the lack of stopping places."

He seemed eager to elaborate. "Gets worse every year. The spots where we could stop are mostly gone, ploughed up or fenced off. Local folk who knew us are leaving the villages 'cos they can't afford to live in 'em no more. We only get hate from the rich gorgios who take their place. And the farm work's not there no more, 'cept from a few folk such as you. Like I said, there's foreign work gangs now doing what we did, and they work for pennies. We mostly deal in scrap metal and gryes, and a few of us make decent vongar. But a lot of us are stuck on fixed sites and don't move much at all. Some have been forced into houses and have no work and have to live on benefits. It's 'bout as bad as it can get. A lot o' young Roms don't know 'bout life on the drom. They're gypsy travellers who don't travel. There ain't no dromengros, no men o' the road, no more. I try to move around as much as I can—in my motor, o' course, not like the old days with a grye and a wag-gon. A lot o' my people get sick real easy now 'cos the healthy outdoor life they once had has gone."

Cath was moved by his candour and the sadness of his story. She realised that he trusted and respected them. She couldn't exactly say why, but she decided in that moment that, come what may, they must not betray him.

"Is there no way you can give yourselves a future?" she asked, expecting to hear more depressing tales. To her surprise he smiled.

"Some of us are buying up land, usually just rough pasture. But we can put our gryes on it and we can stop on it, 'cos we tell the gavvers and the council guys we're protecting our animals from thieving. We get moved on, but there's always someone else to take our place. Some have built bungalows to get round the no-stopping rules, but it's hard to get permission from the councils." He shrugged. "We've a long way to go."

"Have you bought land?" Cath asked the question with no ulterior motive, but she saw him tighten up. Things were getting too personal. "You don't have to answer that," she added quickly. "I don't want to pry."

He relaxed a little at her words. "It's okay. I've bought a few bits here and there. And I want to buy more. It's just rough land no givengros—that's gorgio farmers—are wanting, so I get it cheaper. If we can keep going like this we might get our folk a circuit. We're nothing if we're not dromengros, and we have to find a way to be dromengros again." He laughed. "Even if we have to travel in our motors and not with Open-lots."

"What about fortune telling?" Angie asked.

He stared at her, assessing the depth of her interest. Angie smiled, holding his gaze. "There's still a bit o' dukkerin," he continued, "but not as much. A lot of our folk are on fixed council sites and don't meet as many gorgios now. But real Roms don't feel free living like that. We need our own land, then we can move about like we used to. Like I said, some of us have made a start on that, but it's slow. A lot o' young Roms would like to help, but they've no vongar. I tell you," he fixed her with a piercing stare, "if there was only us Roms on the earth the place would be like new. Whatever folk who hate us say, it's the gorgios and travelling riff-raff that make all the mess. And look at the spoil heaps and the plastic in the sea. We did none o' that. And we could live with rhinos and elephants—we wouldn't be killing 'em for a bit o' ivory. We only take what we need for the day, like travelling folk have for thousands of years."

Cath was impressed with his passion and sense of purpose. "What's your special skill, if you have one?"

He almost laughed. Cat burglar *extraordinaire* he thought. "I'm good with gryes. I think I'm gonna stick with that." He pulled a sombre face. "I was gonna look at a little farm up in the hills that's for sale." He shrugged. "Guess I didn't make it."

Cath prepared tea with the spare electric kettle and ceramic teapot she had brought from the farmhouse. He had answered a few of her questions, but there were more she needed to ask. Why was he on the run? What had he been doing to have the police chasing him? Was he dangerous? Was he violent? Should she keep Angie away from him?

She gave him a key to the cottage, and they left him drinking his tea. Those questions would have to wait for another day.

* * *

Phil Yates was up at first light as usual. He left Dot sleeping and, in his robe and slippers, padded downstairs through the silent house to his office on the ground floor at the back of the property. It had once been the billiards room, but Phil had got rid of the carpets and the embossed wallpaper, preferring a more clinical, sharp-edged business environment.

He and Harry had carried the crates containing the T'ang horses into the office and locked them in before joining their wives in the dining room for dinner, as he had got used to calling their evening meal. He had wanted to unpack the horses straight after they had eaten but had to delay the longed-for moment due to other business. There were arrangements to make for the race meeting on Saturday and a long call to Clive about the fitness of the three horses he was entering. Then, finally, he had spoken with Detective Inspector Nigel Hirst.

Hirst informed him of the accident and the escape of Luke Smith who, at the time, was being brought in for questioning in relation to the theft of "certain valuable artefacts" and the bizarre death of their owner. "A case of the biter bit if ever there was."

"Is it *the* Luke Smith?" Phil had asked, a sickening feeling in his stomach, expecting the detective to tell him the worst.

"I don't know," Hirst had replied. "I'm doing my best to find out. But there's that many filthy gyppos with the same goddamn surname it's going to take a while. I'll get back to you when I know for certain."

"You're a gambling man, Nige, what are the odds it's him?"

"I'd say fifty-fifty, no more, no less at this stage."

Phil had to make do with that. But his confrontation with Sy Boswell and Tam's revelation had awoken the ghosts of the past and increased his paranoia. He had suffered an unsettled night. But this morning, in the pre-dawn quiet, he felt calm at last as he unlocked the office and took the T'ang horses from their packaging.

There they were: four beauties that stood side by side on his desk, reflecting the first of the daylight coming in through the window that almost seemed to bring them to life. He pulled up a chair and sat for a long time gloating over his possessions. They were his now, four magical beings to place around his property to keep him and his world safe. In the distant past kings and tribal chiefs had used the severed heads of enemies for the task of protection. Magical horses, Phil felt, was a far more civilised way.

But the joyful experience had been marred. He could live with the fact that Tam McBride knew that the horses were in his possession because Tam was too afraid to breathe a word. It was the cat burglar he had used that had ruined the experience—and until Hirst confirmed his identity he could not begin to enjoy his new treasures.

He put the horses back in their crates and almost wept with disappointment and frustration. He had to know who the burglar was. He had to find out so that, if necessary, he could be removed. Only then could he begin fully to appreciate the wonder of his new possessions.

As he locked the office door he realised his hands were shaking. Damn that burglar, he thought. Whoever it was, he had to be got rid of. And soon. He couldn't take any chances.

* * *

Tam McBride was woken by the pain in his knees. The bullets had been removed and he had been bandaged up, but then he had to ask the kindly paramedic if he thought it likely he would ever walk again.

"You need to go to a physio," the paramedic had told him. "I'll give you her phone number. She'll help you off the record, but you'll need a full wallet."

In spite of the pain—or perhaps because of it—Tam was angry. What had been the biggest single heist of his long career, one that would provide the final payment for his retirement to the Mediterranean island of his dreams, had become the worst of all possible nightmares. He was lame and an invalid and was under sentence of death.

He had to find Luke Smith. Then, perhaps, he could persuade Phil Yates to pay him for the T'ang horses. If he failed he would have to flee, his retirement plans unrealized—and just hope Phil wouldn't send a hitman after him. But Phil Yates had a long memory, and he was a man who bore grudges. One day, as he was having breakfast in some rundown eatery in downtown Marseilles, a body could pull up on a motorcycle and pop him as casually as a tin man on a fairground shooting stall.

He had to find Luke Smith. But he couldn't even begin the quest until he was well enough to drive again. And where would he look? He would have to begin by mixing in gypsy traveller circles—but if Luke got to know he was chasing him, his own life would be under threat from any young Rom with a clan reputation to make. And he only had till midsummer, less than five short weeks away.

Tam swallowed two painkillers with a glass of whisky. He cursed his unlucky fate. But he wanted more than anything to retire with dignity. He wanted to live on his chosen sun-drenched island. He didn't want to be looking over his shoulder for the rest of his brief life. He had to find Luke Smith. And there was only one man he could turn to in his plight: his dangerous but principled twin brother, Malcolm.

* * *

An hour after sunrise, Cath, sweating from her labours, stepped out of the Cuckoo Nest pig unit. She took off her face mask and gloves. She could hear Charlie's saw blades already running and guessed he was busy with a big order.

She stared thoughtfully across the yard towards the cottages. If the gypsy traveller was going to be hanging around until his knee was fully mended, she had to get to know him better.

He had not left the key she had given him in the lock, so she used her own. Did he expect her to be bringing him breakfast? If so, he would have to wait. To her surprise she heard footsteps behind her. Turning in the doorway she saw Angie approaching with food on a tray.

"Bacon, eggs and fried bread," her daughter announced with a grin. "A breakfast fit for any traveller."

"That's as far as you go," Cath said with a frown. "I'll take it from here." She cut Angie off before she could object. "You're not to be alone with him till we know more about him. I'd like you to make a start on the milking. I'll join you as soon as I can."

Angie frowned. "When's that?"

"Soon."

"That's not an answer."

"It's the best you're going to get."

Cath took the tray from her scowling daughter and waited to make sure she was heading for the milking parlour, then she entered the cottage. Luke seemed not to have heard their voices. He was sitting in the window seat watching an inter-city train as it hurtled by. Although, as far as she could tell, she had made no sound, he must have sensed her behind him. He turned quickly, moving away from the window, his hand on the knife on his belt.

"Breakfast," she said, smiling. "How's the knee?"

He returned her smile, quite ingenuously, she thought with a sense of relief.

He shrugged. "It woke me in the night, but I got back to sleep."

"You should lie flat as much as you can. It'll heal faster."

He smiled again. "Like I said, I like to see stuff on the move. It gives me good vibes. I just don't see why these trains need to go so fast."

She laughed. "I think it's part of our obsession with conquering time."

She put the tray on the window seat, then went into the kitchen and made tea for them both. When she returned he was already halfway through his meal.

"This food's good! You rear it yourself?" Again the open, uncomplicated smile.

"The eggs and meat are ours. The bread's bought from a local baker."

"You do okay. You got a good life. I live mostly on beer and takeaways." He drained and refilled his mug of tea. "You two lovely ladies on your own?"

His question seemed honest enough. Did he expect an equally frank reply? Was he as genuinely friendly as he appeared, or was he a skilled manipulator? She decided to tell him the truth, hoping she wouldn't live to regret it.

"Matt, my husband, fell off a stack three years back and broke his neck."

"Jesus!" he exclaimed. "But the two of you can still run the place?"

She pulled a face. "It's not been easy."

He topped up his tea, left his empty plate on the window seat and sat opposite her on the other dining chair. He accepted one of her cigarettes and they smoked a while in silence.

"I never buy them myself," he admitted. "I'm not a habit kinda guy. I save every penny so I can buy land. If you've a map of England in your house I can show you the places where I've bought stuff. The more I buy, the better chance my folk will have to find somewhere to stop. The way things are now with pollution and all that, I sometimes think the gorgios are gonna sink under it and die out. But we'll still be here. We have to keep up our travellers' skills or we'll go down with 'em."

He had begun to fascinate her. She realised he was a man with a mission. But there was something else about him, something that troubled her, that was dangerous and not at all idealistic.

He was watching her closely. "You won't be a widow long," he said, looking serious.

She felt the sudden intense charge between them, the power in his observation. "You telling my fortune?"

He shrugged and smiled. The moment passed. "It's just a feeling. But I ain't no good at dukkerin. My dai was, God rest her. Couldn't see her own death though."

They were silent again. She studied him as he drank his tea. Then, in one of her rare flashes of intuition, she realised what was bothering her.

"You're looking for someone, aren't you? You're on the hunt."

A sombre cast came over him. Not just in his eyes and face, but his whole being appeared to darken. Even the part of the room where he sat seemed to lose something of its light, as if he was drawing it into himself to nourish his purpose.

"I'm debt collecting."

He didn't elaborate. She felt his energy suddenly turn against her, gently repelling her. She got up to leave, taking the tray with her.

"I'll be back later. Rest. Keep out of sight."

He watched her as she left the room but said nothing more.

* * *

When the goats had been put out to browse, Cath and Angie returned to the farmhouse. Cath washed up Luke's breakfast things while her daughter peeled potatoes for their evening meal.

"You were ages in the cottage," Angie said accusingly. "I thought you must have moved in with him."

"We were just talking. I thought it was a good idea to try to get to know him. He could be with us for a few days."

"And did you...*get to know him*?"

Cath studied her daughter, picking up a strong impulse of resentment. She chose her words carefully. "Oh, I only broke the ice a little. He was very polite and complimented us on the quality of our food." She thought it wise not to mention that their tenant was on the lookout for someone who owed him money.

"You were a long time breaking the ice. It must have been pretty thick."

Cath found she couldn't keep her perceptions to herself after all; the impressions she had gained during her visit to the cottage had grown stronger as the morning had passed. "I get the strangest feeling about him."

Angie stopped peeling potatoes. "What sort of feeling?" Her tone held hints of alarm and curiosity.

"I don't know... Like it wasn't just chance that brought him here. Like it was..." She searched for the word. "Like it was fate."

Angie turned to face her mother. "What are you trying to say?"

"I'm not sure yet. It just seems we've got caught up in unfinished business."

"What business—his or ours?"

"Both."

12

Phil's office was locked and deserted. The filing cabinets, the wall safe, the large desk with its two laptops and fancy desk lamp and his upholstered office chairs stood in the dusty sunlight that streamed in through the east-facing window. A small dining table and chairs stood to one side of the desk. The fruit boxes containing the T'ang horses were stacked in a corner waiting for their new owner to decide on their future.

Phil and Harry returned from the gallops, went straight into the office and sat at the dining table. Maureen brought them breakfast on the hostess trolley and left without a word, not wishing to encroach on their sombre mood. The two men talked as they ate.

"These T'ang horses... I mean, whose idea was it anyway?" Harry asked in genuine puzzlement, glancing at the boxes in the corner.

"I saw photos of them in an antique collectors' mag," Phil said. "I thought they were beautiful, and I just had to have some for myself, to bring us good luck at the races." He felt it expedient to include Harry, but said nothing about their role as protectors. Harry would have scoffed at that. "I wanted to do a private deal and I asked around. I kept it very hush-hush. It was Tam McBride who located them. He said he could arrange to get them for me."

"He never said anything about them being in a private collection?" Harry asked.

"Not a word. He said it wouldn't be a problem to get hold of some. I thought he was going to buy them. There was no mention of cat burglars and snakes! The first I heard of *that* was on the TV news! He told me what he thought he'd have to pay, and we agreed a price, giving Tam a bit of profit. It wasn't the money that mattered to me, it was the horses and their magical powers."

"Don't you think too many people know too much about these horses already?" Harry looked Phil squarely in the eye. "I mean, it must be common knowledge on the antique collectors' circuit that they were stolen."

"Too many people know for sure." Phil's face clouded. "We're gonna have to reduce their number."

There was a knock at the door. Harry opened to admit Nigel Hirst.

"Nige!" Phil exclaimed. "Good of you to come so fast!" He gestured at the hostess trolley. "Grab yourself some breakfast."

"Don't mind if I do." Hirst helped himself to a generous serving of sausages, eggs and toast.

While Hirst ate breakfast, Phil talked on the phone to Clive Fawcett and Harry checked with Brian, the minder, that he was aware he would be accompanying them to the races on Saturday and that they would be staying overnight.

When Hirst had moved on to his second cup of black coffee, Phil felt he'd had enough hospitality. "He's on the run, this gyppo guy? The one you mentioned on the phone last night?"

Hirst's features were set in their habitual expression of bitter distaste. Some who didn't know him would have simply called it a sneer. "He rolled one of our motors. Two of our best officers are in hospital with burns."

"This gyppo guy did that?" Phil asked in surprise.

It seemed that the truth was painful for Hirst to relate. "Well, no, not exactly. Actually they suffered a blowout on a slimy road. We have an eye witness, a local farmer, who saw it all from his tractor cab." He pulled his bitter face. "He didn't do anything to help though, apart from phoning the emergency services."

Phil wasn't sure if Hirst had expected the farmer to risk life and limb. He had a more important question. "You sure this Luke Smith's the one—you know, from back then?"

"He's the same. Fifteen years older, like us all." He smiled crookedly at Phil. "Fifteen years more dangerous."

Phil was starting to fret. "He's looking for us—I know it! He must have found out what happened. He must have found out about us."

Harry introduced the voice of sanity. "You don't know that, Phil. That gyppo might just want paying for the heist."

Phil seemed unconvinced. "Mebbe... Mebbe not. Do your guys think he was the burglar?"

"I'd say we're ninety-five percent sure," Hirst replied. "He was driving a 4 x 4 BMW registered to a Riley Smith when we picked him up. It was just chance really, and our officers seized the moment. The BMW's completely legit, by the way. We're looking for this Riley guy to bring him in for questioning, but we've had no luck so far. He obviously registered the motor from an address of convenience. It's near impossible to keep tabs on these gyppos. There's still a few of 'em that move easily around the country, in spite of being on our nationwide database. Luke Smith's disappeared, and the BMW's just sitting in our compound. Who knows if anyone will ever claim it? We need to know if this Riley has a father named Ambrose. That'll clinch it. The Luke Smith we picked up will be the burglar and the last man in England you want to meet."

Phil was silent for a while, deep in his thoughts. Hirst helped himself to the last slice of toast while Harry moved to the desk and began work on his laptop. Phil turned to the detective.

"We can't take any chances, Nige. We must assume this guy is the one. We have to act as if he was."

"It was a helluva smash," Hirst remarked. "The gyppo could be hurt. Could be hiding out."

"Find him, Nige," Phil said with cold fury. "Unofficial."

"Sure, Phil. Don't worry. It's a priority."

Phil nodded, seeming reassured.

Hirst stood up to leave. "I'd appreciate some company tonight—if you don't need me." He glanced at Harry.

The big man pondered a moment. "I've a sweet sixteen from Slovakia. Or a fifteen-year-old wild thing just in from Riga." Harry brought up their images on his laptop.

Hirst studied the photos. "Thank heaven for little girls, especially from Eastern Europe! I'll take the Latvian." He moved to the door. "Catch you later."

When Hirst's reassuring presence had gone, Phil's anxiety bubbled over. "For Chrissake, Harry, get rid of those T'ang horses." He gestured at the crates in the corner. "There's no luck left in 'em now. Not since that Smith's touched 'em." He seemed almost at the point of tears. "I can't go near 'em." He thought a moment. "Stick 'em in the old ice house. Do it on your own. It's our secret."

Harry knew arguing was futile. Phil, rightly or wrongly, had decided. "Then what?" he asked, hoping Phil had a plan. His reply proved that he hadn't.

"We'll wait a few years, then sell 'em."

"How? There's not that many about, so every dealer's going to wonder if they're hot. If you can't prove convincing provenance, the only thing you can do is give 'em back to Tam. You haven't paid for 'em, have you? You've nothing to lose."

"Tam might not have much of a future," Phil replied coldly.

"So what d'you want to do with 'em?" Harry was beginning to sound exasperated.

Phil waved his arms impatiently. "Just put 'em on eBay—one at a time! Homeless horse looking for new owner!

Harry laughed. Phil joined in, realizing he had unintentionally said something funny. But all the old fears were crowding in on him, like vengeful spirits risen from their graves.

* * *

Cath filled egg trays. Angie was busy at the cooker, grilling bacon and black pudding, frying eggs and bread.

"I could do with some help here, " Cath said irritably. "You can put that food in the oven to keep warm."

"I'm busy," Angie replied tersely. "It's my turn to take him his breakfast and I want him to enjoy it. I don't want to serve him dried-up eggs and curly bacon. We shouldn't give him food that we wouldn't eat ourselves."

Cath was worried. Her shrewd and cynical daughter was still, in some respects, naive and vulnerable. She didn't want to be an over-protective parent, but there were times when caution was essential. "He's too old for you."

Cath's words invaded Angie's head with the chill of a sudden summer snowstorm. "Who says?" she blurted out without thinking. "He's an interesting guy."

Cath realised her suspicions were confirmed. "Look —just don't!"

Angie turned angrily. "Don't what?"

"You know what I mean. He's a gypsy traveller. He'll move on."

"Not if he falls for me. He'll stay here forever!"

Cath stared at the wise, ridiculous girl who faced her. It was like looking in a mirror, seeing herself at the same age, pregnant by Matt, who was twenty years her senior. But at least Matt was settled on the farm, with no thoughts of going anywhere else. This arrangement had suited Cath—but what experience of the traveller life had Angie ever had? Even if Luke fancied her, he'd see her as an encumbrance. "Be warned. You'll get hurt."

"These things you're saying mean nothing. You're only saying 'em 'cos you're jealous!" Angie hurled the words accusingly at her mother. She hadn't the remotest idea if she believed them herself.

"The crazy things you say! He's nothing to me—or to you. He's only been here five minutes!"

"Time has no meaning if you're in love." Angie left the house defiantly with Luke's breakfast tray.

Cath hadn't the heart or the energy to stop her. She just hoped Luke's distrust of gorgios would prevail. Charlie was still busy with an order, his sawblades had been screaming since six am, so there wasn't much chance of him spying on the farm. But they couldn't go on like this; they had to be sensible and more guarded, or things might spiral beyond control.

* * *

Luke unlocked the door at Angie's knock and let her into the cottage with his breakfast. She set the tray on the dining table and sat opposite while he ate.

"You don't have to watch me, y'know," he began a little testily. "Travellers eat same as other folk. We don't stuff the food in our ears! Why don't you make me some tea?"

"I'm sorry." Angie, shamefaced, went obediently to the kitchen. It had not been an auspicious start.

When she returned with the ceramic teapot, she saw he had almost cleared his plate. She poured tea for them both, hoping he wouldn't consider her action presumptuous.

She couldn't bottle up her curiosity any longer. "Will you tell me about gypsy travellers, Luke?" she asked hopefully.

"What d'you wanna know?"

There was no rebuff. He was smiling. She felt a warm glow of reassurance. "Everything. How long have you all been travelling?"

"Forever. I've been told for at least a thousand years."

He was smiling again. She had chosen a subject he liked to talk about. But she was worried for him. "I read a book a while back that said you might be gonna fade away into history."

He frowned, looking very serious. "Dordi, dordi, no, not at all! We'll be here till the last bit o' freedom's gone. Life ain't worth living then anyway." He stood up and looked out of the window, his gaze far away, as he recalled the fireside tales of his childhood. "Old times were best. What they call *Waggon Time*. Them big Readings and Ledge waggons rolling all over England." He turned to her, his face glowing with enthusiasm, as if he had lived through those years himself. "That was the best time for us! That hundred years from 1850 or so. Hop picking. Pea picking. Stopping where we wanted. The true Rom will never beg. He'll work, harder and longer'n anyone else."

"I wish it was like that now!" Angie exclaimed, caught up in his nostalgic mood.

"Don't we all? Blamed for everything now, ain't we? Missing motor or grye, it's always us. Villages full o' townies, worried 'bout their house prices. Gavvers playing their game, moving us on."

She poured more tea, wanting to stay with him there forever, bathed in the magic of his talk.

He returned to the table and drank his tea. "We still do some o' the fairs in our flash trailers. Still raise gryes on fields we've had to buy. Still keep the mem'ry o' the old ways. But it ain't the same."

"Oh...it's so sad." She felt like crying.

"Yeah. Gorgios done their best to box us in. But there's still plenty of us. Guess there's 'bout five thousand true Roms like me. At any rate, as true as you'll ever get these days. Most Roms have a drop o' gorgio blood in there somewhere."

"Five thousand in England?" she asked.

"Yeah. And in Wales. Real black bloods in Wales. They've lasted better there, 'cos they've not been as pressured."

"You'd fill a little town."

"Don't seem so much when you put it like that. But then, I guess, there's all the rest."

"What rest?"

"We have names for 'em, but they got no names for themselves. We call 'em poshrats—that means half-bloods in Romany—and diddecoys. They got a little bit of the real black blood, but it's gotten watered down. Then there's tinkers—Irish and Scots. They're running the fairgrounds and dealing antiques. And there's English guys who been hawkers, basket weavers, farriers and the like. And poor folk who been mumpers."

"What are mumpers? I've never heard of the word before," she admitted.

"They been round a long while. Almost as long as us. They're beggars mostly. Thieves. They got nothing, no tradition. You call 'em tramps. Some of 'em used to do casual work. But that's all gone now. We used to see 'em on the road. But not anymore. They've either died out or gone into cities."

"So where d'you come from, in the beginning?"

"Us Roms come from India. Way, way back. So long back no one can remember. But I've read 'bout it—I *can* read, y'know—and I've learned. We came out through the deserts and the mountains till we got spread round everywhere. There's a good few of us in America, but I don't know how many are true Roms."

"Why did you leave India?"

"No one can remember. It was mebbe 'cos we were given a bad time, 'cos we were successful. Bit like the Jews. Wherever they stop they make a good go of it. So do we if we've half a chance. So we're both hated."

She hung on his every word. "You know so much. I know nothing. I'm dumb as a clod."

"Don't say that." His voice had the ring of sincerity to it. "Weren't for you there'd be no orchards growing. No meat. No eggs. Nothing. Except what grows wild. If it weren't for farmers, we'd have had no work back in waggon time. But back then most folk were poor. There weren't that much diff'rence between gypsies and settlers. Folk in the villages had no 'lectric and only pumps on the roadside for water. They had no indoor toilets and baths. It's only since gorgios got big ideas 'bout thereselves that they divided thereselves off from us and took away our work."

"You think there's room for us all—the clods and the Roms?" she asked, frightened for a moment by what he might say.

He smiled widely. "Course. If you love this earth you got a place on it. You'll do your best to look after it and still put food in your belly. Trouble is there's too many settlers doing nothing for the earth. Only taking. Things have gotten out o' hand."

She stared at him, entranced. "Will things get worse for you?"

"Yeah. Guess they will. But we gotta raise our spirit again. We gotta fight back."

Tears of pain and hope sprang into her eyes when she heard his words. But she had no idea why.

13
_____

Tam had to admit he'd been lucky. He couldn't drive yet, or walk without the aid of crutches, but he had been assured by the physio he would make a full recovery by the end of the summer. However, if Phil Yates had meant what he said, that was too long for him to wait.

He had to track down Luke Smith without leaving his house. It would have been a comparatively easy task with anyone else, but the fact that the guy was a traveller made his task almost impossible. There was no one reliable he could ask who bridged the gap between the settled world and the travelling community. He knew a couple of dealers who had contacts with the Boswells, but neither of them could be trusted. Information cost money, and he would almost certainly be ripped off.

The police had already questioned him about the theft and the strange death of the antiquities' owner. He had denied any knowledge, and his lameness should have been his complete exoneration. But the detectives wouldn't give up. They had raided his yard and office—and even his house—–but of course had found nothing.

And they hadn't found Luke Smith. At least they had, but he had escaped from custody. Now he could be anywhere, and midsummer was drawing closer. He watched the TV news, but the media's short attention span had moved on to other crimes and criminals.

He struggled on his crutches into his office in the large semi-detached house in the city that he was still sadly compelled to think of as home and his official base. One of his nephews and the young man's girlfriend lived there too, rent free for the not-too-onerous task of looking after him.

It was Dougie and Sheila who had rescued him from the woods and taken him to the doctor and the physio. No one else could be trusted to keep his misadventure to themselves. The arrangement was that Tam had taught the pair all he knew about antiques and the world of covert dealing. In return they kept an eye on his security and were guided through small but significant deals he allowed them to do on their own.

His two sons by Morag, his deceased wife, Murdo and Donald, had made lives of their own in Scotland, the former as a university-based archaeologist, the latter a Gaelic scholar and an emerging authority on Celtic studies. They had distanced themselves at an early age from their father's activities and only met with Tam if he made the journey north at New Year or Burns Night. Dougie was more like Tam, an adventurer who had found his niche in the sometimes-shady world of antiques dealing. Sheila thought of herself as a fellow enthusiast and occasional co-conspirator.

Security at Tam's house was no small matter. He had watched in dismay as the town around him changed over the twenty years he had lived there. The wide, once-quiet tree-lined street at the front of the property had become part of the city's inner ring road, filled with traffic at all hours of the day and night. The noise and the headlights were an irritation but just about tolerable. It was the changes at the rear of the house that depressed and worried him.

The large block of rented sixties tenements that had been due for demolition in the year Tam bought his semi were still there. The development of small brick semis that had been planned as replacement housing had never materialised. Instead, the tenements had remained, becoming more dilapidated as the years passed and inhabited now by drug dealers and their drug-dependent customers.

The place was also becoming a warren of low-level pimps and call girls, with almost nightly incidents of violence. If Tam hadn't got a private space with locked gates and razor wire at the back of his house, he would never have kept his Volvo secure or Dougie's Renault van. As it was, he'd had to install steel security shutters over his ground-floor windows and doors.

The changes had crept up on him, as they do in these situations, a gradual but steady deterioration setting in that reduced the market value of his house and made it almost impossible to get rid of the place. Dougie was buying a flat in a quieter area and didn't need Tam's semi. The only thing Tam could do with it was to rent it out, as had the family next door, but their house had already been sublet to a succession of dealers and pimps.

Tam just had to get away, and he had already made plans to buy a spacious villa on his favourite Mediterranean island. But his move to that property was now on hold because of the nightmare situation surrounding the T'ang horses. The only thing he could do in his distress was to commit himself to extreme action.

It had taken him a few days to decide because he had never asked for a favour of this nature before, but at last he picked up his desk phone to contact the only man he could trust to understand his problems and save his skin, a man who would not expect payment but who was a fanatical believer in justice. He dialled Malcolm's mobile and hoped for the best. The conversation between the brothers went something like this:

"Is that ye, bro?"

"No, ye noddy, it's the Grim Reaper. Who the hell else would ye think would be on this phone?"

"Ha'e ye got some spare time? I've got serious problems here."

"Get a new mobile and ring me back on the second number I gave ye. I'm going to ring off."

The phone went dead. Tam shouted for Dougie to bring him a new mobile from the hidden compartment under his bedroom floor, and the ritual began again.

"Malcolm!"

"O' course. I'm thinking ye must ha'e gotten involved wi' a deal that went bad."

Tam explained the complex saga of the T'ang horses and that the only way he could save himself was to find a gypsy traveller called Luke Smith, who filled his client, Phil Yates, with fear of the devil. But he was knee-capped and housebound and no better than a dead man walking—and on crutches into the bargain.

Malcolm listened without interruption, recording the phone call as he always did with business of this nature. When Tam had finished, he asked him to repeat the names and addresses, where known, of "the major players in the sit-iation," which Tam promptly supplied.

"Okay, bro, ye leave it wi' me." Malcolm rang off. His next move was to buy an Ordnance Survey map of the area in question and study it for an hour, at the same time Googling the wider visual layout of roads, lanes and villages. Then he phoned certain individuals who might need his services to let them know he would be away "visiting a sickly relative" until further notice. Justice for Tam was now his sole priority.

* * *

Cath and Angie worked in the barn, fetching clean straw for the goats' bedding. Angie passed a bale of straw from the stack down to Cath, who speared it on her pitchfork. Then, bending and using the fork as a lever, she hoisted the bale up behind her. She walked off with the bale perfectly balanced, the fork taking the strain, its shaft resting on a sacking pad on her shoulder and her hands gripping the fork handle.

In the absence of a working tractor they had to resort to the old ways of doing things. Although she could still manage it, Cath wondered if she would be quite so willing to work this hard in ten years' time. The farm Land Rover was away for its MOT and would not be back until five pm. Rules! she thought. It was a wonder anyone could do anything!

She returned to the barn for another bale and was about to hoist it up behind her when the sound of a motor came from the yard. "Are we expecting anyone?" she asked.

"Might be the law looking for Luke," Angie replied, suddenly apprehensive. She climbed down from the stack and followed her mother into the yard.

Phil and Harry were getting out of the Mercedes as Cath and Angie emerged from the barn. No one noticed Luke, who watched them from the shadows of the tractor shed.

"What's up now?" Cath asked, trying to suppress her mounting anger and fear.

Phil's manner was brusque to the point of bluntness. "I haven't heard from you, Mrs Scaife. Is there a problem?"

Phil seemed to Cath at that moment to be the personification of everything that was wrong with the world: all its covetousness and callous self-interest summed up in one man. She wondered, if she'd had a gun in her hand, if she would have shot him, her hatred was suddenly so intense.

"No," she replied coldly, "there's no problem."

Harry leaned on the car watching as Phil took a couple of eager steps forward. "You'll sign?

Cath shook her head. "We're still thinking about it. Your offer's with our legal advisers," she lied, playing for time. "They'll be getting back to us."

She sensed that Phil didn't believe her. His manner became more insistent. "You don't seem to understand that I'm doing you a favour. No more money worries. I pay the bank. You keep the farm. I bring in a few horses. We're all winners."

No, you're the winner, Cath thought. A legal share of the farm would accompany the clearing of the debt. It would be the thin end of the wedge. He would want more fields, accommodation for stable lads. He would do up the cottages, erect more buildings, level and resurface the yard. He would remove the orchard, the goats and the pigs, and bring in more horses. And every move he made would involve a greater share of the business until he owned it all. He had done it before with other poor souls; she knew the sad stories.

"I'll let you know," she replied. "Please leave so we can get on with our work. I don't want any more hassle!"

Phil and Harry made no move. Angie surged forward and yelled at them. "You heard her! Piss off!"

Phil wasn't used to being shouted at. He didn't like it one little bit. His face darkened. Harry stopped leaning on the car and stepped forward to join him.

"You'd rather the bank foreclose? They will. Then we'll buy the place for a song and you'll be the poorer."

Cath realised that would be their next move: a deal with the bank. They would force her to sell to avoid legal action. There would be no rival offers. They would get the farm, like they had with Birch Hall, well below its paper value. Should she agree just to get him off her back? She would still be able to buy another house and a small market garden. Before she could calm her whirling thoughts Harry weighed in.

"If we pay off your debts, you'll obviously owe us. No one's denying that. But we can sort this out as generous business partners, or you can fight us, though I can tell you now you'll be wasting your time and the little spare money you might be able to raise. We'll give you forty-eight hours to make up your mind."

Phil and Harry got in the Mercedes and drove away. Angie rounded on Cath in fury. "Why the hell didn't you tell 'em—we don't want 'em here!"

Cath was on the brink of tears. "Don't you start as well! Ain't as simple as you think." She sat down suddenly on a bale of straw. "If he buys our debts it won't be long before he owns the whole farm and kicks us out. That's just the way he is. But I can't pay off the bank and he knows it. I can't win, can I? Whatever I do or don't do, this place is lost!" She got to her feet wearily and set off towards the house. "I've had enough of all of you. I didn't wed Matt to end up like this!"

Angie hurried after her. "Mam? Mam—we can fight this! Talk to me! Please!"

Mother and daughter disappeared into the farmhouse as Luke, deeply preoccupied, stepped from the shadows of the tractor shed. He was about to approach the house but ducked back into the shed as Charlie Gibb appeared in the yard.

Charlie strode to the farmhouse door and hammered on it furiously. There was no response. He rapped impatiently on the kitchen window. "I've seen you with that Phil Yates! He'll have you out! Wanna sign with me!" He battered on the door. "No good hiding in there! Ain't no future without me! If I'm a partner here you'll be safe with me. I'll be a good farmer. I'll be kinder to you than the bank or Phil Yates!" There was still no response. Charlie turned angrily away and set off back towards the sawmill.

The sawmill yard was packed as an agricultural auction mart with tractors, stacks of raw timber, new field gates, cut fence posts, hydraulic log splitters, fork lifts and winches.

Charlie strode through the yard and went into the mill. Luke, still slightly lame, followed him through the boggy willow wood, then into the yard. Charlie seemed to have vanished. Luke entered the main cutting floor of the sawmill. There was nowhere for him to hide, so he abandoned any idea of concealment.

The place seemed completely deserted. Machines, belts, blades and benches all stood idle. The wind whistled through gaps in the brickwork high above his head. Curtains of dust hung in the sunlight. The smell of sawdust reminded him of circuses he had visited as a boy with Ambrose, who had been buying up horses that were past their best for the ring.

The scale of the sawmill was awesome. A vast network of beams and rafters rose above him like the construction scaffolding for a new ocean liner. Flights of open wooden stairs disappeared into the mesh of woodwork above.

Luke wandered around, fascinated. Without warning a gigantic sawblade, inches from his hand, screamed into life. He recoiled in shock and surprise. A moment later a blade behind him started up, with the voice of a shrieking demon. He turned, momentarily confused and vulnerable. More blades sprang into life, as if controlled by a workforce of ghosts. Alarmed, he backed away from the blades and left the mill.

High up in the sawmill loft Charlie keyed codes into his mobile that turned off the sawblades. He clapped his telescope to his good eye. "There's something going on here that I don't like," he muttered. "Something that might be bad for Charlie." He picked up Luke's figure in his telescope as he limped through the stretch of boggy woodland back to Cuckoo Nest. Charlie moaned softly to himself, an eerie chilling wail. "Who is he, eh? What's he doing at Cath Scaife's? She's up to something and I'm gonna find out what. Ain't no one gets one up on Charlie Gibb!"

* * *

As soon as darkness had taken silent possession of the farm, Luke crossed the stackyard and tapped on the window of the farmhouse kitchen.

"I thought it was time we did a bit o' strong rockering," he said with a frown as Cath opened the door. "We need to talk honest and plain. That okay with you?"

She let him into the kitchen before she replied. "I don't see why not." She bolted the door behind him and drew the curtains over the window. "I'll take a look at your knee as well while you're here."

Angie came in from the scullery carrying two plucked chickens. "You can eat here with us tonight. May as well have it while it's hot."

Luke sat, as before, with his foot on a milking stool, while Cath examined his knee.

"It's a lot better. Just don't overdo it." She applied more oil and worked gently on the cartilage, then rebandaged the knee.

He watched her in silence while she worked and while Angie took the legs off the chickens and put them in the oven. When Cath had finished, he looked at her accusingly. "What kind o' crazy place is this? Folk coming and going and yelling all day? I'm s'posed to be resting."

"It's turned into a bit of a war zone, I'm afraid," Cath replied apologetically.

"That Sawmill Charlie—the guy's a total psycho!"

"There's others even worse," Cath replied.

Should she say more? He couldn't possibly have any interest in their problems. In a day or two he might be moving on... She glanced at him. His features framed an unspoken question. She took the plunge:

"We had a visit from a local big shot called Phil Yates." She felt his leg tense under her fingers at her mention of the name.

"What kind o' big shot?" he asked.

She met his gaze. "There's only one kind of big shot, ain't there?"

He laughed. "Guess that's true. What is it with this one?"

"Phil Yates wants to pay off our debts and use the place for his horses. It's his way of getting a stud cheap. That's the way the man is—he wants the place without having to pay the market price for it."

"Why doesn't he just rent the paddocks?" Luke asked. "That way you'd still be the boss."

"Ever tried doing a deal with the devil? Bit by bit, year on year, he'd take the place over. We'd be strangers on our own land. I couldn't bear it. I'd sooner do a deal with Charlie Gibb."

Angie's eyes flashed with fury. "Not while I live here! I don't want Charlie Gibb pawing me about! I'd rather we sold up and left the place."

"We've got to do something," Cath admitted. "The bank could force us out at any time. They say there's no future for this kind of mixed farming, but I don't want to change things—and I don't want to see the place cash cropped so it loses its heart. Matt took out the bank loan the year before he died. It was his dream to start a small riding school. It meant new buildings, improved access and, of course, the horses. Before we could get started he died and a farmer down the road stole the idea. He's got a thriving riding school now, and we've got nothing."

Her revelation set Luke thinking. "Why don't you bring this Phil Yates in as a partner? You got the land, he's got the money. Can't you work something out?"

She shook her head sadly. "He's like a worm in an apple. He eats your world away from the inside. He's poison. No one comes off best with Phil Yates."

As they ate their evening meal, the three of them together around the kitchen table, Luke pondered Cath's words. They confirmed what Sy had told him: Phil Yates was a nasty piece of work, a man who usually got what he wanted and who didn't like losing. That sort looked for their opponents' weaknesses and used them like weapons. Anyone with debts or illegal interests was easy meat, bullied and blackmailed into submission. Under the guise of offering solutions they destroyed lives beyond repair. And Phil Yates owed him. It seemed it might prove tricky to get paid for the T'ang horses after all.

"This Yates guy live round here or a way off?" Luke asked the question as casually as he could. He didn't want them involved with his manhunt.

"He owns a Jacobean mansion called Birch Hall. It's a big house about a mile this side of the motorway," Cath told him. "He's been there a couple of years. Before that he was living near Newmarket, so the gossips say."

He knew the Yates place already. He had driven past its imposing gateposts in the BMW on the day before the car accident and had wondered who it belonged to. "I've dikked the place. It's a fair spread. How come a travelling farrier could get to buy a spot like that?"

"There've been all kinds of rumours," Cath said, "mostly about race fixing. But nothing's ever been proved. Folk say he got Birch Hall cheap because the owner was facing charges of horse doping. How Phil Yates's legal people got him off is a mystery. But they had him in a corner, and he had to sell cheap."

Luke smiled his thanks across the table. There was something unexpectedly complicit in the way Cath smiled back.

He's after Phil Yates, she thought. They were on the same side.

14

Luke did not return to the cottage. He waited until the bedroom lights had gone out in the farmhouse then started Cath's old Land Rover and drove away as quietly as he could. Half an hour later he drove past the entrance to Birch Hall. The minor road that ran past the Hall was quiet. It was not used much since the local road layout had been changed when the route of the motorway had been altered. He pulled the Land Rover into woodland and doused its lights.

It was a night of new moon and starlight. A keen-sighted observer might have spotted Luke's figure flitting across the road into the grounds of the Hall. He kept at a distance from the house, studying the layout of front lawn, gardens and outbuildings. Gradually he drew closer, noting the open curtains on the ground-floor windows and the well-lit interiors. Evidently the occupants felt confident of uninterrupted privacy.

He observed the lights and cameras on the corners of the property and was careful not to get too close. He disappeared into the shadows to the east of the house front to watch a Mercedes pull away from the drive and over the front lawn. The vehicle stopped in rough grass at the edge of woodland on the southern limit of the lawn.

Intrigued by this activity, he circled the lawn and moved closer. The boot of the Mercedes was open, and the large figure of Harry Rooke, , wearing a head torch, was carrying small wooden crates down a flight of steps into what Luke guessed was an old ice house. He wondered at first if the place contained a secret weapons stash, but the crates looked familiar. Harry muttered to himself as he worked, and Luke was able to catch a few angry words:

"This whole damn thing's getting impossible. The man's going to overreach himself and we'll all go down! It's happened to civilisations, and it happens to people who don't learn. All this guilt and paranoia. Can't he just enjoy his life and be satisfied? The sooner he finds that guy the better!"

Two Dobermans had ridden across on the back seat of the Mercedes, and they sniffed around on the grass near the car. As Harry carried the last crate down the steps there was a hint of movement in the bushes at the edge of the woodland. The Dobermans growled. Harry locked the ice house door and hurried up the steps. The dogs whined, sniffing the air. Harry shone his torch at the dogs. "What's up, lads?" The Dobermans began to bark.

The bushes swayed in the gentle night breeze, revealing the merest hint of a figure. The dogs took off after it. Harry jumped in the Mercedes and followed.

The dogs raced across the front lawn and reached the drive by the steps to the main entrance. Harry followed them, sounding his horn. He glimpsed a running figure in his headlights for a split second, then lost it again. He sounded his horn continuously.

Brian and Steve appeared on the front steps. Harry left the Mercedes and ran towards them.

"Intruder!" he yelled. "Follow the dogs!"

The three men ran after the Dobermans.

Luke's fleeing figure raced past shrubberies, ornamental ponds and ranges of outbuildings at the back of the house. Two hundred yards behind the dogs pursued. Security lights came on. Luke's flying shadow played fleetingly across the walls of the out-buildings.

Harry, Brian and Steve took out their handguns and loosed off a few rounds at the shadow. The dogs reached the wall at the northern boundary of the property. They whined and cast around in confusion. The three men caught them up. They burst through an integral door onto a footpath that led to the metalled road. When they followed the dogs to the road they saw a Land Rover speeding away into the distance.

"Get a look at him?" Harry asked.

Brian shook his head. "No way. It was just a shadow."

"It was a gyppo," Steve asserted. "It had to be."

Brian agreed. "No one else moves like that."

"Shit!" Harry cursed under his breath.

They leashed the dogs and walked back towards the house.

"A gyppo?" Harry asked. "You sure?"

"We're positive," Steve replied.

* * *

The panelled drawing room at Birch Hall, which was originally the main hall of the Jacobean house, was illuminated by wall lights and two crystal chandeliers. Minor artists' paintings of horses and idealised rural scenes adorned the walls. The room was comfortably furnished with reproduction sofas and easy chairs. A large TV was fixed to the wall, and a well-stocked bar occupied a corner.

Phil, in a gaudy silk dressing gown, sat watching a DVD of *Eagle's Wing*, one of his favourite westerns. He had watched it a half-dozen times before because he was fascinated by the story of the struggle between two men to own a wonderful horse. Dot, indifferent to horses, was fast asleep on a sofa, her head resting on a pile of plump cushions.

Harry strode in, and Phil hit the pause button. "What's all the racket?" he asked irritably. "I'm trying to watch a goddamn movie!"

"We've had an intruder." Harry thought it expedient not to mention that it was almost certainly a gypsy.

The news carried Phil to his feet. "Oh, yeah?"

"A young guy. Fast."

"Get a good look at him?"

Harry shook his head. "We couldn't get close enough."

"On his own?"

"The dogs didn't find a sign of anyone else."

"Did the cameras show anything?"

"Not much more than a shadow. No clear definition."

"Who's on tonight?" Phil asked.

"Steve."

"Tell him to walk round the grounds and to keep checking the cameras."

"Of course. It's routine." Harry didn't tell Phil that the camera on the southeast corner of the house had picked up a clear image of the intruder, but unfortunately his face had not been visible. If he showed the image to Phil it would result in panic attacks and more paranoia.

He wondered again, as so often before, if acquiring the Hall had been worth it. His business partner had become a classic case of the more you have the more you fear losing. No number of new acquisitions was going to cure him. If anything, they would make things worse.

Phil gestured at Dot. "Take your sister up, Harry. I want to see the end of the movie."

Harry picked Dot up effortlessly and carried her to the door. Dot did not wake up.

"She can't go on like this, Phil. We'll have to get her dried out."

Phil showed signs of impatience. "Okay, Harry. We will."

Harry seemed about to protest, but Phil had already restarted the film. He carried his sister from the room.

An hour later Phil entered his bedroom and stared down at Dot in the bed. She hadn't woken up when he switched on the lights, which was unusual. For a moment he thought she was dead, and he had to lean in close to hear if she was still breathing. Relieved, he took off his dressing gown and got carefully into bed. It would be a massive inconvenience to have her die just now. He settled down and fell asleep quickly but after only a short time began to dream.

He was running across a sepia-toned desert in an eerie half-light. It was a little like the dry Mexican landscape of *Eagle's Wing*. There were a few scattered rocks and stunted trees, but no sign of a dwelling. A figure appeared behind him, hardly more than a shadow, but he knew he was fleeing from it. No matter how fast he ran—and it seemed that he could hear his own laboured breathing—the figure kept pace with him.

He reached a rocky defile but couldn't make out if there was water in the bottom. Should he try to cross? Would he drown? He agonised for what seemed like an age. The shadowy figure was closing in. Before he could make a move, a monstrous horse, like a cross between Eagle's Wing and a hideously distorted T'ang figurine, rose out of the defile and towered over him. The horse shook its head wildly and rolled its eyes. He couldn't get past it. He turned to face the shadowy figure, but it morphed into Tam McBride, who shot him in the legs. In terror and despair he turned back to confront the horse that opened its jaws and swallowed him, head first.

Phil woke up, gripping the edge of his duvet like a lifeline. "Goddamn!" He turned to Dot. She was still asleep. "Dot! Dot!"

She woke up and saw Phil leaning over her. "Jesus Christ—what?"

He seemed about to speak but changed his mind.

"What the hell's going on, Phil?"

"It's nothing. Go back to sleep."

"Damnit, Phil! I need to rest. We've got the races to-morrow, for Chrissake!" She turned away and went back to sleep.

He got out of bed, put on his dressing gown and left the room.

In the bedroom next to Phil's Harry was fast asleep in his made-to-measure super-king-size bed. Maureen lay awake beside him. Her mobile bleeped softly. She checked the message, then got carefully out of bed, put on her robe and stole silently from the room, taking the mobile with her.

As soon as the bedroom door had closed, Harry opened his eyes, sat up and stared at his wife's empty place. He swung his massive frame out of bed and stood undecided in the middle of the room. Then he seized a tin of cotton-wool balls and, with a savage grunt, crushed it in fury. The lid flew off and coloured cotton-wool balls exploded all over the floor. He flung the tin across the room, where it whipped his wedding photo clean off the dressing table. The photo smashed to fragments against the wall.

* * *

At four a.m. precisely, Malcolm McBride scooped up his clothes and left his current female companion sleeping. He propped an already-prepared note against her travel clock on the bedside table: *Business—could be some days—please keep the place as tidy us you found it. I'll be in touch.* He knew she was too much in awe of his reputation to take advantage of his absence.

He padded into the sitting room of his generously proportioned flat in Bethnal Green, dressed quickly and checked his travelling bag to make sure nothing had been forgotten. Then he took the lift to the parking floor. His camouflage gear, sniper's rifle and backpack were already in his car. Five minutes later he was heading north in his beloved X-Type Jag on the three-and-a-half-hour drive to see his wounded brother.

Malcolm was a man of principle and a firm believer that any punishment that might be meted out should be in proportion to the crime. In the London underworld he was respected and feared in equal measure. Nicknamed M, in a serio-comic subversion of the Bond franchise, he was the man who was summoned when the balance of power was threatened by wayward and overweening elements. If you were paid a visit by M, he was usually the last person you would see in this unfortunate world—if you were lucky. Mostly his victims didn't see or hear anything.

It was a welcome change to be driving beyond the M25. Malcolm resolved to do it more often. He wanted to retire. The kind of people he worked for these days were mere shadows compared with an earlier generation of men. Those were real men! Men whose word you could trust, who ran their businesses according to old-fashioned values like respect and fair dealing.

You always knew where you were with men like that. If they requested your expertise it was always well-founded. It was to keep the world in balance. No volcanic eruptions. No collision of tectonic plates. Just business as usual. No mess. Not like the state of things now.

Now it was a free-for-all. A muddle of rival factions. Shifting loyalties. Casual killings. Betrayals as common—and as inevitable—as flies on a corpse. A dismal procession of squalid deaths at the hands of characterless men. As the old order faded away these men pushed themselves forward. Men who sounded—and even looked—like each other. Men with no scruples. With no finer attributes than a shorthorn bull in an art museum. He could no longer work for such vapid brutes, such empty men.

The body who died in his snake house was one of these upstarts. A man who enjoyed inflicting pain whether it was merited or not. He wouldn't be missed. The gap he had left had already been filled by a rival faction. What interested Malcolm was the guy's death, which was appropriate. His mysterious nemesis was someone he would like to meet.

It was clear to Malcolm that Tam had suffered an injustice. After rigorous questioning on the phone, it seemed his brother had acted in good faith and there was no justification for the use of such violence against him. Just because the perpetrators *could* didn't mean they *should*. It was his duty to deliver a timely reminder that unnecessary and self-indulgent actions could lead to unpleasant consequences. The balance of power, however provisional and imperfect, had to be maintained, or the world would spiral into chaos.

* * *

The door handle of Luke's bedroom turned with a squeak and a shadowy figure entered the room. Luke stepped from behind the door and had his knife to the figure's throat before he realised who it was.

"Cath!" he exclaimed in surprise. He released her. "I didn't know who you were in that thing." He smiled at her appearance, dressed in her old raincoat. They stood very close. She seemed embarrassed.

"I came to see my patient. How's the leg?"

He laughed. "It's okay, doc. You've got a gift for heal-ing. Us Roms would be proud o' you. We'd call you a true drabhani."

The charge picked up between them. She slipped off her raincoat, revealing her nakedness. He under-stood the meaning of her smile across the supper table.

He threw back the bed covers. "Best get in. Might catch cold."

They slid under the bedclothes. They embraced, cautiously at first, then more passionately, seizing each other with wild abandonment. After a while they rolled apart and lay still.

"You needed that!" she laughed.

He joined in her laughter. "So did you!"

She rested her head on his shoulder. "I know you took the Land Rover." She was silent a moment. "You're after Phil Yates, aren't you?"

"That bastard owes me!" He made no attempt to modify his anger.

"I get the impression he owes you more than mon-ey," she said thoughtfully.

"There's personal stuff," he admitted.

"Want to tell me about it?"

He looked at her, obviously reluctant to say more. They caressed each other for a while in silence.

"Talk to me," she prompted again. "We might be able to help each other."

He rolled on top of her. "You don't wanna know my problems."

She rolled back on top of him. "Try me."

He laughed. "Okay, doc. You win." He studied her. "We were stopped in a reg'lar atchin tan called Hob Moor. It's down the drom a little way from here. We were poovin the gryes—getting 'em a bit o' free grazing."

The more he talked the more animated he became. She watched him with growing fascination.

He sat up, leaning back with the pillow against the headboard. "There was a trailer fire. My dai—my mother—and my sister died. This gavver, this Hirst, he said my mother'd most likely been drinking. She never touched more'n tea in her whole life! He said she was prob'ly the cause o' the fire, as gypsies were all drunkards! I was in court on that day, but I

195

started shouting at Hirst and calling him a liar, so they threw me out."

"You think Hirst was covering for someone?" she asked.

"I do," he replied vehemently. "But I ain't no proof." He paused a moment, then decided to continue. "I think my dadu and my brother know something 'bout why it happened. But they ain't saying."

"You suspect Phil Yates?"

He shrugged. "Mebbe. I don't know."

"You'll need help if you're going to take on a man like that."

"Is that an offer?"

"It's a promise."

An hour later, in the pale pre-sunrise light, Cath left the cottage as a long goods train trundled south on the up line. As she walked back to the farmhouse, she failed to spot Angie watching from behind the bedroom curtains.

Angie sat at the breakfast table, red-eyed and sullen. Cath hurried into the kitchen, fastening her work shirt. She looked at Angie with concern.

"What's wrong with you?"

Angie glared at her mother. "Predator!"

Cath, shocked, was lost for words.

"I saw you, didn't I? Sneaking back from the cottage!"

Cath's anger was aroused. "I've not been sneaking anywhere!"

"Dad will be turning in his grave!" Angie announced accusingly.

"You won't make me feel guilty, young lady, so you needn't try! I've every right to come and go here as I please!"

Angie wouldn't give up. "You're a thief! I wanted him! And now he's lost to me forever!"

Cath laughed. "Don't be such a drama queen. He's far too old for you."

"And I suppose dad wasn't too old for you? Like you were sixteen and he was thirty-six!"

Cath found herself losing the argument. "I'm only looking after him." She cursed herself for offering such a feeble reply.

"Liar! You were gone ages. You've destroyed us!" Angie left the room, slamming the door behind her.

Cath threw her hands into the air in frustration. "Children!"

15

Brian and Steve exercised the Dobermans, as usual, while their bosses ate breakfast. They followed the usual circuit around the grounds, the rear yard and garage area first, then the ponds and shrubberies at the back of the house, finishing with a stroll around the edges of the front lawn. They performed the routine twice a day, with the exception of any days Phil required them to be with him at race meetings and public events. They watched the dogs closely, looking for any change in behaviour that might indicate the presence of trespassers.

Today was one of those rare occasions. The dogs picked up the scent of the previous night's intruder, and the two men let them sniff around until they eventually lost interest in a trail that was becoming increasingly cold.

"Whoever it was he didn't come back," Brian observed. "He might just have been sussing the place for a break-in. Guess we gave him something to change his mind."

"What else would he have been doing here?" Steve asked, puzzled by his companion's attitude.

Brian shrugged. "No idea. But the fact he was here at all—and it was obviously just one guy on his own—makes me wonder."

Steve found Brian's tone slightly ominous. "Wonder what?"

"I don't know," Brian replied. He shrugged. "It was most like just a one-off."

The two men put any doubts aside and wandered leisurely past the eastern wing of the house and on to the wide front lawn.

"You'll be on your own at the races today then," Steve remarked. "Let's hope there's no trouble."

"Harry and Nige will be there." Brian laughed. "Short of an assassination attempt I should think we'll manage."

"Don't tempt fate," Steve cautioned. "The one time we drop our guard will be the day someone has a go at Phil. The number of enemies he's made, I'm surprised there hasn't been some sort of face-off already."

Brian looked thoughtful. "Are you thinking that gyppo last night might be the start of something?"

Steve shrugged. "I don't know. Could be though. Phil's always been jumpy round gyppos, even if they've only been moving their vanners to one o' their fields and we've had to drive past 'em. He looks around all shifty like and gets real tense, as if someone had put the law on him. Watch him today at the races and you'll see what I mean. There's bound to be a gyppo or two around, 'cos this is one o' the meetings they go to."

"I'll be there one hundred percent," Brian confirmed. "I need this job. If we lost Phil, we might suddenly find we're homeless."

"Don't be so damn gloomy! You've got me worried now," Steve confessed. "There's something in Phil's past," he said thoughtfully, "I mean between him and some gyppo." He looked knowingly at his colleague. "He gets that spooked look that comes over him when gyppos are mentioned. He's had a run in with one for sure."

Brian laughed. "You'd better be on red alert this afternoon then."

Steve shrugged dismissively. "I don't expect any trouble. Not in the daylight. If any trouble comes, I'm pretty sure it'll be at night time. But I'll be watching the cameras. And I'll walk round with the dogs. I need this job as much as you!"

"You really happy here then, Steve?" Brian asked. "I mean *really*? Phil and Harry aren't such likeable guys."

"It's crossed my mind," Steve admitted. "We have to clean up the shit Phil leaves behind him. But it's not much and not often. We get well paid to live in a place we could never afford ourselves. And we can have one o' Harry's girls for free whenever we want one. What could possibly go that wrong it would make it all come to an end?"

Brian pulled a thoughtful face. "I ask myself that same question every day. But it will end, won't it, like the other jobs we've had. Something'll happen. It's just a question of when...and how."

* * *

Cath had finished tethering the goats and feeding the pigs with no help from Angie when she heard

Luke tinkering with her old Citroen Estate that she kept in a lean-to shed near the deep-litter houses. Five minutes later she arrived in the lean-to with two mugs of tea. Angie had still not appeared.

They drank their tea in silence. She noticed he was walking normally and seemed to have no pain. She wondered if he would be moving on. His interest in the Citroen suggested he might be getting restless.

"No one's started this old thing for ages. What makes you think you can?" she asked with a challenging smile.

"She'll go, no problem." He laughed mischievously, revealing a hitherto unknown side of himself. "Just needs the right guy to turn her on!"

She climbed into the Citroen and turned the ignition. It almost started. He made adjustments under the bonnet. "Try again."

It started. He adjusted the timing. She got out, leaving the engine idling.

"You must be the right guy."

He smiled. "Guess I am."

She took his hand. "It's yours whenever you like. It's got three months still left on the road tax. The key for the farm fuel tank is hanging by the kitchen coat rack. Just help yourself."

"Reckon I might."

They embraced, holding each other close for some minutes.

"We do that again if I can get the tractor going?" he asked with his impish grin.

"I think *that* would be a cause for celebration!"

No, she thought. He won't be moving on. He had unfinished business here, business with that devil who lived at Birch Hall.

* * *

The last race of the afternoon had ended. Racegoers thronged the winners' enclosure. Phil, in a loud suit, had Dot in an even more garish outfit hanging on his arm. Harry had Maureen on his. Dot smiled at everyone, whether stranger or acquaintance. Maureen tried to look happy. Brian stood a little behind the foursome, keeping the crowds back and watching for any sign of trouble. Hirst hovered nearby, avoiding the cameras.

Freddie Parfitt, the jockey, sat astride Good Times. Clive Fawcett held the horse's halter, while Phil stroked the animal's head and congratulated its rider.

A young TV interviewer and crew waited for Phil to give them his attention. At a sign from Phil the interviewer spoke to the camera. "Another winner for Lucky Phil Yates. Good Times, at 7 to 2, strolled home by five lengths." He turned to Phil. "What's the secret of your phenomenal run of successes, Mr Yates?"

Phil spoke directly to camera, not even glancing at the interviewer, as if he had taken control of the show. "Guess I have an eye for a promising animal. I've been round horses all my life, my dad before me. You could definitely say horse culture is in my blood."

The TV interviewer picked up on what he thought was a promising line of questioning but had to wait until the camera swung back on to him. "Could you tell us a bit about your father, Mr Yates? Did the knack of picking winners start with him?"

Phil tightened up at the question. Dot realised and looked worried.

"What kind of stupid question's that?" Phil eyed the interviewer as if he was unfit for his job. "We're not here to talk about my dad!"

Dot increased her grip on Phil's arm. He noticed. With a visible effort he regained his composure. The young interviewer looked confused and embarrassed. Phil snatched the microphone from his hand and took over completely.

"First of all, I'd like to thank Clive Fawcett, my trainer. And Freddie Parfitt, my jockey. And, of course, Good Times! What a team!"

Phil beckoned to Clive, who took his place on camera. "Clive Fawcett, ladies and gentlemen—the magician!"

"The real genius is standing here at my side." Clive beamed at Phil. "Mr Phil Yates, today's deserving winner!"

Phil tossed the microphone in the direction of the interviewer and moved on, smiling broadly and shaking hands with his admirers. Brian followed close behind.

Harry had lost touch with Maureen, who had somehow managed to attach herself to Phil's left arm, while Dot still clung to his right. The big man seized the moment and drew Hirst aside.

"Many gyppos on your patch these days, Nige?"

Hirst shrugged. "No more'n usual. They're mostly on council sites. There's a bit of thieving, but what can you expect? Most of 'em's got no work. Why d'you ask?"

"We had one snooping last night."

Hirst saw his chance to wind Harry up. "Could be that Luke Smith."

Harry looked troubled. "Hell do I know? We never got close enough. Anyway, I've no idea what the guy looks like."

Hirst took a copy of Luke's mugshot from his wallet and gave it to Harry. "You do now."

Harry studied the mugshot. "Can I keep this?"

Hirst sniggered. "Put it on Phil's breakfast tray. It'll lighten up his day!"

Hirst's comment reopened a well-worn line of thought in Harry's mind. "Phil still thinks he saw a bloke that night. Some long-haired hippy guy. Makes him more paranoid than ever."

Hirst shrugged. "Fifteen years and he ain't come forward. That guy's a phantom."

"Mebbe so," Harry replied with a frown, "but the bastard's bigger than all of us." He felt a pressing need to move the subject forward. "How's the manhunt?"

"Not a whisker," Hirst admitted. "He's holed up someplace. But he'll come out. And we'll be waiting."

Sy and Luke, in smart farmers' caps and all-weather jackets, watched them from the crowd.

* * *

Charlie, in his floppy hat and eyepatch, crossed the sawmill yard with a determined expression and a chainsaw.

He talked to himself as he walked. "I'd make the place pay. I'd be a good farmer."

He climbed on a tractor, stowing the chainsaw in the cab. Then he hitched up the tractor to a crop-spraying rig. "I know what you're up to, Phil Yates," he cried. "But you ain't gonna beat Charlie Gibb." He drove out of the yard.

An hour earlier Charlie had watched the two women leave on their regular Saturday provisioning trip to the town, the daughter looking unhappy and angry. Of the gyppo he could see no sign. When he arrived in the Cuckoo Nest stackyard he noticed the Citroen Estate was no longer in the lean-to. He wondered if the gyppo was using it. Maybe he'd bought it and moved on. The important thing was he had the place to himself for a few hours.

He sprayed the Cuckoo Nest paddocks with grass killer, up and down, up and down, laughing as he drove. Then he attacked the fence posts with the chainsaw. He didn't cut all the way through, so the fences still stood up. He emitted his eerie high-pitched laugh as he worked.

"Think you can get ahead of me, Phil Yates, eh?" he yelled above the noise of the chainsaw. "Ain't no one smarter'n Charlie Gibb!"

Then he drove back to the sawmill, detached the crop-spraying rig from the tractor and swung himself up to the loft, where he clapped his telescope to his good eye and settled down to watch the farm. Still no sign of the gyppo. He must have bought the Citroen and gone.

* * *

Racegoers packed the bar of the *Winning Post* hotel, which stood across the road from the racecourse entrance. Phil, in jubilant mood, bought drinks for everyone.

"Drink up! Come on, guys—they're on me tonight!"

Dot, already drunk, lurched unsteadily at the bar. Harry spotted her and pushed his way through the crowd.

"Get some coffee," he growled into her ear. "It's a big moment. Don't let us down."

She clung to him for support. "What's Phil so scared of, Harry? He wakes in the night. He's so touchy. What's going on with him? You can tell your little sister."

Harry shrugged. "Search me, sis. I'm only the god-damn teaboy."

He knew if he told her the truth it could be curtains for them all; she would never condone their past violence. Better for her to believe their success was all down to good luck.

Dot persisted. "You're with him all the time. You must know what's bothering him. I just wanna help him."

He was no longer listening. He was watching Maureen and Phil laughing with the drinkers at the bar. He noticed the sudden withdrawal of her fingers from his hand when she realised he was looking.

As Phil raised his glass to the landlord, he saw two smartly-dressed gypsy travellers staring at him from the far end of the bar. He recognised Sy from their encounter at the *Coach and Horses.* He knew Sy was a Boswell, but the other guy was not known to him.

For a moment he wondered—could it be...? They were staring at him intently. He imagined he could feel their eyes boring into his brain! He grabbed Brian's arm and pointed, with the idea of sending his minder to ask them their business. But when he turned back to look, they had gone.

"What's up, boss?" Brian asked.

"Those two gyppos stood at the bar—did you see 'em?"

Brian shook his head, noting Phil's unease and recalling his recent talk on the subject with Steve. "I saw no gyppos, boss."

"If you do see 'em, let me know, right? They ain't having free drinks on me tonight!"

Brian cast a glance around the room, but there was no sign of anyone who looked remotely like a gypsy. "Sure, boss, I'll let you know." Privately he wondered if Phil was seeing things.

When Phil looked again towards the end of the bar, he saw a familiar figure staring back at him. It couldn't be Tam McBride—but yet it was! It was no lookalike, *it was Tam himself*! But it couldn't be possible for Tam to have recovered so quickly, he must have died from his injuries out in the woods – and therefore, Phil realised with a shock, this was his ghost!

Have I gone mad, he thought? Was the past coming back to destroy him? He recalled his recent night-mare—was the spirit of Tam McBride after vengeance? He grabbed Maureen's arm. "See there! There!" He pointed towards the end of the bar. "D'you see that guy with curly grey hair?"

"What, Phil? Who?" Maureen was alarmed by his agitated state.

Phil was still pointing. "There! There!" The conviviality had drained from his face. He looked an-guished, his eyes starting from his head. He turned to the landlord. "That man will not drink at this bar tonight!"

"What man, Phil?" the puzzled landlord asked.

Phil pointed. "That man. That—"

But the figure at the end of the bar had disappeared.

Phil suddenly clutched at his throat and collapsed.

* * *

An hour later the doctor had gone from the master suite at the *Winning Post* and Phil, heavily sedated, was asleep. Dot and Harry sat in armchairs at his bedside. They drank strong coffee.

She stared anxiously at the sleeping figure. "What's happening to him, Harry? Is he really ill? Did he have some kind of attack?"

He winced at her choice of words. He tried to reassure her. "The doctor said nervous exhaustion. Nothing to worry about. It's been one helluva day. Three horses and three wins—it's pretty amazing!"

"Mo said he was waving his arms and talking nonsense. D'you think someone spiked his drink?"

He shook his head. "What would they gain from it? I think he's just stressed. The media's given him a rep it's hard to live up to."

But it was nothing to do with that, Harry knew. Phil had made money too quickly and, some might say, too easily. Like all such insecure folk, Phil thrived on media attention. The real problem was his brother-in-law's ingrained superstitious nature that created monsters from the dark that might rob him of his wealth. The sooner he could rid the world of Luke Smith and Tam McBride the better—and present Phil with their heads on a gilded platter.

"Get some sleep, sis. I'll sit with him a while." He handed her his room key. "Tell Mo to shove up."

When she had gone, he took Luke's mugshot from his pocket and stared at it. He had to make that guy his priority. Unlike Phil, he had no problem eliminating trash. As far as he was concerned, he would be doing the world a favour

16

Cath and Luke dressed in the early daylight that flooded in through the cottage windows. They embraced and kissed.

He studied her. "Y'know, you should grow your hair. You'd look really something with it longer."

"D'you think short hair makes me look butch?" She had never asked the question before and was curious to hear his answer.

"Not one little bit. You're a beautiful rawni. But you'd look even better with it longer." He added, with a touch of pride, " our juvals always keep their hair long."

"I had it long once," she admitted. "I don't think it would suit me so well now."

"Why not? Try it, just for me."

"Mebbe I will."

He caught her look of anxiety. Puzzled, he let the subject lapse.

"You know, I've gypsy traveller blood in me," she confessed with a self-conscious smile. "The Taylors from Cumbria and the Prices from Wales. It's a few generations back. I suppose that makes me a diddekai."

"I knew it!" he exclaimed. "You don't get healing skills like yours in the gorgio world. Least not any more. They had them way back when they were poor like us and lived in the villages, but that's gone long ago. You've kept your skills 'cos you're still out here in touch with the earth." He beamed at her. "How far back did you have the blood?"

"My grandfather was a Price," she admitted. "He married a herbalist called Janet Strange. I feel ashamed for letting the bloodline down."

"Don't! The Stranges have our blood." He laughed. "You're almost a poshrat!"

He grabbed her suddenly and hugged her. "Welcome back!"

She felt a warmth and comfort in his embrace she had never known before, not even with Matt. She found she was holding him tightly, reluctant to let go. Eventually they pulled apart and looked at each other, their eyes filled with mutual approval.

"Fancy bacon and eggs?" she suggested.

He noticed her anxiety had vanished completely. "I'd like just you. In a dish. With cream. I'd lick it all up!"

They laughed. He was pleased to see a subtle hint of modesty at his comment. Juvals, he believed, should never indulge in excessive bawdiness, or they risked making themselves look cheap. It was something he had absorbed from talk between his father and Taiso, when they sat around Taiso's campfire years ago. He had understood it to mean that sexual longing should always be clothed in restraint. Not that he and Cath had shown much of that! But their relationship was a private matter, not on public display.

They went downstairs. As Cath was about to leave, Angie barged in with a breakfast tray.

"Oh—God!" Angie exclaimed at the sight of them.

Cath smiled. "Thanks. You've saved me a job."

Angie flung the tray to the floor. "Get it yourself!" She turned on her heel and fled.

Cath hurried after her. "Angie—wait!"

Luke stared at the mess on the floor. He shrugged. "Room service just ain't what it used to be." He rescued the bacon and fried bread. "Looks like I'm on short rations."

Cath hurried back to the farmhouse expecting to find Angie waiting to confront her, but her daughter was not downstairs. She found her in her bedroom packing a travelling bag. "Angelica—stop this!" she exclaimed.

Angie rounded on her mother in fury. "You stop it! You should put a red light over this farm!"

Cath raised her hand to slap her. She caught herself in time. Mother and daughter stared at each other, both shocked. Angie flung herself on the bed weeping, as Luke appeared in the doorway eating a slice of fried bread.

"What did I do?" he exclaimed in dismay. "I can cook my own breakfast if it would stop a war!"

Cath and Luke sat at the kitchen table poring over an old hardback book on gypsy travellers.

"It's my grandfather's book. I've often looked through it. Its images have haunted me," she admitted. "Now everything's falling into place."

It was true. The deep attraction to gypsy travellers she had felt from an early age. Her decision to have gypsies working on the fruit picking, rather than the local women Matt had always used. She remembered telling Matt she thought they would be more reliable, as the locals only came if they had nothing to do that was better paid. Matt agreed to give them a try as long as she organised it, and it worked out well. The fruit pickers were Woods and Boswells, and she had gotten to know Sy through them. They never let her down.

"They prob'ly knew you had some of the blood," Luke said when she told him her thoughts. "Our juvals—and specially the rawnis—are canny like that."

They looked at the photographs in the book. She was struck by the composure and dignity in the bearing of the elders and the radiant self-confidence of the teenagers and children. She told him her impressions.

"That was waggon time," he said, his voice tinged with sadness. "We all know those days will never come again. Now it's just one big struggle."

"You'd call it the gypsy travellers' Golden Age then?"

He nodded, too moved by the old photographs to say more.

She felt a profound sense of loss stealing over her. It was her peoples' loss, her own loss. In gorgios' terms the modern-day plight of gypsy travellers must have been like the sweeping to power of William the First, called by historians "the Conqueror," and the establishment of the feudal system, the so-called *Norman yoke.* Or the apparently unstoppable enclosure movement that deprived the landless poor of the common land they depended on to eke out a living. The gorgios had paid a high price, but they had survived. But would the gypsies?

They put the book aside, divining each other's feelings that they had seen enough images of waggon time for now. The photographs of healthy gypsy children, of vigorous groups of hop and strawberry pickers, were causing them both too much pain to continue.

"I'm going to try an experiment," she announced suddenly. It was time to face her demons and to tackle an issue that had haunted her for years. His presence gave her the strength that had been lacking for so long.

She spread a large-scale map of the area on the kitchen table, then suspended a pendulum above it. She had seen her mother use the technique from the years they had spent on the dry chalk lands to the east, where water diviners were in demand in the digging of artesian wells.

He watched with intense anticipation. He didn't speak, not wishing to break her concentration. The pendulum swung back and forth for a while as she moved her hand slowly above the map. Then it began to revolve. She took a pencil and marked an X on the map.

"D'you know the spot?" he asked, his voice betraying his feelings. "Will we find evidence there?"

She shrugged. "I don't know. Just bear with me. I'm searching for recent burials. The closest I can get is this field. I'd need a larger-scale map to get more detail, and I haven't got one."

He was beset by a rush of emotion. "What d'you think we'll find?"

"I've no idea. The place isn't named on this map, but locals have always called it Hudson's Field. I s'pose 'cause Abe Hudson owned it for most of his life, back in Victorian times. The field belongs to one of my neighbours, and we're not on very good terms, so I hope he doesn't see us and start shouting."

Angie was still sulking, so Luke helped Cath tether the goats and feed the pigs, then he donned Matt's smart all-weather jacket and best cap as he had at the races because, as they were both aware, he was still a wanted man. Then he joined her in the Land Rover, and she followed a narrow back lane for half a mile until they stopped in the gateway to a small pasture. They set off across the field, Luke carrying a navvy's shovel. An old brick barn stood in the middle of the field. He followed her into the barn. The place was empty. It had an earth floor thinly covered with wisps of old straw.

"If I'm right so far, this is where we'll find something." She quartered the barn until the pendulum responded. "I've done my bit," she smiled. "Now it's your turn."

She held his jacket and cap and he began to dig. A short while later they stood at the edge of a shallow grave. In the grave lay the skeletons of a man and a dog.

"Old Musker and Nip," he announced solemnly. "Evidence at last."

"There's no point going to the police, though, is there?" she cautioned. "We'd have to get past Hirst. Once word of our find gets out, he could still destroy the case. These bones don't put Phil Yates at the scene—or anyone else, come to that. It's a suspicious death, but it just looks like some old mumper and his dog."

"Guess you're right," he admitted. "But at least we've found 'em."

He covered the bones again, leaving a little meat and a generous sprinkling of beer on the grave. "We used always to make gifts to the dead," he explained, "even if they were buried in a Christian churchyard. We'd need one of our old rawnis to lay their spirits to rest. Taiso will know one."

They drove on a little further and turned on to a different lane. She left the Land Rover on the verge and they walked down the lane together. The leaves of the oaks and hawthorns in the hedgerows rustled softly in the breeze.

"I knew there were gypsies in the old stopping place," she explained, "so I drove down on the shortcut we've just used to see if their womenfolk wanted to earn some cash plucking chickens. We used to raise a lot of meat on the farm back then."

"Is this Hob Lane?" he asked with intense interest. "I don't rightly remember the place. I only have mem'ries of the fire."

"This is Hob Lane," she assured him. "I suppose Hob's been down here longer'n anyone."

"Let's hope we can get him on our side!" He smiled, though his manner remained tense with anticipation.

As she talked, he imagined her as a stunningly attractive seventeen-year-old, with a mass of curly black hair. She had left her Land Rover in the fading twilight at the end of the lane, shielded from view by a belt of trees.

"The gypsies were camped in the lane by this little wood." They stood on the verge with the wood behind them. Birdsong drifted down through the trees. "I'm finding it hard to believe that violence could happen in such a tranquil spot," she admitted. "But I know what I saw." She pointed. "I could see the travellers' trailer pulled on just there."

She watched as he walked away from her along the grass verge. The sounds of birdsong and rustling leaves faded away as he heard again the voices from fifteen years ago, voices that he would never forget...

"Riley. Luke. Look after the gryes. And your dadu. They's all we got!"

"Let me come with you!"

"Your job's to take care o' your dai, my girl. She's all we got!"

"We're only gonna nick a bit o' gorgios' grass..."

Luke wept quietly, as the nightmare scene replayed in his mind. After a while he returned to Cath, who was still standing on the verge by the little wood.

"Tell me what happened, Cath. Tell me what you saw." His face was filled with pleading. She took a deep breath.

"Old Musker was putting up his bender just a few yards from where you're standing. I remember I waved to him...and he waved back." She struggled with herself for a moment, as the pain of the memories almost overwhelmed her. "Then they came... suddenly...Phil Yates and Harry Rooke, in Nigel Hirst's car."

He visualised the scene as she described it: Hirst's car skidding to a stop on the loose surface of the lane, Phil and Harry jumping out and racing towards the trailer, Hirst leaning against his car, watching...

"I stepped back quickly into the trees," she said, "because I didn't like what I was seeing, and I didn't want them to spot me."

The horrific scene played out in his mind: Harry shooting Nip, then kicking the dog's body aside, Phil throwing a petrol bomb through the trailer's window, the trailer bursting into flames, his mother and sister trapped inside screaming...

Cath, distressed, struggled with her narrative. Luke watched her intently.

"I couldn't believe how fast the flames took hold of the trailer. And I couldn't help. I couldn't help!" She wept, blurting out the story through her tears. "The big man—I didn't know his name back then—turned on Old Musker, who was just standing there staring at him in horror...then he shot him in the head, and Old Musker fell backwards on top of his bender."

She was having too much difficulty speaking. He took her in his arms and held her close. After a minute she began again.

"Hirst was there with the car. Harry threw Old Musker and the dog in the boot. Phil and Harry got in and Hirst turned the car around." She paused, staring into his eyes. "That's when they saw me."

"They *saw* you?" he exclaimed, dismayed.

"I was caught in the headlights. I'd come out of the wood to try to help...I don't know how...and was on the grass verge...just standing here. They must have seen me, but how clearly I don't know. I expected them to come after me, but they drove off. And I ran away." She began to weep bitterly. "I just ran away!"

"Enough," he said. "Let's get you home."

* * *

Cath sat on Luke's bed in the cottage. They had gone there automatically, keeping away from Angie, who knew nothing about the trailer fire except for a few fragments of local gossip. Luke entered the room with mugs of tea for them both. They drank in silence. When they had finished, she leaned her head against his shoulder.

"Okay now?" he asked, encircling her with his arm.

"I don't know how I drove home," she said, her voice still choked with the horror of her relived experience. "I couldn't stop shaking and crying. I wanted Matt to get the police, but he said, if they sent Hirst, we'd be Phil Yates' enemies. I cut my hair short—the way it is now—in the hope I wouldn't be recognised. We had Angie to think of...she was just a baby. The gypsies who came each year to pick fruit used to talk of the tragedy, but we said nothing. I've been ashamed of our cowardice all these years." She wept again and dabbed her eyes. "I still think one day Phil Yates will make the connection and realise I was the witness. I've been living with the fear of that for fifteen years."

He looked at her earnestly. "Would you tell a court what you've just said to me?"

"Matt's dead. Angie's almost grown up. Yes, I'd do it now, if it'll help you get justice."

They sat in silence for a while. An intercity train hurtled past, heading north on the downline. A few minutes later another shot past on the upline.

"Sitting here watching trains makes me wonder," he said with a puzzled frown, "which of us is smarter. The gorgios going past at a hundred miles an hour, or us sat here going nowhere. We've seen some o' the worst stuff folk can throw at us, but we're still here, and sometimes we can even smile. But we'll never forget what happened and mebbe it's made us wiser. But one thing I do know, in both gorgios' and travellers' worlds, there has to be justice; there has to be a reckoning. If there ain't, the human world's gonna spin out o' kilter, like a chavvy's top on rough ground."

17

Charlie Gibb's home was a converted railway passenger carriage that stood close to the sawmill. It was bought by his grandfather from British Railways in the sixties, when large quantities of old rolling stock were being sold off. It was lifted into place by an enormous crane. Buying the carriage had been cheaper than building a house, and planning permission back then had been straightforward. Ted Gibb had been a local character and got his own way with the planning authority. No doubt because he wasn't an albino, Charlie often thought to himself.

Charlie had not yet been born, but he had seen the photographs his teenage father had taken of the grand arrival of the railway carriage. A business and a home had been provided, which had saved

Charlie from competing in the non-albino world. Gradually Charlie had managed the work with his one good eye and, on his father's death from septicaemia following an accident, had the mill put into his sole ownership.

He was happy there, or as contented as his appearance allowed him to be. But he aspired to more than a life in the mill. He wanted to own land. He craved the respect and social status of a farmer, even if he only ended up with a couple of hundred acres.

An electric cable ran from the mill to the railway carriage. He had no Internet, but he watched his small portable TV for an hour or two most evenings. He had never been able to overcome the stigma of his appearance to allow himself to relax after work in one of the few remaining local pubs. Life had marked him as an outsider.

Charlie, in his eyepatch, was seated in an armchair worn smooth and shiny with years of use. He watched *Crimewatch,* a programme he didn't like to miss, as it was a rare chance to indulge in media therapy. Compared with criminals, he felt he was a vastly superior being. It was the next best feeling to being a farmer. On this particular evening an item gripped his attention and he turned up the volume.

Luke Smith's face filled the screen, accompanied by the presenter's voiceover:

"This is Luke Smith, who escaped from custody while being taken in for questioning concerning the death of a retired businessman."

The camera then focused on the presenter and Nigel Hirst, who sat at a table in the studio. The presenter announced that:

"Detective Inspector Nigel Hirst is leading the manhunt."

The camera zoomed in on Hirst, looking sour and vindictive in his crumpled charcoal-grey suit. Hirst took up the narrative:

"Luke Smith is wanted for questioning in connection with a burglary that took place in the Home Counties on (he gave the date) *in which the unfortunate businessman died* (he gave the man's name). *Smith was apprehended but escaped from custody; in the process he may have been instrumental in causing a serious traffic accident. He is believed to be armed and highly dangerous and should not be approached. He has traveller connections and may be hiding out with a criminal element within the travelling community."*

The camera panned out to reveal the presenter:

"Anyone who knows Luke Smith's whereabouts should ring the incident room..."

Charlie was unable to wait any longer. He turned the TV off, crammed on his floppy hat and went out.

He peered through the uncurtained kitchen window at Cuckoo Nest. Luke and Cath sat at the table deep in conversation. Luke picked up a small object that lay on a tissue in front of him and studied it. He wrapped the object in the tissue and put it in his pocket.

"What are you going to do with it?" Cath asked.

"I've a plan, and I think I can use this," he replied, tapping his pocket. "But it's too much to do on my own. I'll have to make peace with my people."

"Have you fallen out with them?" She didn't expect an answer.

"What happened after that fire... Guess I went a bit wild. They think I'm too much of a chancer."

"Are you?"

He looked at her with the serious expression she associated now with his deepest concerns. "Whatever I've done in the past, it's been either to find out the truth of that fire or to get money to buy land for my people to stop on. I've gotta know we've a future as dromengros, as real travellers. We can't go on being picked on by the likes of Phil Yates and Harry Rooke and an endless line o' gavvers."

"You're a kind of Robin Hood, wouldn't you agree?"

He laughed. "I've read a bit about that mush, but I think it was only a story. The old-time witches us travellers know all call him the Green Man, the spirit o' the wildwood, that's inside all animals and everything in nature. But I've a spotted grye called Prince of Thieves I might race against other travellers one day, so I guess I'm delib'rately making a link with that other Robin Hood, the one in the story books."

Cath listened, fascinated. There was so much depth to this man, so much courage and clear vision. She felt humbled. He had spent his adult years risking his life and his freedom for his people, however unorthodox his choices might have been. She had stayed at home, fretting about being discovered by Phil Yates.

Charlie, outside the window and unable to lipread, whined and moaned with frustration. Should he go to the police and report this felon? But that would set Cath against him. He had seen the object that Luke put in his pocket and it led him to a single conclusion. "Ah, Cath Scaife," he hissed, "you're planning to kill me, ey? Big mistake you're making!" He turned from the window and strode away into the darkness, laughing eerily as he went. "Ain't no one can kill Charlie Gibb!"

* * *

Malcolm McBride noted that his camera was fully charged up. He unplugged it and put it away in his camera bag. He added the bag to the items he was assembling in the kitchen of the cottage he was renting for the summer: walking boots, hooded camouflage jacket, field glasses, a large bag of high-protein snacks, two flasks of Douwe Egberts coffee (his favourite beverage), Ordnance Survey *Explorer* maps, his powerful zoom lens and tripod. Yes, he was ready for an interesting day out. He would not take his sniper's rifle. That could wait for a later occasion.

He put the items in the Jag and set off into the maze of country lanes. Flights to the Med excluded, it had been years since he had ventured further than the M25, and he drank in the rural landscape of the North like an elixir. But he found his critical faculties had also woken up and were keeping disapproving pace with his journey.

There was too much monoculture on these farms, he thought, most of the crops destined for distilleries or cattle feed. An inefficient economy. There were too few hedges and trees, depriving wildlife of places to live. He passed through village after village without any sign of a shop or post office, a school or a pub.

Village England was becoming a dormitory for affluent townies, with little evidence of vibrant communities. Landscape as appendage to life in the city. Or as money-making machines for rich landowners. He felt sad. His years inside the circuit of the M25 had blinded him to the tragedy that was being enacted elsewhere.

He arrived at the entrance to Birch Hall. What egomaniac had created such a pompous gateway? A silver-spoon guy, perhaps. Or some merchant adventurer replacing his half-starved tenants with sheep. Or money from the slave trade, maybe. And now it belonged to some race fixer.

The sight of the Birch Hall gateway made him feel angry. The history of the Big House was far too often a history of major crime, of human rights abuse and, in this case, animal cruelty. But crime didn't always have to go unpunished, to be read about in reappraisals of history. Crime should be punished as soon as it was recognised. The human race no longer had the luxury of time; it couldn't wait for history to catch up.

He had once thought of himself as a bringer of justice, but now, increasingly, as a parasite preying on its hosts. How could he bring justice to a criminal underworld that had forgotten its true meaning, an underworld that had slid into the abyss?

Any day, his paymasters could themselves become the targets, as ruthless new players rose to take control. So it would go on, it seemed: justice fallen victim to the greed and casual violence of a world decaying from the inside out. It was time to retire, to make this his last official contract.

But this job had at least a semblance of the values of the old criminal underworld. A wrong had been committed: an outrageous invasion of a private person's space. A death of one of their own had resulted (even if he despised the man). And the prime mover of these unhappy events was the owner of this ancient pile. Without this player's presence, his brother's suffering would not have occurred. He hoped his final job for the mob would also be the first and last for his wounded brother. It was time for Tam, like himself, to retire and leave the insanity behind.

There was no sign of surveillance cameras on the trees by the gateway—the race fixer obviously felt as secure as a Norman baron in his mediaeval castle. But he was about to change things. He got out of the Jag and took photographs from a variety of angles of the entrance to Birch Hall. Stage One was almost accomplished. He returned to the Jag and drove off to consider Stage Two. Everything in life should have structure.

* * *

The days passed at Birch Hall without any troubling incidents. Phil and Harry decided it was time to pay a belated visit to their private gym in a large ground-floor room at the back of the Hall that had once been the library. Phil, in gaudy gymwear, went straight on to the treadmill. Harry, in shorts and T-shirt, went to the bench. Hirst arrived ten minutes later and perched insouciantly on the exercise bike.

"Have you ever wondered," Hirst began, "that the guy you thought you saw that night might not have been a guy at all?"

Harry stopped pumping iron. Phil slowed the treadmill.

"Well, have you?" Hirst repeated cuttingly, as if he was questioning a suspect.

Phil looked tense. "Go on."

Hirst smiled crookedly. "Might have been a woman."

Phil stopped the treadmill and got off. Harry sat up.

"Wasn't a gyppo woman," Hirst continued, "because they died. It was either a New Age hanger-on or someone local. Who d'you know with long hair from back then?"

Phil scowled. "No one. I looked."

"At the women?" Hirst asked.

Phil's temper flared. "I *looked*!"

Hirst shrugged. "Just a thought."

Steve tapped on the door and entered. "Mail for you, Phil." He handed Phil a medium-sized plain brown envelope, then left quickly before anyone had time to find him extra duties.

Phil looked at the envelope. All it bore was the name *P Yates* followed by a postcode. He tore it open. It contained a photograph of a black hearse entering the gates of Birch Hall. The house could be seen at the end of the drive. "What the hell's this?" He showed it to Harry and Hirst.

"Looks like someone's giving you a warning," Hirst said with a smile. "It ain't a gyppo this time. They don't have the smart software to create something like this."

Harry turned the photograph over. "I guess this guy thinks you owe him."

Phil snatched the photograph from Harry. On the back was printed the bleak message: *300K AND COUNTING.*

Phil roared one single word "Tam!!"

Harry shook his head. "It can't be. Tam could never do this—not in the state we left him in. He'll be living on painkillers for months."

Phil objected. The figure at the *Winning Post* bar flashed into his mind. "It can't be anyone else. He might still be a cripple, but he's paying someone to put the frighteners on. Whoever took this photo *was here*!"

Harry and Hirst looked at each other. "You're right." Hirst sniggered. "Maybe next time he'll send you a pic with a hearse *leaving* Birch Hall, with your good self laid in an open coffin! You could frame that one!"

"Fuck off, Nige!" Phil retorted scornfully.

Hirst got off the bike. "I'll leave you to figure it out." He moved to the door. "Catch you later."

"Mebbe we should have got rid of Tam while we had our best chance," Phil gave voice to his fears.

"It's only a pic, Phil. What more can he do? We're as safe here as Churchill in his War Room!" Harry put the photograph back in its envelope. "If it'll make you feel better, I can pay Tam a visit."

Phil shook his head. "You're right, Harry. It's only a photo. The clown's just trying to punch above his weight. Let's forget him." He paused, frowning thoughtfully. "Mebbe Nige has a point though—we didn't look hard enough for that witness."

Harry disagreed. "Nige is just winding you up—you know what he's like. No witness, no case—and it's a cold case now anyway. Very few are revisited."

Phil stared from the window, which looked out on to a wide paved courtyard and the range of garages that had once housed Broughams and Landaus. "We'd lose all this if the truth came out. This beautiful place. This piece of old England. Don't you care? You're tied into it as tight as me."

Don't remind me, Harry thought. But *that* can be changed. Before he could think of a suitable protest, Steve stuck his head around the door again.

"Phil, Charlie Gibb to see you."

Phil scowled. "I thought that weirdo might turn up."

Phil, in a purple tracksuit with a towel draped around his neck, sat at his office desk. Charlie, in his eyepatch, hat and work clothes, sat opposite. Harry, in T-shirt and joggers, stood watchfully by the door.

"Got a problem, Charlie?" Phil asked, jutting his chin out aggressively.

"I got a claim on Cuckoo Nest," Charlie stated firmly. "Cath Scaife and me gonna be partners. That's agreed. Ain't no competition."

Phil was surprised and disappointed that the albino showed no sign that he was intimidated by the setting, by the obvious trappings of wealth and power. He leaned back in his chair and studied Charlie with a smile. "Is that so?"

"I'm gonna pay off her debt," Charlie announced. "That's what's gonna happen."

Phil suppressed his irritation. Why was he even talking to this idiot? His mind beat an insistent tattoo: *Get rid—Get rid—Get rid.* "Too late, Charlie. She's signing with me. I made her an offer she can't refuse."

He turned away on his executive's swivel chair and looked out of the window in order to demonstrate his indifference to Charlie's case. But he was painfully aware that his deal hadn't been finalised.

Was it possible this weirdo could get in ahead? He turned back to his visitor.

"Tell you what, Charlie. You work for me. I have the paddocks and cottages. You have half the profit from the crops. All winners, yeah?"

Charlie's good eye narrowed cunningly. "Sure you want them paddocks?"

Phil smiled patronisingly. "What are you trying to say, Charlie?"

"Paddocks ain't no good."

"They were okay when I last saw 'em."

"Take another look," Charlie hissed.

He stood up to leave. Harry, at the last moment, let him pass.

"Hell's he on about?" Phil asked as the door closed behind Charlie.

Harry shrugged. "Guy's crazy, ain't he? Talks rubbish. It's a wonder he's able to run that sawmill."

"Mebbe he's smarter than folk think. He could know something about Cath Scaife and be blackmailing her."

"Like what?"

Phil shrugged. "Hell do I know? Some dodgy busi-ness deal, most like. Cash sales that were un-recorded. Diseased stock that was illegally buried. Mebbe they have cocaine orgies down there!"

"I think he's just bluffing," Harry said dismissively. "The guy's a fantasist."

Before Phil could reply his mobile rang. "Nige—what?" He listened for a full minute, then turned to Harry. "Nige said some delivery guy he knows saw a gyppo down by Cuckoo Nest. Sounds like our man." His mood changed completely. "*That's* what Charlie Gibb has on Cath Scaife—harbouring felons! Harry, let's spoil their day!"

18

After a leisurely bath, Luke busied himself in the cottage bedroom packing a travelling bag he had borrowed from Cath.

Angie burst in. She looked at the scene in disbelief. "You can't leave—you've only just got here!"

"Important business trip," he replied without elaboration.

"Are you going robbing?" she asked eagerly. "Can I come?"

He shook his head. "I'm finished with all that. I'm gonna see my dadu. No gorgios allowed." He smiled. "Specially not pretty ones."

He picked up his bag and moved to the door. She grabbed his arm.

"I want to be with you, Luke!" she blurted out. "I need you!"

"Well, you can't have me," he replied sternly.

"Why not? We'd make a great couple."

"I'm spoke for."

"Mam's too old for you," she said resentfully.

"You're far too young." He kissed her tenderly on the forehead. "But I still like you a lot."

"Do you, Luke?" She was filled with a flood of warmth and sexual excitation.

"You're the second-best farmer in the world!"

She looked disappointed. "Only second?"

He gave her a hug. "Take care of the farm, Angie. I'll be back soon as I can. Ask Cath about your gypsy connections." A moment later he had gone. She sank down on the bed, smiling wistfully.

He sat in the Citroen Estate in the stackyard. Cath leaned in at the window.

"Keep out of bother, Luke. You've got half the known world after you!"

He laughed. "They won't find me."

They kissed. He pulled out of the farm gate and drove away. The receding sound of the Citroen's engine was blotted out as an intercity train sped past. When the train had gone, the sound of the Citroen could no longer be heard.

A feeling of emptiness enveloped her. Would the police catch him, she wondered? Would she ever see him again? In spite of their feelings for each other, the very nature of the modern world could throw up a new set of obstacles to keep them apart. As well as arrest and detention, there was the chaos of the beleaguered gypsy world, where any number of problems could demand his involvement and delay him.

She did her best to suppress these negative thoughts. Of course he would come back. They had Phil Yates to deal with. She had to help Luke to get justice. And they were linked by blood. That was a truth no problems were big enough to destroy.

* * *

The Mercedes sped through the country lanes, Harry at the wheel and Phil beside him. Brian and Steve sat on the back seat. Hirst followed in his unmarked police car.

Cath had only just gone back into the house when the Mercedes swept into the stackyard. Hirst parked in the gateway, blocking the exit.

Phil, Harry, Brian and Steve approached the farmhouse. Cath came out again, grim-faced.

"This is harassment!" she shouted. "Get off my land or I'll call the police!"

"Be my guest," Harry replied with a humourless smile as Hirst strolled into the stackyard. "You're not as important as you like to think you are. Today we have a warrant to search the property."

Hirst joined them and produced the search warrant. "Catherine Scaife, we have reason to believe you may be harbouring an escaped felon."

"What nonsense is this?" she replied angrily. "I'm harbouring no one!"

Hirst ignored her. He turned to Brian and Steve. "Take a look around the house, lads. Shoot on sight if you see him. We'll split up and search the buildings."

"Where are the other police officers?" Cath demanded to know. "This search is illegal!"

"Shut it, mouthy bitch!" Steve snarled. He slapped her hard across the face and she fell awkwardly, unable to prevent the back of her head from hitting the yardstones.

Angie, returning from the cottage, grabbed a yard broom and attacked Steve. "Leave her alone, you fucking thug!"

Brian clipped her on the jaw with a nicely timed right-hand jab. She sprawled on the yard and lay still.

Phil was in his element, dealing out orders like a rigged deck of cards. "Watch over 'em, Steve. Bat 'em again if you need to. We'll take a look round the farmyard. Bri, do the house."

Brian took a handgun from his belt and entered the farmhouse, while Steve stood over Cath and Angie. Harry and Hirst headed for the buildings. Phil set off to investigate the paddocks.

As Harry and Hirst, handguns drawn, checked the barn, Angie dragged herself to her feet. Cath still lay where she had fallen.

"What the hell have you done to my mam?" Angie yelled. She made to grab the yard broom again, but a blow from Steve sent her backwards against the garden seat. Her nose began bleeding, and she spat blood from biting her tongue.

"Shut up and stop there!" Steve snarled. He slapped her across the side of her face, a blow that set her ear ringing.

Cath came to and sat up. She stared at Angie and then at the minder. "What have you—?" Before she could finish her question, Steve slapped her again.

"Sit next to your brat and shut up! If you move, you'll get this." He produced a knuckleduster from his pocket. He had no intention of using it, as it would leave obvious signs of blows, but it had the effect of silencing the two women.

When Phil arrived in the first paddock his smile of happy anticipation turned to furious horror at the sight of the grass, which was brown and withered. "Charlie fucking Gibb!" he exploded. He kicked the nearest fence post in outrage. The entire structure collapsed, right around the field, like a row of dominoes. Phil stared aghast. "CHARLIEEE!!!"

High up in the sawmill loft Charlie watched events at Cuckoo Nest through his telescope. The entire roof void of the mill rang to his wild laughter. "Serve you right, Phil Yates!" he yelled. "And there's more where that came from! Ever fancied getting a shave with a chainsaw, eh?" He laughed again. "Ain't no one smarter'n Charlie Gibb!"

Back at the farm, Harry and Hirst, having found no sign of their quarry in the buildings, approached the lineside cottage. The locked door flew open with one well-aimed kick from Harry.

Hirst glanced in the kitchen and sitting room, then joined Harry upstairs. He pulled a sour face, prodding Luke's heap of washing with the toe of his shoe. "He's been here. I can smell a dirty gyppo anywhere."

"We gonna wait?" Harry asked. "We'll box him in with our motors by the farm gate."

"I can't." Hirst looked apologetic. "I've a meeting with the Super in an hour."

The two men put their guns away.

"Next time we bring the dogs," Harry said decisively.

Hirst drove away to keep his appointment. Cath and Angie still sat side by side on the garden seat, with the addition that Steve had bound their wrists with gaffer tape. Phil, Harry and Brian joined him. Harry shook his head at Steve's enquiring glance.

Harry ordered the women to be unbound and to stand up. He towered over them threateningly. "That gyppo—where the hell's he gone? Be smart now. No lies."

"He's a traveller," Cath replied huskily. "He worked a while and then moved on. It's what they do. You know that."

"Moved on where?" Phil asked sternly.

"How should I know? They don't tell us gorgios anything." She could always pull that one now, she thought.

"Travellers work for you a lot, do they?" Phil asked with quiet menace. He stared at Cath intently, unnerving her.

"What if they do?"

"Soft spot for 'em, ain'tcha?" Phil persisted.

"They're just people. They work hard. They don't cause me any trouble." She left the implication hanging in the air.

"Lie for 'em, would you? Cover up for 'em?"

Phil's eyes bored into her. She grew increasingly uneasy.

"Look, I hardly know these people. They just come here to work in the orchard. That's all."

Phil turned away with a knowing look. "Okay, that's it for now. Let's go." The four men got into the Mercedes and drove out of the stackyard.

Cath, fearful, watched them leave. Angie helped her to shuffle slowly back into the house.

The four men in the Mercedes were silent for some minutes, thinking about the recent events.

"That was a goddamn waste of time," Harry said gloomily. "What's happened to the paddocks?"

"To hell with the paddocks!" Phil snarled. He was silent for a moment. "Harry, I know now. It was her."

Malcolm had watched the Mercedes leave Birch Hall with the four men. A short while later the two women drove off in a Range Rover, probably to the increasingly distant shops. He had observed that chauffeuring the women was one of the minder's tasks—but not today. The men had more pressing business by the obvious haste with which they had driven away.

He put his field glasses in his backpack and took out his camera and zoom lens, fixing them to the tripod that was already set up. He took a dozen photographs of the main housefront, closing in a little with each exposure until the final photograph showed only the main steps and entrance. Then he put the camera and zoom lens away and took his sniper's rifle from its case.

The rifle was a Dragunov SVU-A that he had used for long-distance work for the last five years. Although it wasn't the lightest sniper's rifle on the market, he found its accuracy at distances of over half a mile to be impressive. He estimated that from where he stood to the main entrance of the house was no more than six hundred yards, well within the Dragunov's capabilities.

The ammunition he was about to use was a special kind of dum-dum bullet that he had obtained from a longstanding contact. The bullets were designed to cause maximum damage on impact. He had already decided on his targets from his survey with the field glasses.

The conditions were perfect, with no wind and a uniform layer of altostratus at twenty thousand feet. He adjusted the bipod and PSO-1 scope and swept the housefront a couple of times before he was satisfied that both he and his rifle were as one.

He proceeded systematically to destroy the heads and raised arms of the statuary that stood on the front terrace: fifteen shots, thus using only half of his thirty-round magazine. He surveyed the damage in his field glasses and felt pleased. The occupants of the house would realise that he could pick them off with ease. He looked forward to seeing their reaction.

He had set up two concealed cameras in the trees with a clear view of the front of the house, one camera for daylight and one for night vision. He controlled them from his laptop. He hoped for a bit of amusing viewing when he got back to his cottage.

He packed up his gear and returned to the Jag, which was hidden among bushes fifty yards from the road. He knew the vehicle would be safe, as it wasn't keepered woodland; there were no signs of feeding stations for pheasants or other game. Phil Yates owned the adjoining timber but did not indulge in rough shooting. Perhaps the man had a soft spot for wildlife.

He returned to his cottage and spent some time making adjustments to his photographs. Then he drove five miles to post the second of his brown envelopes in a village with a bright red post box but no sign of a post office. Stage Two was complete. The shape of Stage Three would depend on his target's reaction.

* * *

When Phil arrived back at Birch Hall he thought his heart would explode from the sense of outrage that gripped him. This guy, whoever he was, was not going to stop. He found Dot staring glumly at the damage. She was not the hysterical type, which was a relief. Maureen, who was given to fits of excitement, was nowhere to be seen.

"Where's Mo?" He hoped she hadn't fled in a state of terror.

"Hiding under the bed, whaddya think?" Dot replied, without a change of expression. She added, as an afterthought, "or she might've run away to Tenerife with the postman—or anyone who seems remotely like a human being."

Harry was already scanning the woods in his field glasses. "This guy knows what he's doing," he said thoughtfully. "He must have a helluva rifle. Dumdums over this distance are notoriously inaccurate. But he wants money, not dead bodies. You'll have to offer to cut a deal. We don't know who he is or where he's based. All we think we know is he's working for Tam. You'll have to put a white flag or some such out front. He'll be in touch for a meeting. That's when we'll get him."

Harry's cool-headed advice, as so often, quietened Phil down. He took control immediately, addressing

Brian and Steve.

"Okay, guys, get the dogs and take a good look round. Start with the woodland opposite. Anything that isn't where it should be, you let us know. Then clean up the mess out here best you can." He was still coldly furious but calm. There was nothing else he could do. They'd had tough situations before, but they'd always come through as winners.

He was already thinking of the trap they would set. He knew the location he would choose. But would the shooter agree? Could they tempt him out of his comfort zone? Or would he start picking them off one by one until they gave in? But that kind of violence only happened in the movies.

They could simply conceal a tracker among the money, and Nige could haul him in with Bri and Steve in police uniforms. A quiet arrest and a body disappeared in a moortop quagmire.

But what if there were two or more of them—could his guys handle a firefight? Would it be easier just to pay up and have done with it? The idea upset him. He was Phil Yates—and folk always did things his way!

No, he was not going to give in. He felt sure the shooter was a lone gun. If he wanted his money, he'd have to come and get it.

19

Luke drove south for eighty miles, using A roads rather than the motorway. If by some stroke of bad luck he was spotted, a motorway was one of the worst places in the world to find yourself trapped on. He located the old brickworks in the gathering dusk. Leaving the Citroen behind a broken-down wall, he made his way on foot through the derelict site looking out for gypsy patrins.

The old brickworks covered a large area, too far from big towns and main roads to be an attractive proposition for housing. Ruined buildings were dotted about among heaps of spoil, rusting machinery and expanses of puddles. A feral tomcat hissed at him from the gaping entrance of a broken drain. He mimicked the call of an interested female and the animal cautiously approached him, allowing him to stroke the sensitive areas behind its ears. One wild spirit recognising another.

He noticed a big Datsun pickup parked discreetly behind what had once been an office block and workers' canteen. Near the pickup was an arrangement of broken bricks in the rough form of an arrow. He followed the direction indicated by the patrin until he caught a fleeting impression of Riley's shadowy figure moving ahead of him. He followed the figure through the gathering darkness.

Ambrose and Riley were seated on old pallets by a small fire shielded by the walls of a roofless building. The two men got to their feet as he approached them.

"Good to see you, son." Ambrose embraced him.

Riley grasped Luke's hand. "This had better be good. It's taken us half the day to shake off the law. And it's all 'cos o' you. You got every gavver in the whole of England dikkerin for you."

Luke smiled. "Greetings to you too, bro. Still happy in your life, eh?"

The three gypsy travellers settled themselves around the fire.

"What is it you want us to know?" Ambrose asked.

"I've found out who burned our trailer," Luke began. "Got evidence that'll send 'em down. A witness, too, if needed."

Covert glances passed between Ambrose and Riley. The latter stood up, furious.

"The hell you have! How many times have we told you it was an accident! Why do you have to invent some new madness? Just let it go!"

"Be silent, Riley," Ambrose commanded. "Let Luke finish."

Riley resumed his seat. He glowered at his brother.

Luke continued. "Phil Yates, Harry Rooke and that bent gavver, Hirst. Think they might be likely candidates?"

Ambrose and Riley tightened up. They made no comment.

Luke stared at them, incredulous. "Ain't you naught to say?"

"You must understand, Luke," Ambrose began, "it was a difficult time."

Riley shifted uneasily. "We had to make a choice."

Luke looked at them, hurt and offended. "Damn—you know! You've known all along! But you never said a word to me!"

"It was for your own good," Ambrose replied. "You'd have done some crazy thing and ended up mullo or in jail."

"Was that your way o' caring for me?" Luke asked. "Pretending it was an accident? I never believed you...and it near destroyed my faith in you." He looked his father in the eye. "Tell me, Dadu. Tell me the truth now."

Ambrose sighed. "It all started twenty years back," he began. "Your mother and me, we'd gone down to Stow Fair, hoping to do a spot o' business. We left you three chavvies with your Uncle Taiso."

As Ambrose talked, Luke pictured the scene. Groups of gypsies were doing deals over horses, some slapping hands in agreement, others shaking their heads and walking away. Clifford Yates, a forty-five-year-old travelling farrier, approached one of the groups leading a lively piebald vanner. Phil, a mean-looking twenty-year-old, was with him. Clifford called out to Ambrose to give him a price for the piebald.

Ambrose and Clifford argued over the vanner. The haggling grew rancorous. Ambrose eventually turned away, gesturing dismissively at Clifford and Phil. "He's been rough used, I can tell," I said to them. "He's not worth half what you're asking."

Riley put more wood on the fire as Ambrose continued his narration. "I fell out with Clifford and Phil over that deal at Stow. They were trying to cheat me. I thought it was over—and so it should have been. But later that day they came back."

Again Luke pictured the scene as Ambrose talked. Mireli was cooking on a camp fire outside their trailer. She was pregnant. Ambrose fetched her a full water jack.

Clifford and Phil suddenly appeared with the piebald vanner. Clifford came at a run, whacking the horse's rump so that it galloped through Ambrose's camp. Mireli had no time to move out of the way.

Ambrose struggled with his story. "That grye knocked your dai down and she fell on the water jack... She lost our unborn chavvie...and near died herself... It was murder, and I wanted revenge. But it took me two years to catch up with Clifford and Phil."

Luke was drawn in by his father's vivid description. The old brickworks was left behind, and he was standing in a wild grassy valley dotted with elder bushes and hawthorns. Ambrose and a gypsy traveller in his mid-thirties named Nat Boswell faced Clifford and Phil.

"It was early evening, but not yet dark, when Clifford and me squared up. Nat Boswell and Phil Yates were seconds."

In his mind's eye Luke saw Ambrose and Clifford strip to the waist. They began to bare-knuckle box. A scattering of gypsy travellers and their friends, which included Tam McBride, watched from the bushes.

The fight was fierce, with each man striking the other several hard blows. Both men were sweating copiously. Ambrose, the younger by twelve years, was getting the better of it, and he called for Clifford to give up. But Clifford cursed him for a coward and refused to tell Phil to throw in the towel, and so the fight continued. Eventually Ambrose knocked Clifford down, and he did not get up again.

"I felled him stone dead," Ambrose recalled. "Never meant for to kill him, but that's how it was." Luke saw Phil, screaming with fury, running at Ambrose with a knife. Nat Boswell and Tam McBride restrained him.

Ambrose drew his tale to a close. "Phil took Clifford's body away to bury it on a bit o' land they had. He's hated me and my blood ever since."

They sat around the fire in the old brickworks, considering the implications of Ambrose's story.

"Phil swore revenge. Three years later, him and Harry Rooke burned our trailer." Ambrose looked sternly at his sons. "But I don't want no more o' this. No more tit for tat killing."

"Phil Yates is a crook," Luke objected. He thought of Cath and Angie. "He wrecks folks' lives. Someone has to stop him."

"And you're the great hero?" Riley sneered. "You're the Rom who's gonna do it, all on your own! They'll cut you up and feed you to their dogs!"

"Riley's right, son. You go on with this killing there'll be never an end to it," Ambrose declared with passion. "I want my fam'ly to spill no more blood. This blood for blood thing has to stop."

Luke disagreed. "It ain't as simple as that. It ain't just about us now. How many more juvals and raklies, mothers and daughters, fam'lys and chavvies gonna be destroyed 'cos o' this guy?"

"That ain't none of our business now, bro." Riley's words hit Luke like a slap in the face.

"Mebbe it ain't yours, brother," Luke replied, "but happen it could be mine."

" Speak with Taiso , Luke," Ambrose implored. "Don't try anything on your own. Taiso's gotta decide. If he likes what you're saying he might help you. But go peaceful. Don't make out you got all the answers. Remember, he's been going down the drom twenty-five years longer'n you, like a real dromengro. Will you promise me you'll do some serious rockerin' with him?"

Luke looked at his father for a long silent moment before replying. "I promise to do as you ask, Dadu. I promise to do serious rockerin' with my uncle Taiso —if he'll let me."

Ambrose smiled. "It pleases me to hear you say that, son. I'll speak with Taiso tonight and tell him you're jalling the drom to meet him."

"Never speak till he lets you, bro," Riley advised. "Don't commit the sin o' pride in his presence."

Luke nodded. "I hear you."

The three men clasped hands in the firelight.

When Phil returned from the gallops, he found a second brown envelope waiting for him. The envelope was addressed as before to *P YATES* and with only the Birch Hall postcode. It contained a doctored photograph of the front elevation of the house, but instead of shattered bronze statuary there were four slender Corinthian columns, their elaborate capitals decorated with acanthus leaves and scrolls.

On the top of each capital was a severed, blood-dripping head, arranged from east to west in the following order: Maureen, Harry, Phil and Dot, all clearly recognisable. At the foot of the main steps, a pair of slavering ghouls feasted on the remains of four headless bodies.

Phil hurtled out of the main doors and down the steps, waving the photo at Harry, who was about to start cutting the grass of the front lawn on a big ride-on mower.

"He wants to destroy us all!" Phil yelled.

"Who does?" Harry climbed off the mower and looked at the photo. He turned it over, noting the neatly printed words *350K AND COUNTING*. "He's just having a laugh, Phil. Like I said: He wants money, not stiffs. Get Brian and Steve to rig up a white flag."

Phil calmed down a little. "Why are you mowing the grass? We have staff to do that kind of thing. Where the hell are they?"

"They're patrolling the boundary with the dogs," Harry explained. "If that guy's out there we'll get him. I'm cutting grass while I wait for them to make contact. The dogs are bound to pick up his scent, as he must have been out there watching us for days." He waved his arm in the direction of the woodland to the south.

For a moment Phil felt uncharacteristically contrite. "You've got everything covered as usual. Sorry I got wound up." He spotted something moving at the southerly edge of the lawn. "What the hell's that?"

Before Harry could reply the answer became obvious. A large adult hare streaked across the lawn with the two Dobermans in pursuit. The hare knew exactly what it was doing as it jinked to the left, then to the right, each time increasing its lead on the dogs, who overshot their quarry by several yards at each change in the hare's direction.

The hare's lead increased from ten to twenty yards before it vanished back into the woodland. The dogs would have continued their vain pursuit, but Brian and Steve appeared. After a few minutes' frantic chasing they managed to leash and quiet down the dogs.

"If you're gonna go after hares, at least do it with the right dogs," Phil said, amused by the antics of the Dobermans. "Well-trained Bedlingtons crossed with those two and we would have had him." He added, scowling: "Ain't much of a patrol, is it? More like something out of Mack Sennett's Keystone Cops. We're turning ourselves into idiots!"

He glanced up as a Microlight passed low over the woodland to the west of the lawn. Damnit, he thought, there's always some idiot spoiling the peace of the countryside. What the hell will these morons come up with next—a zip wire from Skiddaw to Scarborough? Will we all be happy then?

He went back into the house. Harry waved the minders over and told them to give the dogs a drink, then find an old white sheet in the laundry room.

* * *

Malcolm had decided it was too risky to remain in the woodland. In spite of his skills of concealment and surprise, the odds were not in his favour, even if their dogs were a pair of clowns. He had nothing to prove. The long procession of dead men who had never glimpsed the agent of their demise was suffi-cient testament to his abilities, whether in the use of firearm, blade or garrote.

He hired a Microlight and overflew Birch Hall. He had flown in this manner many times over the Kent and Essex countryside and considered himself an accomplished pilot, although he hadn't flown for a good few years.

He passed through the skies above Birch Hall and was just in time to see the hare chase, which he pho-tographed. On his way back he noted that a piece of white material had been fastened to a couple of posts and placed out front on the edge of the lawn. They had seen sense at last.

If this hadn't happened, he would perhaps have had to shoot one, or both, of the dogs—and he felt very bad about such things. But he had never messed up a contract, and this would be no exception. They would pay what justice demanded. It was simply a question of *when*, not *if*.

Overflying the North of England in this way, he was very much aware of the landscape as a living being. A single once-beautiful fabric, too often thought-lessly marred by the actions of *homo sapiens*, the wise man. He realised he had reached a point in his life when he didn't much like anything he saw, or anyone he worked for, with the exception of his brother.

Getting justice for Tam was a fitting way to end his career and begin to put something in the other side of the scales, to restore his personal equilibrium. Planting trees, perhaps. Helping hedgehogs. Shooting recalcitrant farmers who had the gall to pronounce themselves custodians of the landscape, when all they were concerned about was profit. He laughed. Shooting greedy farmers—now that was something he could quickly get used to!

20

I t was the first day of Appleby Horse Fair, and a
vast encampment occupied Fair Hill to the north
of the town. There were livestock transporters, expensive mobile homes, trucks of all kinds, pickups
and horse trailers, plus a variety of motors including
several Mercedes. There were a few Travellers' Spe-
cials, but these were outnumbered by less ostenta-
tious (and cheaper) models. There were one or two
Open-lots, but they had arrived on the backs of
trucks. Very few persons attending the fair these
days travelled in the old way with vanners and
waggons.

To an outsider it was hard to believe that the world
of gypsy travellers was not thriving. But over recent
years, Appleby Fair had changed. Many Roms felt it
had been hijacked by a spurious non-traveller ele-

ment who were mainly concerned with harness racing. The majority of these people were Irish. They had fine horses, it was true, but they were not Romany travellers.

Those Roms who made a substantial part of their income from buying and selling horses now carried out their transactions elsewhere, in locations known only to themselves. The majority of poor Roms, who at one time looked on Appleby Fair as a place where they could meet with widely scattered friends and relatives, now kept in touch with each other by mobile phone and met privately. They no longer felt at ease at Appleby Fair.

Gone were the days when fairgoers pulled their waggons on to the verges of the lanes around Appleby and greeted others of the blood by countless campfires. Those convivial times had become a distant memory among the elders. They felt they'd been treated like cattle, confined within a fenced-off enclosure on the Hill. They were already fenced off enough by the gorgios in their day-to-day lives.

Folk still washed their horses in the River Eden at fair time, and visitors still took their photographs from the bridge. But few of the riders were Roms.

Taiso had decided not to go to Appleby Fair this year. A number of families from several clans had been welcomed instead on his own land in the wild landscape an hour's drive south of Appleby. Luke and Sy planned to visit him later in the day but wanted to spend a few hours at the fair first.

Sy ran through the crowds, leading Luke's lively spotted stallion Prince of Thieves on a rope. He called as he ran: "Dik akai! Dik akai!"

After leading the stallion for a few hundred yards he stopped, and a dozen young Boswell men gathered around him. Sy kept up his call for another minute until he felt he had attracted a big enough crowd mostly of young Irish lads and the increasingly numerous fairground riff-raff.

"I'll sell this grye to the mush who can stay on his back for a full minute. He's gotta be the best rider at Appleby Fair!" Sy looked around at his audience. "Who's gonna be the first?"

Several of the Boswells attempted to ride the stallion bareback. Prince of Thieves bucked and kicked and threw them off one by one in a matter of seconds.

"You put a hex on that grye!" a Boswell discreetly placed in the crowd called out. "No one can ride him!"

Luke called out from another part of the crowd. "I can ride him!" He stepped into the space in the middle of the gathering. "I bet any mush a tenner I can ride that grye. I fall off in less'n a minute I give you twenty back."

A dozen young Irishmen held up ten-pound notes. Two serious-looking raklies collected the money and made a show of noting the punters' names.

Luke walked up to the spotted stallion and blew on its nostrils. He seemed to speak to it, or whisper, although no words could be heard, and his lips barely moved. It was all part of the mystique he was creating for the occasion.

Then he stroked the animal's nose and rubbed its chin. A moment later he vaulted on to the back of the stallion. The animal bucked and kicked briefly, then became still. Luke walked it a little way, turned and walked it back.

"Minute's up!" Sy called out. "You're the winner, mush."

"He charmed it! I seed him!" a brawny Irish lad shouted. "He rubbed a potion on its nose!"

Luke dismounted and held out his hands. "Money back if you can smell a potion!" A few Roms tried, but no one could.

"Deal's a deal, guys," Sy said. "If he'd lost, you'd be the happy ones, eh?"

The Irish lads shook their heads and walked away. A few looked angry, but the young Boswells encircled Sy and Luke and the angry men gave up and wandered off.

"Gorgios call this teamwork, don't they?" Sy laughed.

Luke patted Prince of Thieves. "I told him we were gonna have a bit o' fun! He knew what he had to do from the start!"

"Did you charm him?" Sy asked.

"I don't need to. He was reading my mind."

Sy wasn't sure if he should believe his friend or not. Luke was pleased to see he had everyone guessing.

"Let's test him," Luke suggested. "I need to know I can ride him anywhere."

The group of Boswells, riding their horses bareback, accompanied Luke and Sy down to the River Eden, where a few Irish girls were washing their horses. Some swam their animals in the deeper parts of the river. Luke on Prince of Thieves and Sy on a bay mare rode their horses into the Eden. The other Boswells joined them. There was banter and laughter, a great good-natured Romany spectacle, like those in days gone by that would soon be lost in the mists of time.

Luke took Prince of Thieves under the town bridge, then rode him into the deep pool on the south side of the river. Horse and rider were almost completely submerged.

"Trying to drown him, mush?" Sy called out, laughing.

Luke laughed too. These were rare moments of happiness. He was so much at one with the animal he felt the stallion might really be picking up his thoughts. He decided to swim him across the river to where Sy was sitting bareback on the mare. Prince of Thieves set off at once, without Luke urging him or saying a word.

"He's a magic animal," Luke stated with evident pride. "He can do anything! He knows what I want to do before I've had the idea myself!"

"Ever thought that mebbe it's the other way round—that he had the idea first and you just picked it up?" A young Rom called Royston laughed at Luke's look of surprise.

They rode their horses from the river and dismounted.

"Are you ready now, mush?" Sy asked.

Luke smiled. "Never been readier."

The two men clasped hands.

"It's time we were on the drom to Taiso's," Luke decided.

* * *

As dusk descended on the trucks and trailers pulled on to Taiso's land, outdoor cooking fires were lit, horses were tethered and water jacks filled. The entire place was surrounded by trees, most of which had been planted by Taiso and his extended family to baffle the prying eyes of gorgios. Taiso had built a bungalow at one end of the site, but he preferred to live in his trailer and to cook outside, unless the formidable Pennine weather closed in.

Luke walked through the encampment, leaving Sy and his relatives to take care of the bay mare and his spotted stallion. He approached a new but modest trailer, in front of which a small cooking fire burned brightly.

Taiso, Luke's uncle, a little taller and darker than Ambrose, his younger brother, sat by the fire. He stood up as his nephew approached. Luke stopped at a respectful distance.

"D'you think you might be the prodigal son?" Taiso asked, not smiling.

"That's for you to say, Nano," Luke replied with equal seriousness.

Taiso gestured to a vacant folding chair that had been set ready by the fire. "Best sit."

Luke obeyed the invitation, and the two Roms became quickly immersed in quiet conversation about traveller times gone by and their thoughts on the years to come. An hour passed with the two men remaining uninterrupted. Luke realised his father had phoned his elder brother and briefed him on the situation, and Taiso had spread the word that they must be left alone.

They talked at length about justice and the need for self-respect among gypsy travellers. The trailer fire was discussed in this context, and Luke was invited to express his honest opinion. Then they talked of his future, and Luke mentioned Cath and her struggle with Phil Yates. He was careful to stress her gypsy credentials and his own hopes that this was the woman with whom he wished to form a long-term "law-abiding" relationship.

"She has the blood, Nano," Luke said. "Our rawnis know it and tell the raklies to work for her."

"And Phil Yates is causing her trouble?"

"He is. And she's afraid of him."

"He's put her in a bad narki, has he?"

"He has. It's his way." Luke thought he could not do better than quote from Cath. "He's like a worm in an apple. He eats folk's lives away from the inside."

"I've heard about that mush. He's a traitor to his surname." Taiso spoke with fierce emphasis. "It was a surname we once respected."

They talked a while longer until Taiso took out his mobile and made a call. They were joined shortly afterwards by two older men, both of whom Luke recognised as Boswells, who listened to Taiso's brief whispered words and then left. Gypsy telepathy in action, Luke thought with a smile.

When the men had gone, Taiso placed more wood on the fire, and this seemed to be an unspoken signal that his private conversation with Luke had ended. His extended family, Roms, jukels and a few raklies, materialised from the darkness and gathered to one side of the fire. All eyes were turned to Taiso and Luke. No one spoke, the silence broken only by the crackling of the fire.

Taiso placed his hand on Luke's shoulder. "Luke has come to speak with me tonight. He has told me a story that brought tears to my eyes. He's asking for our help. We won't disappoint him, will we?"

Luke left Taiso alone with his people, removing himself from the fire and sitting on the earth at the edge of the circle of firelight. He watched the activity around other campfires, at the juvals and raklies coming and going, preparing the evening meal; at groups of Roms, talking and greeting each other; at the chained dogs, the jukels, mostly lurchers, either sleeping or, like himself, silently watching.

After a while, the womenfolk became busy with cooking around Taiso's fire and the men disappeared into the trailer. Every few minutes young Roms, obviously summoned, tapped on the trailer's door and were quickly admitted. Luke noted that Sy was the first of them. Another half-hour passed. Then Sy and the other young Roms left the trailer. Five of them, including Sy, formed a small group on the far side of the fire. The other young men melted away into the bustling darkness of the encampment.

Sy beckoned Luke to join them. Luke clasped hands with the other four young gypsy travellers, two of whom he knew well and the others by name and acquaintance. They formed a small group of their own, eating their evening meal together. It was made clear to Luke that they understood the situation facing him and were willing to help at his direction. Sy said his two sisters would join them in the morning.

A group of musicians with squeezebox, fiddle and guitar materialised from the darkness and played exuberantly, attracting folk from other family sites. Amos Wood joined them with his violin. Some of the gypsies danced, including three of the young men in Luke's group. He was pleased they did, as a clandestine gathering of six men might excite curiosity and gossip.

The musicians moved on to play at other campfires. The members of Luke's group bade him *kushti rardi* and he was left alone with Sy. They talked quietly for a while, Luke outlining his plans for bringing Phil Yates to account.

"It's just ideas at the moment," Luke admitted. "We'll have to watch how things develop."

"It's complicated," Sy said eventually. "I've never heard of a group of us doing anything like this. There's a lot we don't know."

Luke laughed. "Gypsy travellers are good at handling the unexpected. It's what we do every day. We've got faster brains than most gorgios. We're at our best when we've got a challenge."

"You truly think we can do this?"

"Taiso does. And so do I. I think we've got no choice."

Sy stood up. "We'll be on the drom at first light—unless you want to race your grye."

"I'm not racing him here this year," Luke informed his friend. "I've other plans for him," he announced mysteriously. "I'll meet you at first light."

Luke was left alone with his thoughts. Six young Roms taking on a group of ruthless men with guns and dogs. About equal odds, he reckoned.

* * *

Cath's day had gone badly. Her face was bruised and swollen. Her head ached, and she felt ill. Somehow she had helped her daughter with the animals, but after a frugal evening meal, she had given up the struggle and taken to her bed.

Angie sat on a chair at the bedside. She had a black eye. "We can't give in to these bullies, Mam, can we? Maybe Luke will come back and help us."

"He's got his own problems," Cath replied, her voice sounding weak and far away. "I don't see why he should feel beholden to us."

He could have been arrested again for all she knew, or busy pursuing his mission to buy land for his people. Now he had gone, she didn't feel like a person with gypsy blood anymore. She didn't feel like anything, just the pain in her head and despair in her heart. They were alone and friendless, with hardly more value than roadkills picked over by the crows, their neighbours, until they vanished completely.

She had an idea she should speak to her accountant to try to find a way of getting rid of Phil Yates. But she had no strength to pursue it.

"Fancy a cuppa?" Angie suggested.

"More'n anything." Cath grimaced. Smiling was painful.

Angie looked apologetic. "I've been out of order. I'm really sorry."

"That's okay."

Angie took her mother's hand. "We're pals again?"

"Of course. But we need to pull together now. No more arguments. No more of those moods."

"I promise." Angie kissed her mother on the cheek. "I love you, Mam."

"I love you too."

"Cuppa time."

Angie left the bedroom and went down to the kitchen. She found Charlie Gibb sitting at the table. Drawers had been pulled open in the sideboard and he was glancing through the papers he had removed with his one good eye.

"Hell are you doing, Charlie?" she exclaimed.

He waved a fistful of papers at her. "You can chuck these in the fire. Phil Yates don't want this place no more. You gotta sign with me now."

"To hell with you, Charlie!" she shrieked. "I'm gonna kill you first!"

She grabbed the shotgun, which was propped against the wall near the window. Charlie, with a cunning leer, stepped quickly through the back door. Angie rushed after him with the shotgun.

She hurried across the stackyard, but she was way too slow. She heard Charlie's laughter, far ahead of her, fading into the night. She gave up and stood for a moment in the yard. The place was filled with jumping shadows cast by the moon as it raced through tufts of broken cloud. The wind rattled loose woodwork in the barn and whistled through gaps in the walls of buildings. Sheets of corrugated roofing grated against their fittings, and cables slapped against woodwork in the gusty wind. Slightly spooked, Angie returned to the house.

Back in the kitchen she leaned the gun in its place by the wall and locked and bolted the door. She boiled the kettle for tea, filled the teapot, then put it on a tray with two mugs and a jug of milk. She went upstairs and pushed open Cath's bedroom door.

"Here I am at last!"

Silence.

"Mam?"

Cath was not there. The bed was empty, the bedroom in a mess, clothes and shoes tossed about. Angie, fearful and confused, put the tray down on the dressing table.

"Mam? Where are you? What's going on?"

The door slammed shut behind her. She turned in alarm and screamed as Brian grabbed her.

Before she could gather her wits, a hood was thrust over her head and her wrists were bound. She heard a muttered conversation and realised the second voice belonged to the thug they called Steve. Then she was half dragged, half carried down the stairs and across the stackyard. She could smell the night air through the hood.

She was bundled into the back of a vehicle and felt it lurch as it turned around in the uneven yard. Then she found her voice.

"No, no, no! This is wrong! We're not going anywhere! You're gonna let me out and leave us alone!"

Another lurch then the vehicle levelled out and picked up speed.

Us, she thought. *Us*...? But where on earth was her mother?

Then she was screaming. "Mam! Mam! Where are you? What have you done with her, you fucking morons?"

She heard two male voices laughing. And she knew she was heading towards the worst hours of her life.

21

Phil put on his dressing gown and picked up his mobile. Dot woke at the sound of his voice and watched him sleepily.

Phil stared from the window as he talked. As he looked out over the front lawn he wondered if he was in the cross hairs of the sniper's rifle sights. But he knew it was unlikely. As Harry had said, the guy wanted money not dead bodies. "Morning, Clive... Fine morning it is too. How's my lovely boy?... Take good care of him... See you at the gallops." He rang off.

"One day I'll wake up and there'll be a bloody horse at side o' me," Dot said grumpily.

He scowled at her. "Been watching too many movies." A recurring thought struck him. He gave it a try. "Why don't you come up to the gallops? Fresh air'll do you good."

"I went up last year," she replied dismissively.

Phil turned to her in exasperation. "Dot, please—show a bit of interest."

"What in? I didn't know I was gonna be wed to a goddamn horse!" She turned over and went back to sleep.

He gave up and left the room.

In the next bedroom Harry studied himself in the full-length mirror, flexing his muscles. Maureen woke and turned to face him.

"Happy fortieth, birthday boy!"

He stared at her reflection in the mirror. "I wish you meant it."

She replied without hesitation. "Course I do. Why shouldn't I?"

He turned to face her. "I could pop the pair o' you, easy as a bag o' crisps. Think about that."

Her gaze hardened. "But you won't do that, will you, Harry? 'Cos then where'd you be?"

Without a backward glance, Harry put on his dressing gown and walked from the room. How long could he go on like this? Another month? A week? A day?

During the long hours he spent alone, managing his own and Phil's business interests, the more his thoughts were drawn back to the day of the trailer fire. Something had gone wrong for him—for them all—on that day. It was as if his actions had left him exposed to the slow cumulative drip of a terrible nemesis.

It had become obvious in the fight with the young Irish guy, when he had felt the strength go out of his limbs until he was plodding around the ring like a directionless drunk. It had continued with his slow but steady loss of libido, which had led to...he couldn't bear to spell out the humiliating details. It had been followed by his increasing indifference to race winners, to the amassing of wealth, even to loss of interest in life itself.

It was as though a curse had been placed on him that day, as though he had crossed an existential line and awoken the implacable spirit of justice or fate that lay in wait on the other side. He was not a superstitious man, but he felt increasingly that some old gypsy rawni had laid a malediction on him that was impossible to escape.

There was nothing he could do. No atonement would be sufficient to lift the curse from his life. He had to watch himself become an utterly empty man.

* * *

Phil, Harry and Clive watched the horses exercising on the gallops. No one spoke. It seemed to Phil that the three of them leaning there on the car park fence had been somehow shut out from the everyday world that went on around them, the world of galloping horses, of sunlight breaking through cloud, of hope and expectation.

Or was it just himself? What had happened to cut him off like this? Was this the prelude to a stroke or heart attack? It seemed that Harry and Clive standing each side of him were mere memories, light years away on the far side of an unbridgeable void.

He cleared his throat, but it too sounded distant, as if he was hearing a sound made by a separate person. Then he found himself walking in the lane that led from the road to the car park. There was a figure coming towards him...a figure that he felt had been approaching him for a very long time. The distance between himself and the figure was decreasing steadily. He could make the figure out more clearly now. It seemed to be composed of flapping garments, although there was hardly any wind. It wore a hood, but he could see no face within it, only a swirling darkness that...

He felt something pushing at his elbow and a noise that might have been a voice but was making an unintelligible babble.

"Phil! Phil, come back to us!"

He looked at Clive, who was staring at him in wide-eyed concern.

"What?" he managed to ask. He noted that his voice sounded almost normal again.

Clive was still staring. "You gave us a fright, old son."

"It was a thirty-second cat nap." Harry was smiling, explaining. "He's done it a few times. Nothing to worry about."

But Phil knew that it wasn't a cat nap. It was a vision of death coming towards him. He had seen it before in odd moments, but it was always in the distance. Now it was closer, narrowing the gap.

* * *

Dot and Maureen ate alone in the breakfast room. They had decided there was no point trailing through to the dining room, as they would have finished eating long before their husbands returned.

Dot confronted her second slice of toast and marmalade, then decided that attempting to consume it was an unequal struggle. She poured herself coffee and laced it, as usual, with brandy.

Maureen was still at her sausage-and-mushrooms stage and hoped that her companion would not start talking until she had eaten it while it was hot. She realised sadly that was not going to happen.

"We should get away for a holiday," Dot announced. "Just the two of us. It'd teach these self-absorbed fellas a lesson. They might even realise we were no longer around. Whaddya think?"

Maureen swallowed her last piece of sausage. She hated talking with her mouth full. It reminded her of her parents and seemed now to be unbearably uncouth. She didn't want to talk about a holiday either, unless it was permanent. "I don't know. Where were you thinking of going?"

Dot replied without smiling. "Somewhere without horses."

"Like an island in the Med?" Maureen suggested hopefully.

"Don't matter where. Just as long as it's too small to get horses on."

* * *

The little group of gypsies had stopped on the edge of an abandoned airfield. It was a place they all knew well, as they had raced their horses on its grassy perimeter many times in years gone by. The place was deteriorating slowly, cracks in the tarmac widening and clumps of couch grass encroaching.

The encampment was made up of Luke and Sy, plus May and Minnie, who were Sy's sisters, and the four young Roms from the meeting at Appleby Fair: Royston, Farley, Bennett and Kingsley. They sat around a small fire, finishing breakfast and drinking tea. Farley had a lurcher bitch lying quietly at his feet.

A number of vehicles were parked nearby: Luke's Citroen Estate, Sy's big Toyota pickup, a Ford Transit van with its back doors wide open and a small Ford truck. A horse trailer partitioned for two large horses was hitched to the pickup, and a living van was hitched to the truck. A heap of large logs lay in the truck, and a motorcycle occupied the back of the Transit. Prince of Thieves, quietly grazing, was tethered on the grass at the edge of the tarmac.

Luke got to his feet and threw his tea dregs on the fire. "We all ready? Let's be jalling the drom."

He went to fetch Prince of Thieves, and Sy put the animal in the horse trailer. Royston and Farley got into the truck and Bennett into the Transit. The others joined Luke in the Citroen, the sisters sitting on the back seat. A few minutes later they had gone, leaving no sign they had ever been there, except for a small heap of smouldering ashes at the edge of the tarmac.

* * *

Luke pulled the Citroen into the cover of bushes well away from the sawmill and Charlie Gibbs' telescope. The four gypsies, keeping to the cover of field hedges, made their way to Cuckoo Nest for the last quarter-mile on foot. Something was amiss there, Luke had realised, as his repeated calls to Cath had not been returned.

He left his three companions, Kingsley, May and Minnie, at the edge of the orchard and approached the farmhouse alone. The goats had not been put out to browse, and the noise from the pig unit suggested restive and hungry animals. The Land Rover was parked in the stackyard, but the back door of the house stood wide open.

When he stepped silently into the kitchen, he found Charlie, in his floppy hat and eye patch, peering into the wall cupboards and muttering to himself. "Nice place. I'll like it here. Gonna be a good farmer."

Charlie's soliloquy was interrupted as powerful hands grabbed him from behind and slammed him face down on the table. Luke pulled back Charlie's bleeding head and held his knife to the albino's throat.

"Where's Cath and Angie?" Luke demanded. "What the hell you done with 'em, you goddamn psycho?"

"Weren't me! Not me!" Charlie blurted out. "They took 'em. Them two fellas. Last night."

"What two fellas?" Luke asked angrily, pulling the albino's head back until the man could hardly speak.

"Them fellas... who work...for Phil Yates. Mean fellas. They had guns."

Luke's heart sank. Had Phil Yates finally recognised Cath as the witness to the trailer fire? "Did they shoot 'em or what?" he asked sternly.

"They tied 'em up...and put 'em...in a Range Rover. I was watching 'em...from the trees. Then they took 'em away."

Luke threw Charlie out of the house. "Get the hell outta here! It's private land!"

Charlie fell in an undignified sprawl on the yard stones, his hat sent rolling in the mud.

"Keep away from here!" Luke yelled. "I see you here again I'll cut your goddamn head off!"

Charlie got to his feet and shambled away, muttering furiously to himself. "Ain't no one does that to Charlie Gibb! Ain't no one! No one!"

Luke and his companions spent the next hour milking and tethering the goats, feeding the pigs and collecting the eggs from the deep litter houses. The girls had worked on the farm picking fruit and knew their way around. They left the milk in the dairy and carried the eggs to the kitchen, as Luke had seen Cath do. Then he left the three of them on their own to guard the house.

"Don't let anyone near the place on Cath Scaife's orders, unless they're making an official delivery. Any problems you ring me."

He left them his mobile number. Then, just to be safe, he left Sy's as well.

"What we gonna do if things get rough down here?" Kingsley asked. "There's not enough of us to fight back."

"Lock the house and take cover in the orchard," Luke advised. "You can get out the front door that can't be seen from the yard. The key's in the lock. Then ring me and Sy. And keep out o' sight o' that loony in the sawmill!"

He ran back to the Citroen and drove away. The unexpected had happened already, and he hadn't even begun to put his plan into action. He was beset by bad feelings about the day that lay ahead.

One thing was certain: it was going to be all or nothing now.

22

Cath and Angie were tied to wall fittings in one of the outbuildings at Birch Hall. They were gagged, dehydrated and exhausted. They had no idea where they were and were unable to move or call for help. Angie had quickly realised that weeping caused frightening breathing problems. There was nothing they could do so they had no choice but resign themselves to their fate.

After his usual visit to the gallops and a leisurely breakfast alone with Harry in the dining room, Phil decided it was time to pay the women a visit. He had them completely under his control and decided to have a bit of fun with them while he waited for Tam's hitman to make contact. When they had dealt with him he could decide what to do with the women.

One thing had now become clear: Cath Scaife would have to transfer ownership of her farm to him if he cleared her debt to the bank. Once that had been done, despite whatever promises he made to them, the women had no further value. They would take them to the ravine and dispose of them, like they should have done with Tam.

He entered the outbuilding and stood for a moment watching them. "Beautiful morning out there." He closed the door and switched on the light. "Pity you can't see it." He took his revolver from the shoulder holster he wore under his jacket. "I should have realised it was you who was watching that night, Cath Scaife. Can't think how it could have escaped me. Best not take any more chances, eh?"

Before Cath had time to close her eyes, he put the gun to her head and pulled the trigger.

Click.

Cath started to shake uncontrollably. Angie struggled in vain against her bonds.

Phil laughed. "Maybe next time it'll be loaded. Or we could play Russian roulette. We could start with two bullets in the chamber. Makes it more exciting, don't you think?"

He turned to Angie. "Perhaps you could shoot your mam. Or she could shoot you. When there's only one of you left I s'pose I'll have to take over. Won't be so much fun then, will it? The excitement lasts while there's still the chance you could live another minute longer, maybe even two. But you'll be going into the unknown, the pair o' you, sooner or later."

He stood for a few minutes watching them, enjoying the surge of power that filled him. Maybe he should film their game of Russian roulette and create his own live action snuff movie. He could put it on the Internet and charge one dollar a hit and make an easy million in only a few hours. Folk had become so bored and degenerate they would simply lap it up.

But he'd need Harry's expertise to protect his online identity and to take the movie down before he was ratted out. And he didn't want to share this experience with him. Stealing Harry's wife was one thing. Giving him the power of blackmail so easily was another matter entirely. He put his gun back in the holster and turned off the light, then he went out and locked the door, leaving the women in darkness.

* * *

Brian watched the two Dobermans in the rear yard dog pen. The animals were restless, sniffing the air and whining. Their morning feed remained untouched.

Steve ambled up. He glanced at the dogs. "What's wrong with them?"

Brian shrugged. "Dunno. They've been like this for the last half hour."

"Mebbe we've got an intruder. Could be that guy who shot up the statues."

"I was thinking we should let 'em go. The guy would never be able to handle the dogs and us as well. If we caught him Phil would give us one helluva bonus. Whaddya think?"

"You ready for a firefight?" Steve asked with a questioning smile.

"I'm always ready."

"Okay then. Let's do it."

Brian opened the pen and the dogs raced away. He and Steve chased after them. The Dobermans careered across the front lawn, leaped the boundary fence and disappeared into the woodland beyond. Brian and Steve, two hundred yards behind, arrived at the fence, got their breath back and listened.

"Hear anything?" Steve asked.

Brian shook his head. "Not a damn thing. So there ain't a shooter out here. There'd have been one shot at least."

"If he was using a silencer we wouldn't have heard it, " Steve reasoned. "He could be looking for us now."

Brian objected. "He might've shot one, but the remaining dog would've barked. No one could shoot two Dobermans in total silence."

"Mebbe the dogs were after something else," Steve suggested.

"Like what?"

"What would make you run that fast?"

"Cops, mebbe. Money."

"I mean, if you were a dog?"

Brian laughed. "Only one answer to that, ain't there?"

They whistled and shouted, but to no avail.

"Damnit, we've lost 'em," Steve said. "Phil will go nuts."

They wandered about half-heartedly in the woodland, calling and whistling, but eventually gave up.

"They must've gone a fair distance," Steve decided. "I've been told dogs can smell a bitch in heat more'n a mile away."

Brian pulled a reluctant face. "We'll have to get the motor and go looking."

"We'll tell Phil they busted out," Steve said. "We'd better sabotage the pen as evidence."

They retraced their steps to the pen at the back of the house. Royston and Bennett watched them from the nearby shrubbery.

* * *

The lurcher bitch was tied to a slender goat willow among briar-infested woodland to the south of the house. The tranquillized Dobermans lay nearby. Sy and Farley, invisible among the summer leaves, listened to the racket kicked up by the minders.

Farley shook his head. "Gorgios, eh? They're all dinilo."

"We're lucky those guys aren't Roms," Sy thought. "They would've dikked us. Then we'd have problems."

They settled down to observe the solitary stranger, who was dressed in army camouflage and carried field glasses and a backpack. They watched him make his way silently through the woodland to the west.

"That mush is dangerous," Farley concluded. "He's a gorgio, but he knows his woodcraft."

"He must have been the shooter," Sy replied. "Someone's had a bit o' fun picking off those statues!"

"He ain't got a rifle now," Farley observed. "But he's on the hunt. We'd best keep dikkerin him. Did Luke say anything about this mush?"

Sy shook his head. "He mebbe don't know him. We better watch he don't spoil things for us."

"Mebbe Kingsley can dikker him. When will he be joining us?"

"Soon as he thinks it's safe to leave the raklies. Could be any time."

"I don't like that mush," Farley admitted. "He's a killer."

Sy agreed. "A killer he is for sure. Best not give him no space to breathe. If Kingsley don't come, I'll be dikkerin him. If I have to, I'll put him to sleep like those two jukels."

Farley agreed. "You'll need double the dose. He'll sleep like the dead till we're outta here!"

* * *

The woodland near Birch Hall was a very different place compared with the day before. Today there were people about who looked to Malcolm like gypsies. He had watched the activity with the Dobermans in his field glasses and was impressed by the speed and efficiency with which the two dark-complexioned young men had dealt with the dogs. He realised these people, whoever they were, had some kind of plan and knew precisely what they were doing.

He had no wish to get mixed up with them and decided to find a quiet part of the wood where he could lie low and observe events. It was obvious the gypsies were about to make moves against the occupants of the big house. That in itself was interesting. They may be about to make his own task a lot easier.

He hadn't posted his third photograph, even though it was grotesquely comical, with the two guys chasing the dogs who were pursuing a gorilla with a bag marked *SWAG* on his back and an approximation of Phil Yates tucked under his arm. Perhaps the time for photographs had gone.

The thought occurred to him that these gypsies might simply be staging a burglary, in which case he might have to step in and relieve them of the loot. But how many of them were there? Two or three might be manageable. Four or more might not. He was annoyed by the sudden intrusion, but somehow he had to turn it to his advantage. As far as he knew, no one was aware he was there. He had to keep it that way.

He wondered if one of the gypsies was Luke Smith, the cat burglar his brother had mentioned, who wanted paying for the heist of T'ang horses. Fair enough, the guy should have his fifty large, but only if he behaved himself.

* * *

Royston and Bennett watched Brian and Steve as the minders loosened a section of the Dobermans' enclosure to create evidence of the dogs' escape. A movement caught Royston's attention and he looked up to the roof of the Hall, where Luke sat watching from among the chimney stacks. Luke gave them a signal to keep observing, then disappeared from view.

Luke's climb on to the roof of Birch Hall had been easy, as the soft sandstone of the wall on the west elevation of the extension was riddled with weather-eroded hand and foot holds. Once on the roof he could keep an eye on arrivals and departures at the Hall and on his two mobile units to the south and north. But he found his feelings divided between his desire to get long-awaited justice and his urgent need to find Cath and Angie. He couldn't search for them openly. He just had to hope Phil or his heavies would give their location away.

He had heard the story of the missing girls who were found by chance six months after their captor had been shot dead by police. They had drunk their own urine and blood, but had eventually died of starvation. Don't kill the messenger, he thought—at least not till you've checked out the message.

The afternoon light was slowly changing, replaced by the longer shadows of early evening. On all sides of the Hall the grounds lay apparently deserted. A light rain billowed across the house front, then cleared to leave the moon, like a lonely voyeur, perched on the eastern skyline.

One by one, the first-floor lights in the Hall went off and the ground-floor lights came on. A taxi and a Range Rover arrived with the few select guests for Harry's birthday party and were greeted on the steps by Phil and Harry and escorted inside.

Neither Phil nor Harry had desired an extended guest list, Harry because he despised the people who worked for him, Phil because he was paranoid about anyone he couldn't trust finding out details of his private home life.

The ground-floor windows on the south side of the Hall were open to let in the mild evening air. The sounds of conversation and laughter drifted out. Nigel Hirst, Clive Fawcett and his wife Samantha, Freddie Parfitt, the jockey, and Julie, his girlfriend, left their birthday gifts in the panelled drawing room, where Harry dutifully opened them, trying to find a fresh comment to make for each unwanted gift.

Phil had opened the bar, aware that drinks would quickly dispel any awkward atmosphere and loosen sluggish tongues. The talk picked up and naturally revolved around horses; Phil was relieved that Dot managed to appear interested without saying any-thing that would embarrass him. At least, not yet.

Eventually the head of the hired catering team, en-gaged by Phil for the occasion, announced that the food was ready. The guests took their seats in the dining room, where an ornate antique oil lamp burned in the centre of the long table.

The courses came and went, no one eating much, as Phil, Freddie and the ladies were watching their waistlines and neither Harry nor Clive wished to appear unduly gluttonous. As the remains of the fourth course disappeared into the kitchen Dot drained her wine glass and refilled it for the fifth time. Harry watched her across the table, wondering when her mask of sobriety would slip.

Hirst, in a new uncreased suit, got to his feet. "Here's to you, Harry. And to the next forty. May we all still be sitting here!"

Everyone raised their glasses and drank. Harry stood up and cleared his throat. "Thanks, Nige." He glanced around the room, noting the upturned self-indulgent faces, the quality decor and furnishings. "Guess things could be worse, 'ey?" He waited for the polite laughter to quieten. "Thanks to you all for coming today and for your gifts and good wishes."

"It's my birthday next week," Samantha announced. "We should do this again at our place."

Her attempt to hijack the occasion was promptly demolished by Dot.

"What makes you think we'll have enough stamina? We haven't finished with this one yet!"

The laughter was spontaneous but brief, as Samantha's discomfiture was quickly realised.

"I tell you what," Dot continued with crushing brutality, "if we have any leftovers from tonight, we can bring them with us. Might save you a few quid!"

The potential disaster was saved by the arrival of the fifth and final course, a spectacularly colourful "fresh fruit trifle, our chef's very own creation." The tense atmosphere dissipated, much to everyone's relief except Dot's.

"Ooo, Harry," Dot cooed, "you should take a photo of this, before we start slinging it into each other's faces!"

Hirst ate a small amount then excused himself, whispering in Harry's ear. "I've a little rendezvous." He raised his eyes to the ceiling. "I thank you for that. I'll catch you later." He left the room.

Phil pushed his empty bowl aside. "Okay, folks. It's party time!"

Everyone followed Phil into the sitting room, which was yet another panelled reception room, where Brian and Steve had pushed the seating back against the walls. Phil played a compilation CD of *All Time Favourite Hits*. Harry danced with Freddie's girlfriend. Maureen danced with Freddie. Clive and

Samantha danced with each other. Phil and Dot sat together on a sofa watching benignly. Phil took Dot's hand. She smiled at him blissfully, drunkenly.

Brian arrived in the doorway in his outdoor jacket. Harry hurried him into an empty reception room.

"Dogs back yet?" Harry asked impatiently.

Brian shook his head. "Not a sign. Looks like they're having their own party."

"You and Steve check round," Harry ordered. "And look in on those farm women. Phil wants to visit 'em later. Make sure they're conscious. Give 'em a drink of water."

Under the reception room window, pressed flat against the wall, Royston and Bennett crouched, listening.

23

Handguns drawn, Brian and Steve patrolled the grounds in the moonlight. They followed the pathways around the eastern end of the house, then through the shrubberies at the back. They checked the outbuildings and garages. As they searched, a supple breeze blew in and filled their world with confusing movement.

"I don't like this dog business," Steve complained. "We're blind as moles without 'em."

Brian agreed. "If it wasn't windy the moonlight would help, but it's all jumping shadows and wafting leaves. An entire SAS unit could hide out here and we wouldn't be any the wiser."

"Best look in on those two females when we've walked round again," Steve decided.

"We can have a bit o' fun, can't we?" Brian suggested. "I mean, who's gonna know?"

Steve laughed. "Nice one, Bri! That'll wake 'em up!"

"We'd best check the western extension first though, hadn't we?"

"Guess we should. And round the back of the garages. We don't want an interruption when we're visiting the ladies!"

Royston and Bennett tracked them from the shadows.

* * *

After the birthday celebrants had danced for an hour, they returned to the dining room, where the catering team had placed a large cake on the table. Phil opened champagne and filled their glasses while Harry cut the cake.

"Drink up!" Phil beamed at his guests. "The night's still young!"

Dot raised her glass. "Here's to Harry! Best big brother in the world!"

They all clinked glasses and drank. Harry blew out the candles on his cake to a self-conscious ripple of applause.

Dot lurched against the table. "Only forty once, ain'tcha?" Maureen had to steady her in case she fell into the cake.

Phil paid off the caterers in cash. They left promptly, relieved to get away at a reasonable hour.

The guests sang *Happy Birthday*, followed by *For He's a Jolly Good Fellow*. Harry did his best to maintain a smile.

To Phil's disappointment, Clive and Samantha decided to leave.

Clive was apologetic. "I can't do late nights and early mornings anymore these days, I'm afraid."

The truth was a little different. Although Phil had put on a good show, Samantha was bored to the point of desperation, and her husband had decided to go in order to avoid another *faux pas*. He was aware she found Dot blindingly coarse and Maureen a vacuous mute, so a dignified but hasty exit had become expedient. Freddie and Julie had come with Hirst in a taxi, but they decided to leave too, rather than sink into a booze-filled morass and then have to phone for transport in the cold sad small hours.

They sat in Clive's Range Rover at the foot of the main steps with Samantha behind the wheel. Phil saw them off, keeping up his image of the attentive host. Clive looked at the headless statuary standing on each side of the steps. They seemed bizarre and even macabre under the outside lights.

"What happened to your statues?" he asked with puzzled amusement.

"Some drunken idiot took a dislike to them," Phil replied with a grin. "I'll be getting some new ones made to replace them."

Clive smiled. "Will they be drunk-proof?"

"I'll be having them made of tungsten steel," Phil replied. He hardly cared what he said about them anymore.

Clive couldn't think of a reply to Phil's unexpected comment. He was saved by Samantha revving the engine impatiently. "We'll be off then, Phil. Thanks for a very fine evening." He heard a chuckle of amusement—or was it contempt?—escape from the lips of his driver.

Phil waved them off. "Look in on Good Times for me, Clive!"

Clive waved acknowledgement. Phil watched the Range Rover pull away down the drive and suddenly felt intolerably lonely. He didn't have any real friends; he just had money. If he went bust tomorrow, he'd be no one. Lucky Phil Yates would not be gracing his hangers-on with any more reflected glamour. He would be remembered for less than fifteen minutes. The name of his horse would outlast his own.

Sy and Farley noted the farewells from the bushes at the side of the drive. Farley's lurcher bitch watched silently with them.

"Luke will have seen 'em leave. It's time we made our move," Sy decided. "Hope Royston and Bennett know it's time they took over out here."

They melted into the darkness. As they made their way through the dancing moon- shadows at the back of the house, Kingsley silently joined them.

"We're all here," Kingsley whispered. "We locked up the farmhouse and came in the Land Rover. Luke phoned us to say we might be wanted here and to bring the farm vehicle."

"Where are those two gorgios?" Sy asked.

"Chasing mullos in the bushes back there." Kingsley pointed. "It's Royston and Bennett having a laugh. Luke told me he's going in and he'll open the back door soon as he can. We'll leave the two gorgios to Royston and Bennett."

"They're getting motto in the big room," Farley said. "We could get in the house and they wouldn't know we were there."

"Where's the bike?" Sy asked.

"In the bushes at the top of the drive all ready for you."

"And the truck?"

"In the trees opposite the gateway with the pickup."

"Right. I'm away on the drom with the pickup," Sy announced. "Farley will be with the truck. See you later, mush."

Sy and Farley vanished into the night. Kingsley waited patiently by the back door.

* * *

Luke entered the first floor of the house by roping himself to a chimney and abseiling across the housefront to an open window. Once inside, he re-trieved the rope in case anyone spotted it. He had only a general idea of what was happening outside, as it was far too risky to make any but the most ur-gent phone calls. These were moments when a deeper level of awareness took over. The gorgio world called it telepathy. But it wasn't just a mind thing, it was a gut thing, a *knowing,* developed only in those who lived dangerously.

He found himself in a bathroom that led directly into Phil Yates' bedroom, which was obvious because of the clothes. He sat on the bed and chanced a quick call to Sy, who briefed him on the situation in the grounds.

He located the back stairs, went down and opened the door to the rear yard. Kingsley was waiting for him.

"What d'you want me to do?" Kingsley asked.

"Wait here. I'll text you '- "ok "when I want you with me."

Then Luke was gone back upstairs to explore the bedrooms. He had to find Cath and Angie and get them back to the farm where they might be safe. Anything could happen now at Birch Hall and he didn't want them involved.

But he couldn't find them.

A search of the top floor revealed a number of empty rooms that had once been servants' quarters. They contained a few stored items of furniture and a half-dozen paintings covered with cloths. Returning to the first floor, he looked in all the rooms. There was nothing remarkable in them except for the two handguns he found in the bedside drawers of the two occupied bedrooms, which he had already identified as Phil's and Harry's. The guns were both fully loaded. He put them into the side pockets of the small rucksack he was wearing, then proceeded to the last room on the landing, near the head of the main staircase.

The door was locked. His pulse quickened—this must be where Phil had put Cath and Angie. He pressed his ear to the woodwork, as the noise from the ground floor was growing louder, *Green, Green Grass of Home* followed by *Moon River* drifting up the stairs.

But yes, there it was: a female voice, whimpering, pleading, crying.

* * *

Hirst and the Latvian girl lay naked on the bed, engaged in a sado-masochistic sex act. The girl's clothes were scattered on the floor and her hands were tied to the bedhead. Hirst's suit was casually tossed over a small bedroom armchair, his shoulder holster and service weapon lying on top of a tallboy.

The girl, in pain, began to weep."No, no!" She began to cry more loudly. "You stop now. You stop please!"

Hirst slapped her face, which made her weep even more.

"Cry all you want, girlie," Hirst laughed. "The more the better!" He slapped her again much harder. The girl screamed.

Luke, who had found an adjoining bathroom that he guessed had once been a dressing room with a separate entrance from the landing, appeared in the communicating doorway. There was no sign of Cath and Angie, but he recognised Hirst at once.

"Having fun?"

Hirst froze at the sound of Luke's voice. He leaped from the bed, aiming an arcing fist at Luke's head. Luke stepped back and cracked Hirst on the jaw, the power of the blow increased by the detective's forward momentum. Hirst crashed to the floor as Luke whipped out his knife and cut the girl's bonds.

Hirst dragged himself to his feet. "Who the fuck are you?" he snarled, glaring at the dark-skinned intruder.

Luke kept the Latvian girl behind him, shielding her from further harm. "A mullo from the past. And you're that criminal gavver Nigel Hirst."

"Luke Smith!" Hirst spat the words out as if they had burned his tongue.

Luke tossed his knife in the air and caught it again, tempting the detective into making a move. But Hirst, for the moment, seemed to prefer to talk.

"It's Phil Yates you want, not me. He was the one who burned your trailer."

Luke showed no emotion. "I'll get round to him later."

"What d'you want with me?"

"Justice. You did the driving, you were involved, so you pay the price."

As they talked, Luke watched Hirst's eyes. He saw them shift to the left towards his handgun on the tallboy. The gavver was about to make his move, but Luke was ready.

Before either of them could do anything, a shot rang out, seeming deafeningly loud in the confines of the bedroom. Hirst fell backwards against the dressing table. A glance was enough to tell Luke that the man was dead, shot in the head midway between the eyes.

He coaxed Hirst's service weapon from the two-handed grip of the Latvian girl, who had calmly removed it and taken revenge for them both. It was no chance shot, either—Luke realised the girl knew how to shoot. He texted "ok" to Kingsley, then opened the bedroom door. The next moment Kingsley stepped into room.

"That was quick," Kingsley remarked drily, looking at Hirst's body. "Who's the rakli?"

Luke wiped the girl's fingerprints from the gun using Hirst's pristine pocket handkerchief. "She needs our protection. What vehicle can we spare?"

"Only the farm Land Rover," Kingsley replied.

Luke thought a moment. "It's a good thing we've got it. Get Minnie and May to take the rakli back to Cuckoo Nest and stay with her. The rest of us have everything still to do here. And it's far too dangerous for raklies—we don't want any more womenfolk taken prisoner."

"It wasn't too dangerous for this one!" Kingsley indicated the Latvian girl.

"That gavver was careless," Luke said. "Others might not be."

He tried to explain to the Latvian girl that she would be safe with them but was surprised when she showed resistance.

"She thinks all guys are monsters," Kingsley remarked.

Luke recalled the tales he had heard at horse fairs and traveller gatherings in the recent past of French and other European gypsies getting their girls pregnant and selling the offspring to childless couples for anything from five to fifty grand. Gypsy traveller babies were good-looking, and there was a ready market. There were other stories almost too harrowing to believe. That men of the *kaulo ratti* had to resort to extremes like this filled him with despair.

"You must be with us," he told the girl. "If the police catch you, they'll send you back to your country. Then the bad guys will get you and bring you here again."

Something in the earnestness of his manner must have convinced her. She looked trustingly into his eyes. "Okay. I go with you." She began to get dressed. He would have to tell Taiso what had happened and leave the girl's fate in his hands.

Luke arranged Hirst's body on the bed and placed the handgun in his outstretched fingers. It was not a convincing suicide, but there was nothing more he could do for now. Then he wiped any surface the girl might have touched to remove her fingerprints —and also his own. Phil or Harry or both of them were running a prostitute racket, and he had to find out more. He guessed the girl's passport would be locked away in Phil's office.

"Your friends, the other girls—where are they?" he asked the Latvian.

"In big house in city."

"How many?"

The girl held up six fingers.

Luke was repelled by this information to such an extent that he felt defiled just being in a house owned by such men. And this dead cop had been in on it too. If he could locate the girls' passports, who would he give them to? Maybe he should try to free the girls himself. But then what? He couldn't find hiding places for them all—and there was a limit to Taiso's tolerance.

He was unable to get more out of the Latvian, and Kingsley was impatient to leave. As they made their way along the landing and down the back stairs, the strains of *For He's A Jolly Good Fellow* drifted through the house.

Hirst was dead and a young girl had been saved, but where were Cath and Angie? Was there a basement in the place? Were they locked in the ice house? He was at a loss where to search for them next.

24

Brian and Steve walked briskly past the shrubberies at the back of the Hall. They had wasted half an hour being led a frustrating dance by foxes in the trees at the back of the garages that they had mistaken for intruders. Without the dogs, of course, it was near impossible to tell the difference. That the foxes were really gypsies had never occurred to them.

"That wind's getting stronger," Brian observed. "You could hide an entire platoon out here and we wouldn't hear a thing."

"That suggests to me that those farm women can scream all they like and no one will notice," Steve said with a laugh. "We should visit 'em now, while they're all pie-eyed in the Hall."

They suddenly found themselves confronted by two shadowy figures dressed in dark clothing and wearing cat masks. The element of surprise worked to the figures' advantage. Before the minders could make a move, Royston and Bennett had them hooded and tranquillized. They took their hand-guns, bound the minders' wrists and ankles and gaffer-taped their mouths for good measure. Then they rolled them unceremoniously into the shrubbery.

* * *

Unknown to Royston and Bennett, Cath and Angie were still tied to wall fittings in the outbuilding a mere one hundred yards away. Cath seemed uncon-scious, her head slumped sideways. Angie tussled with her bonds, got a hand free and removed her gag.

"Mam? Mam!"

Cath did not respond.

Angie freed her other hand and began untying the cords around Cath's wrists. "Mam—speak to me!" As she unfastened the last of Cath's bonds, her mother fell to the floor. Angie knelt beside her. "Mam —wake up!"

Cath was dehydrated and unconscious. Angie felt her way to the door but found it was locked. Unable to find the light switch, she hammered on the door with her fists and shouted: "Help! Help! Somebody help me!" But her cries, like so much litter, were carried away by the indifferent wind.

The effort of shouting was too much for her dry throat and resulted in a coughing fit. When she had recovered, she knelt by her mother again and tried to rouse her. Cath didn't respond. Angie felt her mother's hands and forearms. They were cold. Was her mother dying?

Water, she thought, I must find water! Although she searched the walls by touch and at last located the light switch, she found no water anywhere in the building, no tap, no sink or cistern. She panicked and beat again on the door, but as before, there was no response from outside.

Blood, she thought. Blood! She pricked her finger on a hairgrip and smeared the slow trickle on her mother's lips. It was better than nothing, but still not enough. Her mother's lips were not as dry, but she made no attempt to swallow the blood. Water! she screamed to herself. Water! Water! Water! But the building was as dry as the central Sahara.

She sat on the floor and leaned back against the wall, then pulled her mother against her and cradled her head like a sleeping child's. At least she could try to keep her mother warm. Sometime soon a rescuer would come.

She had to believe it or succumb to despair. She realised it was night time, as the few tiny cracks around the doorframe no longer showed up as they had earlier. No one would come to rescue them at night.

Hope vanished. Her spirits dropped like stones into an abyss. Their only visitor would be Phil Yates with his gun.

* * *

Phil hurried into his office and went to his wall safe. Before he could tap in the code, his mobile rang.

"Clive—what's up?"

Clive explained that he had gone home, made himself a strong coffee, then walked across the yard to the stable block that was hidden from his line of sight behind the feed store and a range of garages. To his horror, he found that the padlock securing the door of the stable block had been severed with a bolt cutter and the loose box that should have contained Good Times was empty. He had yard lights but no cameras, so there wasn't going to be any visual evidence of the thieves.

"Someone either knew we'd be out or simply got lucky." This was an explanation that covered most possibilities, but neither he nor Phil were thinking clearly.

"Christ!" Phil exclaimed. "I'm on my way!"

"We're not going to find him in the middle of the night!" Clive objected. "He could be miles away by now."

"I'm coming anyway. Why don't you phone the police?"

"I will. But they won't turn up till daylight, and they might not be interested in a stolen horse, no matter how valuable it is." But he was talking to no one. Phil had already rung off.

As Phil ended the call, he saw the figurine of a T'ang horse catching the moonlight in the centre of his desk. He approached the figurine in disbelief and stared at it, as a sensation like ice-cold water trickled from the back of his neck all the way down his spine.

How could a figurine possibly be here? What did it mean? Good Times was missing and had been replaced by a T'ang horse! What kind of diabolical magic was this? The horse's expression—the turn of the head, that eye, those teeth!—seemed to be mocking him.

Was it taking its revenge because he hadn't asked permission to become its new owner but instead had shut it away out of sight like a prisoner in a dungeon? There was more going on here than could be explained by mere logic. He had caught his foot in an invisible tripwire that had awoken the world of sympathetic magic! When did this happen? Where? How?

He left the office and burst into the drawing room, where Harry was stuffing the packaging from his gifts into a bin bag and Dot was dozing on a sofa.

"Who the hell's been into my office?"

"No one," Harry replied. "You locked the door—I saw you. Didn't you have to unlock it to get in?"

Of course he had. Or had he? He couldn't remember. For a moment Phil felt his carefully managed world was beginning to slip away from him. He banished the disturbing notion from his mind. "I thought you locked those T'ang horses in the old ice house?"

"So did I," Harry replied.

"One's got out!"

Harry laughed. "Well, you said yourself they're supposed to have magical powers. *You* put it in the office, Phil. You must have done it in your sleep." At least it was a change from screwing Maureen.

"I did not!" For a moment Phil was unsure. But no. No. If he was sleepwalking, he would have realised. "I did not, I tell you!"

Phil's mind was leaping from one nightmare scenario to another; he couldn't control it. Was Harry taking the piss—had he put the horse there himself? He knew where the key to the ice house was kept...

"Good Times is gone! I'll be back later." He made for the door. Harry didn't offer to help.

"Phil!" Dot called after him. "What the hell are you putting horses in the ice house for?"

He ignored her and hurried from the room.

"He never ran after me that fast!" Dot poured herself a large whisky. She sagged forlornly on the sofa.

The Mercedes was out the front, but he couldn't remember leaving it there. Had his possessions taken on a life of their own? Phil leaped into the driver's seat, turned the key and flicked on the headlights. The figurine of a T'ang horse stood in the middle of the drive, turned sideways-on to the car. The figurine glared back in the headlights, revealing the same mocking expression.

"Oh—Jesus!"

He stared at the figurine in rising fear and climbed out of the car. He walked towards it but found he was unable to touch it. Was it cursed? Had Luke Smith and his clan laid a malediction on all the figurines? Was he, Lucky Phil Yates, trapped in their web? Was his so-called luck being turned against him? Was he going to start vomiting hair and needles? Were all the horses in the world plotting to kill him?

He hurried back to the Mercedes and drove around the figurine. A moment later he glanced in the rear-view mirror. To his horror he saw that the drive was empty—there was no sign the figurine had ever been there. That was the only proof he needed: he was trapped in a world of illusions created by vengeful horses!

Luke tucked the T'ang horse figurine under his arm and watched the Mercedes speed away down the drive. With Phil out of the way, they could move on to the next stage of his plan.

But again he was torn between pursuing his revenge and searching for Cath and Angie. He had managed to force the ancient lock on the door to the ice house and had found the figurines but no captives. He had located no basement door either. Where were Cath and Angie? He began to despair of ever finding them—and their captor had just driven away...

He phoned Farley. "It's time."

* * *

Dot was slumped unconscious on the sofa. Maureen shook her gently but was unable to rouse her.

"Dot? Dot—wake up!"

Harry strode in, mobile in hand. "Can't raise Bri and Steve. If they've cleared off for the night without permission, they can pack their stuff and go for good!" He saw Dot. "Damn! She don't look well."

"It's your fault all this," Maureen stated accusingly.

He resented her hostile tone. "Hell d'you mean?"

She continued undaunted. "Dot saw through you, y'know. You and Phil. All the scheming. The dirty deals. How many lives have you ruined, Harry?

Look at her. All she wanted was a caring guy. Not all this..." She waved her hand at the expensive furnishings. "This place is your bloody power trip! It's you that's pathetic, not her!"

He hit her. She fell, striking her head on a heavy oak side table, then lay still, bleeding profusely. He stared down at her. After the failed Viagra and his deepening sense of sexual futility, he realised he felt nothing. He picked Dot up and carried her from the room.

He took her down the long corridor that ran the length of the ground floor until he reached the back entrance that led to the courtyard and garages. His Range Rover was parked in the yard. He laid Dot gently on the back seat. She was still out cold.

"Time to get you dried out." He doubted that she could hear him.

He got in the Range Rover and drove from the yard. He'd had enough. When he had got his sister sorted, he intended to sever himself from all connections with Phil. The man had become impossible to endure, with his towering ego and endless suspicions. He had the impression lately that Phil had started to lose his grip, with his chronic anxiety, his fluctuating moods and his constant need for reassurance, not to mention the thirty-second blackouts and physical collapses.

They should never have burned Ambrose Smith's trailer. Phil's triumphant revenge had been short-lived and had morphed into paranoia. Was Cath Scaife really the witness to the fire, or was Phil just looking for a scapegoat?

It had got to the point where the man didn't trust anyone—and from this evening's evidence, he had even begun to doubt himself. Harry had visions of a near-future fallout. Well, he'd get in ahead. He would see his legal guys first thing in the morning.

He caught sight of something lying across the drive and slammed on his brakes. Dot, unnoticed, rolled off the back seat on to the floor. What the hell was happening? Was it his turn to start seeing things?

A scatter of two dozen large logs completely blocked the drive entrance. He got out of the Range Rover and stared at them. What was going on? Had the minders done this as a final *fuck you*? But surely not. He couldn't believe they had abandoned the place. Were they running some lucrative racket he wasn't aware of?

He tried Brian's mobile, but there was still no response. Steve's was the same. Had they also picked up bad vibes from Phil and decided to pull out? But they knew too much about the private business of the Hall simply to walk away. He'd find them and sort them out.

Someone was just begging for trouble. Whoever it was, they had raised their nemesis!

25

Harry began carrying the logs from the drive. He had shifted around half of them when he noticed a figure in a cat mask watching him from the grass at the side of the drive.

"Who the fuck are you?" He remembered he had left his handgun in his bedroom, but no matter, he'd sort the idiot without it.

"A ghost from the past," the figure replied. He raised his mask.

Harry remembered Hirst's mugshot. His fury boiled over. "Luke Smith!"

Luke took a step closer. "Comeuppance time, Harry."

Before Harry could make a move Sy, also masked, materialised behind him and cast a skip net over him as Kingsley roared up on Bennett's motorbike. Harry tried to fight his way out of the net but fell with a cry of fury. Luke and Sy roped the net closed and hooked it to the back of the bike.

Luke looked down at Harry. "Can't let you have all the fun, can we, birthday boy?"

Harry tried in vain to fight his way out of the net. Luke and Sy stood over him as Kingsley revved the bike.

"D'you think we should chuck this dinilo in one of the ponds back there?" Sy asked. "Hang a couple o' rocks from his dick?"

Luke stared down at the man in the net. "Hear that, Harry? Ain't a nice way to die. But mebbe not as bad as being burned alive in a trailer."

"How much d'you want?" Harry spluttered. "I'll pay."

"You bet your dumb life you will," Luke replied savagely. "Where've you hid Cath and Angie?"

Harry made no reply. Kingsley revved the bike.

"You let me go and I'll tell you," Harry offered.

"You tell me first and I'll think about it," Luke replied.

"Forget it," Harry growled. "Let me go or you'll never find 'em."

Harry thought of his sister lying in the Range Rover and urgently needing his help. But he knew Luke Smith might never free him, even if he told him where the farm women were being kept. Stalemate.

Luke knew if he freed Harry the big man would almost certainly lie and do his best to fight back. He would be a hard man to beat, even with three against one. He decided the best way was to soften him up.

At a signal from Luke Kingsley set off down the drive on the motorbike, dragging Harry behind him.

Harry screamed.

After half a minute Kingsley turned the bike and roared back.

"Feel like telling me now?" Luke asked.

A spirit of defiance had arisen in Harry. He had no intention of selling himself cheap. These people had no standards, no principles. He was dead whatever he told them. He would say nothing. He almost felt like the young powerhouse he used once to be. It was a great feeling, overwhelmingly welcome. "Fuck you, you goddamn scum!" he roared.

Kingsley set off again down the drive.

Harry yelled defiantly in the spirit of his reborn inner strength.

* * *

Half an hour later, all the logs had disappeared and the drive and lawn were deserted. The Range Rover's engine was still running, the driver's door wide open, but Harry was nowhere to be seen.

There were signs of movement inside the Range Rover. With considerable difficulty, a sequined arm hauled a body up off the floor. Dot's head appeared above the passenger's seat then vanished again, as the tightness of her dress inhibited her movements like a self-imposed straitjacket.

Her head appeared again, slowly followed by the rest of her. She dragged herself onto the back seat, managed to get the back door open, then collapsed head first on to the drive.

She lay still for a minute, then began crawling along the grass at the side of the drive, leaving a trail of sequins behind her that glittered under the moon like a snail track. Slowly she headed towards the house with the laborious exertions of a small bug crossing the expanse of a Herdwick carpet. She paused to rest, as small bugs do, then began to crawl forward again…

* * *

Malcolm had lost track of the gypsies. They seemed to be working in small units, picking off the occupants of the house and bringing them back to the dining room. He had been impressed with the gypsies' speed and efficiency, working in silent harmony in the darkness where even SAS teams might have struggled.

He understood that this was their natural environment and had been for centuries. Evidently some of them still possessed the skills of their forebears with only their night vision and common purpose to guide them. No wonder police and gamekeepers had found them difficult to apprehend.

There had been time, in the gypsies' absence, for him to explore a little of the house. He had found a female, the one called Maureen, in the drawing room and the naked body of a dead man in a first-floor bedroom. He had identified the man from items in the jacket pockets of his suit as Detective Inspector Nigel Hirst, obviously a bent cop in Phil Yates' pay.

He had carried the woman and the cop to the dining room to join the three men already there. An hour earlier he had watched from the corridor as Harry's birthday celebrations were in full swing. He almost laughed. How lives can change.

It wasn't clear what the gypsies intended to do with the collection of persons in the dining room. But he had ideas of his own. He had no wish to fight the gypsies; they had made his own task a lot easier, but he was happy to use his stun gun on them—and his Walther if he had no choice—if they came back to the house and caused him problems.

Phil Yates had driven away earlier, and he had to wait for his return. In the meantime, he must find out where the man kept his liquid assets—probably in a safe in an office or study. And he had a humorous notion of what to do with the occupants of the dining room...

After twenty minutes of determined effort, Dot reached the steps of the main entrance to the house. She crawled up the steps, slow and deliberate, like some scaly vertebrate taking its first hesitant excursion on land. The doors of the main entrance stood wide open, letting in the exuberant night wind, as if the place had been suddenly abandoned. Gripping the door frame, she dragged herself upright and staggered into the house.

She located the dining room and stumbled through the door. In an attempt to regain a semblance of dignity, she straightened her sequined dress and patted down her dishevelled hair. She succeeded in covering everything she touched with mud from her grimy hands.

The main lights in the room were turned off. The fancy antique oil lamp burned in the centre of the table, shedding its soft homely light on a scene difficult to imagine outside the pages of a horror novel.

Brian and Steve sat on opposite sides of the table, their arms and legs taped to their dining chairs, their mouths sealed with gaffer tape and their foreheads glued to the top of the table. Malcolm was not in the least concerned that they should see him. He was going to shoot them anyway when he was ready.

Harry, plastered with mud, sat at the head of the table, the remains of his birthday cake before him. On top of the cake were a few lit candles, their flames guttering in the draughty wind that now frisked unhindered through the entire house like an anarchic free spirit.

In addition to the cake, half a dozen glasses and bottles of liquor stood on the table, as if those who had not already collapsed were still determinedly drinking. A closer inspection revealed that Harry would not be drinking anything at all, as his forearms were glued to the table, his mouth covered with gaffer tape and his legs taped firmly to his dining chair. The tape had been the gypsies' idea. The glue and the unavoidable use of his stun gun were Malcolm's.

Maureen sat opposite Harry at the other end of the table. Dried blood covered the side of her face and neck and had soaked into her gold-coloured dress, turning the silk into a muddy brown. Her eyes, wide open, stared at her husband. Hirst sat next to her with the dark bullet hole in the centre of his forehead. Both he and Maureen were, of course, dead. They required little gaffer tape or glue, only sufficient to keep them upright.

When Harry saw Dot, he struggled massively and tried to cry out. The oil lamp rocked dangerously, threatening to topple over. Oil spilled on to the table.

Dot swayed towards the table and steadied the lamp. "Careful, Harry! You'll be causing an accident!"

She sat at the table, reached for whisky and a glass, poured herself a drink and drained the glass in one gargantuan gulp. She lit a cigarette but lost consciousness immediately, falling face down on the table. Her cigarette went flying, rolling along the table. It lay there smoldering by the spilled oil from the lamp.

The spilled oil caught fire. Flames licked along the table. Harry struggled. The oil lamp fell over, spilling more oil. The flames spread.

Malcolm stood in the doorway. He studied the scene for some moments before he could decide on what action he should take. He abandoned the idea of the Walther. Instead he took his camera from his backpack and photographed the bizarre tableau. He sent a copy to his paymasters and another to Tam. He accompanied the former with the cryptic message *up north they go one better than Russian roulette.* To Tam he said *six down and one to go.*

He might even describe a similar scene in the film script he was writing—and part financing—on the hilarious misadventures of the London mob. It was to be his literary swansong. He wondered if his new bosses would be smart enough to understand the script. Better if they waited for the movie.

The gypsies had done a good job, but they had not delivered Phil Yates. However, he would easily find him. He was looking forward to meeting the man who had inflicted on his brother such pain and humiliation.

He wished to point out that actions of such indulgent cruelty invited a proportional response to maintain the forces of the universe in equilibrium. He wanted to make it clear that justice was a natural mechanism that no one could escape. Karmic law, no less. Hubris and nemesis, or what you will. He was merely the cosmic instrument on this occasion.

Phil Yates would not escape. The force of his single-minded purpose would bind them together as effectively as shared leg irons.

* * *

In the outbuilding, Angie and Cath lay huddled together on the floor. It was the only thing Angie could think of doing to keep her mother alive. She had no idea how long they had lain there, but gradually Cath's body had begun to feel as if it was absorbing warmth from her own. Her mother's pulse had definitely grown stronger.

Angie had nothing except sounds on which to place her attention. Outside the night had become wilder.

She could hear the wind shrieking through gaps under the roof tiles and buffeting the walls like huge spectral fists. She could hear nothing for the sound of the wind. No footsteps, no voices. It was as if they were trapped in the most remote building on the planet. A weather station in the north of Greenland, perhaps. Or an abandoned frontier post of the Foreign Legion.

What had happened to Luke? Her last contact with him seemed ages ago, way back when he was leaving for a meeting with his father. Had he moved on with his life and forgotten them? Would she never see him again? Her mother had mentioned *unfinished business* that had drawn the three of them together.

She wondered what on earth this business could be. Her mother had never said. Was it over already? Was this the inevitable conclusion? Were they doomed to die in this nameless place? Was their farm just a fading memory?

She had searched the interior of the building but had found no key to the door. On inspection she had realised there wasn't even a lock. The place must be padlocked on the outside. How many people had keys? The two thugs, perhaps. And Phil Yates. No one who would help them. She had switched off the light, but there was no sign of day-light in the cracks around the door.

Night seemed so much longer when you were waiting for it to end. But when the daylight finally arrived, Phil Yates would come with it to play his ter-rifying game with the gun.

26

B efore Luke drove away from Birch Hall to catch up with Sy, he had decided to divide responsibilities. Farley had set off to Cuckoo Nest with his lurcher bitch and the truck and living van to keep an eye on the raklies and watch out for Sawmill Charlie. Kingsley, Royston and Bennett were asked to look for Cath and Angie. Harry had remained resolutely mute and the two minders had shrugged and denied all knowledge.

Luke had told his three companions to search for a hidden room on the top floor of Birch Hall that he might have missed. If they couldn't find one, they should look for a door and a staircase leading to a basement. Then he thought of the age of the house and of the religious conflict that had existed back then. He had read about it in visits to the library in his search for more information on gypsy history.

Had the first owner of Birch Hall been a Catholic sympathiser? Did the house have a priest hole? Had the Catholic mass been performed in a secret chapel hidden somewhere in the building? He had phoned Kingsley and tried to explain his feelings, but the three travellers he had left behind hadn't grasped what he was trying to say. He had become convinced that Cath and Angie had been hidden in a secret room. He asked Kingsley to find it.

Look under carpets for trapdoors, he advised, that might lead to a secret place big enough to hide two people. Kingsley had assured him they would, and he'd phone Luke if they found one. But no phone calls came. Luke wondered if Kingsley thought he was crazy. The young gypsy's knowledge of history went no farther back than waggon time.

There was Phil. The man who knew the truth. But how could he wring it from him without revealing his desperation? If Phil sensed a weak spot, Luke knew the cunning devil would use it against him. He would realise he had one ace left. And Phil Yates was a gambling man.

* * *

While Clive drove despairingly around the district in the dark looking for a glimpse of Phil's stolen horse, the animal's owner had arrived at the stables with the forlorn notion that Good Times might escape from his captors and come back of his own accord.

Driven by his inherent paranoia—which was exacerbated by what he believed were his recent supernatural experiences—Phil's first action was to check the loose boxes, although reason told him it was a pointless exercise. Only one loose box was empty, the name *GOOD TIMES* printed above the door. Phil switched on the light and entered the loose box. Two T'ang horse figurines stared up at him from the floor.

"Aaaaah—no!" he cried in disbelief. As he burst from the loose box, beset by a growing certainty that his life was now subject to the caprice of magicians, he heard a tattoo of hooves from the darkness at the far end of the yard. He hurried from the stables and ran eagerly towards them.

Luke appeared in a cat mask, seated bareback on Prince of Thieves. Sy, also masked, led Good Times on a rope.

"Get the hell away from my horse!" Phil cried in shock and outrage.

He tried to approach Good Times, but Prince of Thieves reared up and lunged at him. He knew immediately, from long experience, that the two men were gypsies. Their clothing, the way they moved, their jet-black hair above the masks, all spoke of the type of people he had met at horse fairs in the days when his father was alive.

"Damn you, you filthy gyppo!" Phil roared. "Give me my horse!"

Luke removed his mask. "The name's Luke Smith, Boswell clan."

Phil stared at Luke in fear and dismay. He took out his mobile. "I'm getting the police!"

Prince of Thieves lunged at Phil again and he dropped the phone. The stallion crushed it with a hoof.

Luke smiled. "All alone now, ey? Just me and you." He took Phil's revolver from his pocket and held up a crushed bullet in his other hand. "Shot any jukels lately? Or maybe some old mumper?"

Phil gathered his wits quickly, his survival instinct working flat out. "I don't know what you think I've done, but I've got nothing to do with dogs or tramps. You're accusing the wrong man."

Luke stared at him in cold fury. Cath and Angie had been taken prisoner by this cocky little fellow. Somehow he had to outsmart him.

"I've got witnesses. Too afraid of you back then 'cos they were young. But they'll testify now. You'll spend the rest of your short life in jail. Just think of the folk you'll meet in there who you've cheated. D'you think you'll last more'n a month?"

Phil was wrong-footed. Was this a bluff? How could he know? How many witnesses were there to that accursed fire?

Luke pointed the revolver at Phil. "Mebbe I'll get justice now. It'll save you having to face all the poor sods still inside who've got time 'cos o' you."

Phil backed away in terror. "Please..." he pleaded. "You've got the wrong man."

Luke kept up the pressure. "This is the gospel according to Luke: You're going down—and I've got the evidence!"

Phil stared at him with hatred and mounting dread. He had always feared he would lose the little empire he had built—and now, in the mocking shape of this gypsy traveller, that moment had arrived. But he wasn't called Lucky for nothing. He was a risk taker who only needed half a chance to turn the tables on his rivals. "Why don't we sort this out the old-fashioned way?" he suggested.

Luke sensed a trick was coming. He decided to let the fellow play his hand.

"Are you a sporting man, Luke Smith?"

"What've you got in mind?"

"D'you think your horse is fast? I'll wager mine's faster. Let's put 'em to the test. Winner takes all."

Luke felt his combative instinct rising to the challenge, though his reason fought against it. Sy had raised his mask and was shaking his head in warning.

"A ride to the death, d'you mean?" Luke asked.

Phil smiled as guilelessly as he could. "Why not?

Luke glanced at Sy, who had a look that told his friend to back off. But he had the best horse he had ever seen, and it was a master of rough country. All his opponent's mount had done was gallop around a racetrack. It was no contest. He also had Phil Yates' gun and would use it if he had to.

"I accept."

Sy reluctantly released Good Times. Phil seized the horse's rope.

"Have you really got the balls, Phil Yates?" Luke goaded. "Or are you just a nasty little bully? My grye will ride yours legless."

Phil sprang bareback on to Good Times. "I can out-ride a filthy gyppo any day! And I have the best horse in the whole of England!"

"You're gonna have to prove it!" Luke replied. He gave Prince of Thieves his head and raced from the yard.

Phil, on Good Times, followed.

* * *

The moon, sailing high in a clear sky, cast an eerie glow over woodland, fields and lanes. Luke rode hard on Prince of Thieves. Phil pursued him. They rode across hillside pastures, through woods and wild grassy valleys, down empty lanes, through sleepy farmyards, the distance increasing until they had ridden more than a mile.

A few times Phil drew level with Prince of Thieves, trying to force Luke into danger, into briar-filled tangles of woodland undergrowth, barbed-wire fences at the borders of fields, crumbling quarry edges that led to sickening drops. Each time Luke changed direction and Prince of Thieves drew ahead.

They arrived at a river, Prince of Thieves several lengths clear of Good Times. Luke descended at a gallop towards a low point in the bank, riding full tilt into the water. Phil followed, Good Times blowing hard and tiring.

Prince of Thieves swam strongly, easily pulling ahead of Good Times. Half way across the river a Ming ch'i, the gigantic spirit-form of a T'ang horse, reared from the water. Good Times panicked at the sight and thrashed around, threatening to dislodge his rider.

"Steady, boy! Whoa! Steady!" Phil cried. Had he created this? Was this vision a product of his guilt? Or were the T'ang horses getting their own revenge?

Good Times was thoroughly spooked. Phil lost his grip on the horse. The spirit form vanished.

Luke, who had not seen the Ming ch'i, turned Prince of Thieves and trod water. Phil floundered in the river.

"Help me! Help me!" he cried in desperation.

Luke tried to reach him. Phil grabbed his outstretched arm but contrived to pull him from Prince of Thieves. They fought in the water, all the while drifting downstream in the quickening current.

The horses clambered to safety on the far bank. Their riders were briefly visible, heading downstream towards the thundering water of a weir.

The river at this point was squeezed into a narrow channel, forming a deep torrent that poured over the weir's edge and fell twenty feet into a churning cauldron of water and foam. Luke and Phil appeared briefly at the curling edge, then they vanished into the seething chaos below.

They emerged from the raging water a hundred yards downstream. Phil, drowning, began to sink. Luke grabbed him, dragged him to the bank and hauled him out. They lay on the bank regaining their breath. The horses appeared, walking calmly towards them.

Luke got to his feet and stood over Phil. "D'you wanna go on? I had you beat fair and square. But we can race till your grye's heart gives out if you want."

Phil seemed reluctant to continue. He looked up at his rival. "Why did you save me?"

"I want justice," Luke replied sternly. "I'd rather have you alive in a law court than dead out here."

Phil sat up and eyed Prince of Thieves. "It's one helluva horse you've got there."

Luke smiled. "I know. But he ain't for sale. D'you wanna go on or not?" he asked again.

"I can't," Phil admitted. "Good Times was blowing back there. He's a bit winded. You've got the better animal for rough ground."

"So you admit defeat?

Phil nodded. He seemed resigned. "I'm sorry for what I did back then. You'd better shoot me now and take my horse. I owe you that at least."

Luke was surprised by the man's confession. He sounded sincere, but was it just some new trick?

He seized the moment. "Where did you put Cath and Angie Scaife?"

"I can show you," Phil replied with a cunning smile. "But you'll have to let me live a while longer if you want me to do that. You won't find 'em otherwise. You'll have to leave 'em to die."

They stared at each other, Luke furious, Phil seemingly amused. Damn the man, Luke thought, he knows I can't find them. What kind of dance is he going to lead me now?

Phil laughed quietly. Who's the dinilo here, he thought. I've got my life back and I intend to use it!

Before either man could make a move, the southern horizon was illuminated by a vivid orange-red glow. Phil lurched to his feet.

"It's my house!" he cried. "My beautiful house!"

Exhausted as he was, he flung himself on to Good Times and plunged back into the river. Luke charged after him on Prince of Thieves.

27

They arrived together in the gateway of Birch Hall, Good Times blowing badly and Luke easing up on Prince of Thieves to stay with him. They rode past Harry's Range Rover, the burning house ahead of them. It seemed to Luke that Good Times was hardly moving, while Prince of Thieves was as strong as ever. But Phil had forgotten about their race. His entire attention was fixed on his burning house.

The front of the house was an inferno, the blaze fanned by the insistent wind. Phil leaped from Good Times as did Luke from Prince of Thieves. Both horses panicked and shied away from the blaze.

"NO! NOOOOO!!" Phil yelled at the sight of the destruction. He sprinted up the main steps, but Luke felled him in a flying tackle. Possessed by what seemed like a madman's strength Phil struggled free and hurtled headlong into the burning house. In a second he was swallowed by the conflagration.

Luke stared after him helplessly. Before he could make a move he heard Kingsley's voice behind him. Turning, he saw Royston roping the horses and Bennett approaching down the drive in the Citroen, with Sy following with pickup and horse trailer.

"There's a gorgio robbing Phil Yates' safe," Kingsley announced. "Best sort him."

"You didn't find the juval and rakli?" Luke asked, without any remaining hope.

Kingsley shook his head. "We searched the house, but there were no secret rooms. And we found a big wine cellar. But we've still got to look at the garages and sheds, there's a helluva lot of 'em."

"You and Bennett get searching," Luke decided. "We'll deal with the gorgio."

The fire had spread through the entire front half of the house and had begun to consume the rooms to the rear of the building on the west side, fanned by the gusting wind. So far the rooms at the back on the east side, including Phil's office, were untouched, although smoke had begun to billow through them.

Luke entered the house by the courtyard door and found the door to the office open. A figure in army camouflage was in the process of examining the door of the wall safe. The figure turned to face him.

"Tam!" Luke exclaimed in astonishment.

"Not Tam," Tam's double replied. "I'm fifteen minutes older than my twin bro'—and I'm here to make sure justice is done for him."

Luke recovered himself quickly. "That makes two of us."

Malcolm studied the wild looking gypsy that stood before him. "So ye's the thief that took the T'ang horses?"

Luke feigned bewilderment. "*What* kind o' horses?"

"I'm not going to argue," Malcolm continued. "By rights I should plug ye where ye stand. I'm only interested in justice for my bro'. Ye's put yersel in my way."

Luke found himself staring at Malcolm's Walther PK380 that was fitted with a silencer. "What the hell have these horses got to do with you?"

Malcolm enlightened him. "I happen also to be working for certain vested interests who take a very poor view o' what happened to one o' their top guys, namely the gent who died mysterious-like in his snake house. Can ye tell me about that?"

"I know nothing about snakes," Luke replied. "My job was to get four antique horses for a nameless buyer, who turned out to be Phil Yates, the owner of this house." He thought it worth adding that he hadn't been paid. "The last I saw of these horses was when Tam packed them up for delivery." Had Tam told his brother he had attacked him? Luke wondered, looking at Malcolm's gun. "I don't know if Tam's been paid, but we both risked jail to get those horses." He said nothing about facing death in the psycho's vivarium.

"No one's been paid," Malcolm stated dourly. "I'm here to collect the loot and ye's not in a position to stop me. If there's fifty large spare, ye can have it. O' course, the safe might be empty."

"You'll be making a mistake, twin brother," Luke replied calmly. "I'm here for as much vongar as I can get. If you shoot me, my cousin, who's standing behind you, will cut your throat."

Malcolm laughed. "There's no one behind me, horse thief. No one sneaks up on Malcolm McBride."

"This'll be a first then," Sy said coldly, pressing the flat of his blade to the back of Malcolm's neck. "And there's plenty more Roms out the back who'll be happy to do the same."

"Why don't we agree a deal?" Luke offered, ready to roll under the office desk if Malcolm refused. "If there's anything in that safe, we'll split it fifty-fifty."

For the first time in his life Malcolm realised he was in a losing situation. He hadn't dealt with gypsies before, and he saw that this pair had him beaten. The man behind him had appeared so silently he could have materialised out of the floor. He lowered the Walther.

"Fair enough. But ye won't even get into that safe without me. It's one o' those fiendish wee wall safes that no one can open without the code or a key. I ken ye've got neither. So we've no choice but blow the door off."

Luke and Sy stood back and watched Malcolm as he carefully placed his charges. Then all three of them moved to one side as the Scot blew the safe door clean out of its housing.

"I can see you've done this before," Luke said, genuinely impressed by Malcolm's expertise.

The Scot laughed. "I've done it once or twice. Let's put the loot on the desk and see what we've got."

The safe was relieved of its contents and the large amount of cash and other items were dumped on Phil's desk and assessed. Malcolm took the bonds, the gold bullion and 350K in cash. "That's payment for my bro', ye ken." Luke and Sy helped themselves to the rest of the cash, stuffing it into Luke's rucksack. Luke also took the passports of Harry's escort girls. He had no idea what he would do with them, but they would be lost to the fire otherwise.

The amount of smoke in the room was becoming unbearable and the flames were getting closer to the doorway. The heat was growing intense and they had to shout to make themselves heard above the roar of the fire. But they held their nerve until their task was finished.

Sy hurled Phil's swivel chair through the office window and the three men made their escape by the only route that remained. Luke and Malcolm shook hands.

"My regards to Tam. No hard feelings."

"None o' this ever happened," Malcolm replied and promptly disappeared into the night.

As he put his rucksack on the back seat of the Citroen, Luke's despair over the fate of Cath and Angie overwhelmed him. Even if he was now a millionaire, it meant nothing. It was an intolerably bitter irony that the people he had cared most about in this life should be condemned to identical fates. Was this some kind of message? Was he destined to be alone for the rest of his days? Was it dangerous folly for him to form relationships?

He felt like flinging his rucksack into the flames. His dark mood was interrupted as Kingsley sprinted up. "The juval and the rakli—we've found 'em! We got no time!"

Luke and Sy followed Kingsley towards the complex of blazing outbuildings at the back of the house. Luke wondered if they were already too late.

* * *

Cath was not responding to Angie's attempts to rouse her. The roof of their prison had begun to burn fiercely, the voice of the fire consuming Angie's pitiful cries for help and denying all hope. The heat was intense. Angie made one last despairing effort to attract attention.

She beat on the door. "Help! Help us! We're in here!"

Luke, Sy and Kingsley sprinted towards the buildings. Bennett was waiting for them.

"They're in this one," Bennett said, "but I can't break the lock."

Angie's desperate cries could just be heard by keen gypsy ears, rising above the ferocious roar of the flames.

"We're in here! Help us!"

The building was at the back of an open cart shed that contained the big ride-on mower, making its existence almost impossible to detect in the dark. The door was secured with a large padlock. Luke blew the padlock apart with a shot from Phil's revolver, then kicked the door open and found Angie on the other side. Cath was lying on the floor, her back against the wall. She appeared to be unconscious. Angie threw herself into Luke's arms.

"Oh, Luke—it's Mam. I think she might be nearly dead!"

Blazing material from the burning roof supports was showering down around them. The entire roof seemed about to collapse, threatening to bring the pantiles crashing down on top of them. All eyes turned to Luke.

He ran to Cath. Her pulse was weak but regular. He lifted her in his arms. "Let's go!"

They hurried from the building as sections of blazing roof and debris from the back of the burning house crashed down behind them. The petrol vapour in the mower's tank exploded, barring the entrance to the hidden outbuilding with flames. They had only just been in time...

The convoy of vehicles made its way up the drive, Luke in the Citroen with Angie cradling Cath on the back seat. They were followed by Sy in the pickup, towing the big horse trailer containing Prince of Thieves and Good Times. The rear was brought up by Bennett on the motorbike, with Royston and Kingsley in the Transit.

Two bedraggled Dobermans appeared from the darkness and seemed pleased to see the gypsies. Sy opened the passenger's door of the pickup and the dogs leaped in. As he explained to Luke later, he would either sell them or use them as breeding stock, crossing them with greyhounds to produce more lurchers, the dog of choice for most gypsies.

They turned out of the drive and headed for Cuckoo Nest. A minute later, three fire engines with sirens blaring approached from the opposite direction. They had made a twenty-mile journey along winding country roads to get to the scene from the nearest fire station.

Cath and Angie were safe, but the irony of the situation was clearly evident to Luke. Fire had destroyed his family's trailer, but it had also consumed Birch Hall. Was this an example of cosmic justice in action?

One final detail lodged itself in his mind: There was no sign of Harry's Range Rover that had been left on the drive. Who had taken it? Against seemingly impossible odds, had Phil somehow managed to escape?

28

The orchard at Cuckoo Nest was filled with shifting patterns of dappled sunlight, as the late morning sun shone through breeze-blown leaves. Beyond the fruit trees, Sy's sisters were busy picking strawberries for the shop in the local town. Royston and Farley were fixing the fences around the paddocks, where a new growth of bright grass had begun to carpet them once more.

In the stackyard Bennett and a young gypsy youth worked on the tractor, which had at last been coaxed into life, while Kingsley and Angie flirted with each other as he taught her to ride Prince of Thieves bareback. The stallion considered Luke's friends to be his friends now, and he behaved respectfully to them all.

Zanda, the Latvian girl, had decided to throw in her lot with the Boswells. She was busy in a pair of Angie's overalls, painting the dried-out exterior of the barn an earthy shade of burnt umber while Sy painted the higher parts from a new alloy extension ladder. He noticed how capable she was, working quickly and quietly with a practised economy of physical effort. She never stopped and didn't seem to tire. From peasant stock, he thought, used to hard work from a young age, like folk in England used to be.

The pickup and horse trailer were pulled to one side of the stackyard, next to the truck and gypsies' living van. It was like a new world to Cath and Angie, as the farm's transformation took place, but without ruining the unique character of the place. Cath, slowly recovering from her ordeal, had never seen Cuckoo Nest this busy, not even in the years when Matt was alive. She and Luke watched the activity.

"So the gavvers have decided that the burning of Birch Hall was no accident?" he said without the least trace of guile.

"It's been all over the papers and TV," she replied. "The police are talking revenge. Gangland-type murders. Something to do with the theft of expensive horse figurines and the strange death of their owner."

He pulled an incredulous face. "It's all a mystery to me. Out o' my league completely. I know naught about gang wars." This was partly true. The fire inspectors had blamed an oil lamp as the cause of the blaze that had reduced Birch Hall to a shell. But when he and his companions had dumped Harry, Brian and Steve in the dining room, the lamp had seemed safe enough.

He wondered if Twin Brother had started the fire. Was total annihilation the injunction placed on him by his bosses? If so, they were as extreme as the tales he had read about the Sicilian Mafia. And what of Phil Yates, now named by the police as the missing seventh person who was wanted by the law for questioning? Had he got clean away in the Range Rover—was he planning his future under a new identity?

He pushed these thoughts from his mind as he walked with Cath across the stackyard.

"Y'know," he mused, "I like it here. I could almost settle down."

She seized on his comment eagerly. "Stay with us, Luke. We'll help you clear your name."

He resisted the temptation. "Best if I go to my uncle Taiso's. He knows folk who've got connections with top legal guys. I can afford to pay them." He smiled at her. "You up for a traveller wedding when I get back?"

Both delight and doubt fought for control of her emotions. "Will your people accept me?"

"They'd better! We can get wed on Taiso's land. It's only an hour's drive from here. He'll want to give us a proper wedding feast—everyone with the blood will be there. My dadu will come, and he'll be happy for us."

They hugged each other in a long embrace. "What happened with those passports?" he asked. "Are those girls ever gonna be safe?"

"Well, Sy seems to have adopted Zanda. I don't know if they'll become an item, but he's found out that her great, great grandparents were Kalderash gypsies from Hungary who were killed by the Germans in the war. He said she drew her family tree for him in the dust on the barn floor."

It takes one to know one, he thought again. It wasn't just his earnestness that had persuaded the girl to go with them, it was something deeper: the connection of the *kaulo ratti*. He studied the girl across the stackyard. Though her hair wasn't as dark as his own, it was the shape of her face, the set of the eyes, the litheness of her build that gave the clues of her lineage. Sy had realised straight away.

"How come she ended up with Harry Rooke?"

"Sy said she was an orphan. She told him that criminal gangs buy or abduct the good-looking girls from the orphanages. And most Roma girls are attractive."

Luke thought again about justice. Whose side would Malcolm McBride be on in a country where corruption was the new normal? Would he become a vigilante and shoot the officials?

"What about the other girls?"

"They're being looked after by social workers."

"Will they be sent back?"

She sighed. "That's difficult, 'cause no one knows who they really are or where they're from. Their passports are in bogus names with false dates of birth. They keep saying they were offered jobs, but the employers' names are complete fictions. They could be lying about their real names too, so trying to track them down on missing persons lists is impossible. Their details will be circulated through the Baltic states, but the girls all say they want to stay here. We've opened a real can of worms. No one knows what to do with them. They're staying in a hostel, but they could vanish under the radar at any time."

"They wouldn't be here if they had something worth going back for."

"Suppose not."

He realised that Zanda must have anticipated this mess, so she seized her chance with the Boswells. Smart girl.

* * *

Later that day, when Cath and Angie were packing the strawberries in the farm kitchen, Luke arrived from the cottage with their borrowed travelling bag. He dumped it on the table. Cath and Angie peered into the bag. It contained bundles of fifty-pound notes.

"I thought I'd relieve Phil Yates of a bit o' lucre. He owed me anyway. This should help clear your debts and get Sawmill Charlie off your back. I've given some to my cousins already, so the rest's yours."

Cath and Angie flung their arms around him and kissed him.

"You're free," he said laughing. "Great feeling, ain't it? You've struggled enough on your own. I think it's time you had a bit of assistance." He summarised the arrangement they had been recently thrashing out. "If my people rent the fields for their gryes and you have the rest, the fruit and the milk and meat, we're all happy, ain't we? And there'll always be some of us stopping here to see to their gryes and to help you out if you need 'em."

"We might not be too popular with the locals," Cath said. "But we'll just have to live with that."

"You never know. My people won't cause trouble. The locals might get to see we're clean hard-working folk. Like I said, if you put the earth first, travellers and settlers should get on."

"Let's hope so," Cath replied. "It's an experiment."

"It's time these bloody locals saw a bit further than their nose ends!" Angie declared. "It'll do 'em good. I'll bet if there is any trouble it'll come from them." She had been told by Cath that they had gypsy traveller blood, and the revelation seemed to have acted like an elixir. Her daughter had decided that she had to get wed too, and had homed in on the twenty-year-old Kingsley. Poor soul, Luke had thought with a smile. He'll have to get used to doing as he's told.

On his way across the stackyard, Luke met Bennett pulling up in the Transit. He had taken a break from tractor repairs to buy beers and an evening paper at the small supermarket in the town.

"Learned anything?" Luke asked.

Bennett showed Luke an item in the paper. "They're still on the lookout for Phil Yates. Some dinilos are saying he might've started the fire himself so he can get the insurance. You could give 'em a call and tell 'em he was with you!" Luke joined in Bennett's laughter. "And they're looking for a missing Range Rover," Bennett continued. "You sure that Malcolm mush never took it?"

"How would he get it away? He'd have his own motor, so there'd have to be a second driver," Luke reasoned. "I'm sure Malcolm McBride was on his own. I got the feeling he was a lone wolf kinda guy. We gotta believe Phil Yates escaped. He mebbe knew a secret door we never found and was long gone once he saw he was finished. We'll have to spread the word, get our folk to be dikkerin him."

Sy joined them, having finished painting the barn. He thought it unlikely Phil would ever surface again. "He's a marked man. The top gavvers are wanting to know how that Hirst mush was shot with his own weapon. Ain't no one'll ever do business with Phil Yates now. What's he gonna do—go back on the road with a Brush waggon and be selling carpets?" He shook his head. "Ain't nothing left for him."

Luke made no comment. He had a feeling Phil Yates would bounce wherever he landed. But he had no desire to pursue him. He'd leave that to the professionals.

They crossed the yard, walking past the newly-completed range of loose boxes they had created from a row of old cart sheds. "Prince of Thieves and Good Times are best mates ever since that ride to the death between you and Phil Yates," Sy commented, watching the two stallions grazing together in the orchard.

"It's kinda strange, you calling it a ride to the death when neither of us has died," Luke mused. "I've a feeling Phil Yates is laying low and will come back for the grye. These stables gotta be locked of a night in case he thinks he can nick it!"

Sy reassured him. "Me and Kingsley will be round all winter, lodging in the other kenner. We're gonna be kerengros! We'll be bringing some gryes down from Davey, and we'll have to ride the Prince when you're away and Good Times, too, to keep 'em on form." He laughed. "I like the thought of riding Phil

Yates's winner! But, o' course, we'll be looking out for prowlers."

"You better include Sawmill Charlie," Luke advised. "I'm surprised he ain't been down, shouting and waving his arms! Mebbe we've scared him off!"

* * *

As he spoke, Charlie was up in his loft watching the farm. What he observed made him moan and jabber in fury. "I don't like it. Them gyppos are all over. Cath Scaife's planning to get rid o' me, I know it. They're gonna put me on the bench and saw my head off! Make it look like I've had an accident. But they don't know who they're taking on. Ain't no one ever gonna kill Charlie!"

He clapped his telescope to his one good eye and watched the farm a while longer. Then he swung himself down to the cutting floor, where he was fulfilling an order of new fence posts for Cath. He talked to the sawblade as it whirred and screamed.

"Cath Scaife depends on me now. And she'll depend on me in the future. She's got a bit o' help, but they'll leave her. And I'll still be here!" He smiled as he worked. "One o' these days I'll be a farmer. One o' these days I'll have respect! I'll put a man in here to make fencing—but Mister Gibb will be growing lavender! I'll have a tea room for visitors. I'll have tours of the farm for townies. I'll—"

His private monologue stopped as reality caught up with him. He adjusted his eye patch and pulled down his floppy hat and continued cutting fence posts in silence.

* * *

While everyone was busy around the farm, Luke dug a pit in the floor of one of the empty loose boxes. He lined the base and sides with boards treated with wood preserver, then brought the T'ang horses from the cottage and packed them carefully in a solid-sided box. He lowered the box into the pit and re-floored the entire loose box with paving slabs that he had found lined up in a corner of the barn, bought years ago for some forgotten purpose. He got Bennett to help him as soon as he had finished his work on the smoothly running tractor.

"Why are we doing this?" Bennett asked. "An earth floor will do, won't it?"

"We're using stuff that's already been got and paid for," Luke replied. "Makes good sense to me."

They found they had enough paving slabs for three loose box floors. This pleased Luke, as the floor above the T'ang horses would not be the only one that was paved and therefore it would be less likely to arouse suspicion. He had no idea what to do with the figurines and was annoyed he had ended up with them. He found them strange and a little sinister and wondered if he should ask one of the old Boswell rawnis to exorcise them.

Perhaps they had formed a magical attachment to Good Times. Well, he would put the chestnut stallion in the loose box above them. Maybe that would make them all happy.

Next morning the gypsies, except for Luke, Sy, Zanda and Kingsley, left at first light and took the truck and living van with them. Sy and Kingsley, with Angie's and Zanda's enthusiastic assistance, moved into the second cottage, which was rent-free now, of course.

Sy and Zanda set off with the horse trailer to Davey Wood's land to fetch two more vanners to Cuckoo Nest. Luke and Kingsley were alone at the farm finishing off the work on the loose boxes, which were for valuable non-vanners, like Prince of Thieves and Good Times.

They had not had time to complete the locked tack room that would extend from the front elevation of the range of loose boxes—Luke envisaged that most of the horses kept at the farm would not be ridden bareback, so they had to create a space for saddles and harnesses. The doors of the occupied loose boxes were still not secured with temporary pad locks, a task they had planned for that morning.

To their amazement they found Good Times' stall was empty. A search of the farm produced nothing.

"That damn fella ain't finished yet," Luke said angrily.

Phil Yates had returned for the horse as Luke had predicted. The man had lost no time, but had obviously set himself up in some new place equipped with stabling for his prize chestnut stallion.

He must have had help, as it was at least a two-man task to get the animal away in the dark small hours while eight gypsy travellers were sound asleep! The night had been a stormy one, with everything that was loose making a clatter, perfect for the task of stealing a horse...

But someone had to hold the animal while his accomplice padded its feet so it made no sound crossing the stackyard. And someone else had to supply a horse trailer—towed no doubt by the missing Range Rover.

Luke cursed himself for underestimating his enemy.

It seemed Phil Yates had got himself the makings of a new team. How long would it be, Luke wondered, before he tried again to abduct Cath—or maybe to get rid of himself? One thing was certain: Phil Yates was fighting back.

Luke did not believe the man's confession, volunteered as they sat on the riverbank after their race. The more he thought about it the less credible it seemed. Phil Yates was a man who thought only of himself. His rapid rise to affluence would have been at many other people's expense. But he simply didn't care; he thought he could do as he pleased and would never be held to account for the hurt he caused. He would have forgotten he had even made that confession. Such a person would never change.

The phone call Luke received later that day from Malcolm McBride put the matter more succinctly. Luke was working with Sy, Zanda and Kingsley on the new tack room when Angie called him to the farmhouse.

"There's a strange man wants to speak to you," Angie said, looking intrigued. "He says his name's Twin Brother. He gave me a number for you to call him back."

Luke and Malcolm talked for some fifteen minutes. The gist of the conversation developed Luke's own inchoate thinking with regard to Phil Yates and justice. The Scotsman talked about cause and effect, action and consequence. "It's a fact of existence, a law o' physics, ye ken." As regards Phil Yates, Malcolm said, a counterweight would be placed one day, by human or "invisible" forces, in the other side of the scale.

So should he get justice, Luke asked, by hunting the man down? Or should he wait for hidden powers to do the job for him? "I'd be grateful if ye'd leave it wi' me, Luke. The fella's not worth fighting o'er."

There had to be a reckoning, Malcolm agreed. Justice was a natural mechanism "built into the invisible structures o' creation, ye ken." It "supplies life's checks and balances, even if we dinna ken it." It was a vital attribute of the mystic fluid, the "vril or whatever folk wish to ca' it," that held the universe together. "Dinna fash yoursel though, Luke. I'm creation's humble journeyman in the case. That villain will pay for the hurt he's done ye all."

Malcolm would give no further elaboration, so Luke went back to work on the tack room and waited for events to unfold.

29

Phil walked slowly around the moorland farmhouse and outbuildings, taking in the ancient slab roofs and massive stone walls that befitted the degree of exposure and remoteness of the place. He had only seen the property once on the day of his purchase, and the detail of its construction hadn't completely sunk in. Winter here would be difficult, he could see that, but he would cope if he had to. However, he hoped to be long gone by then. For now it was an ideal hideaway.

He owned other properties than this, a couple of warehouses, a small block of flats, a few semis and HMOs and a dozen terraced houses, as well as shares in many businesses, but nothing in his property portfolio suited him so well as this: a place in which to vanish and begin a new life. He had no radio or TV, but his assistants updated him on events and brought him a box of new mobile phones. He had spent most of the day talking on them and rearranging his affairs.

His lawyers were liaising with the fire service and were pressing for a decision in the official category of *a primary fire in a dwelling that involved fatalities and was caused by unknown factors*. But there was still disagreement as to the cause of the blaze. The oil lamp was now considered a secondary factor to arson—but the question was still open as to who started the fire. A fire inspector's decision was pending, but it was hampered by the police murder enquiry. It seemed there would be no decision and no insurance claim any time soon. Phil was furious.

He was troubled by thoughts of the dead. Would he attend their funerals? No, of course not, far too dangerous. The Boswells and the police would be hunting for him. Would he mourn? Yes, he would, but briefly. However, it was a final severance, and there was no point dwelling on what couldn't be changed. He missed Harry's cool head for business, but he would cope. At any rate, his accountant would. He was appalled that the police could think he might have started the fire himself, when it was either Luke Smith or members of the London underworld. But there was nothing he could do to establish his innocence.

He couldn't do anything without money. His bank accounts had been frozen, and the fire insurance seemed a near impossibility. He had other channels of funding, of course, but capital would be slow to accumulate. He had thought that he would go across to Ireland and buy a place as grand as Birch Hall. When he was ready, Good Times would be shipped over. Then he would start his life again. But at the moment this was a fantasy.

He had toyed with the idea of going to America, but he had no idea about the ease or otherwise of race fixing there. He had blood relations in Ireland. He would be welcome and protected if he threw a bit of money around. His accountant was busy freeing up his offshore funds. But before he could go anywhere he had to clear his name, otherwise he would be travelling in disguise as a wanted man, and Lucky Phil Yates would be history.

He had rushed into the doomed Birch Hall with the intention of taking what he could from the office safe. But by the time he had fought his way through the blazing rooms, he had discovered that gypsies were already there, along with a shadowy army-clad figure, who seemed intent on blowing off the safe door. He had no gun with which to confront them and had been forced to abandon the attempt and escape through a ground floor window. He was furious that gypsies had beaten him to it. Along with the gold and the bonds, there was a small fortune in cash in the safe. One day he would make Luke Smith and those gyppos pay. One day. There had to be justice.

It was three in the afternoon, Good Times' second exercise hour of the day. At least his handsome chestnut stallion knew who he was! He saddled up and set out across the moor. He was observed by nothing more sinister than nesting curlews and a skylark. Perfect. He had vanished from the world and would rise again, quite literally, like a phoenix from the ashes. All that was missing was a touch of his legendary luck.

Good Times was unusually placid. He didn't notice this at first but as the minutes passed, the feeling crept over him like the invisible early hints that you were coming down with flu. The horse had been fed and rested and groomed after his cross-country race with Luke Smith. He looked to be in his usual healthy condition. But something was missing.

"What's up, boy? Are you poorly?"

The animal's usual response to the tone of his voice was absent: no soft whinnying, no slight shake of the head. He was mystified. By the time he had turned to come back his impressions had clarified. It was as if Good Times was quietly waiting for something. But what?

* * *

Malcolm observed the moortop farm through his field glasses. The Range Rover, under which he had attached a tracking device while it was still on the drive at Birch Hall, was backed into an open-fronted cart shed attached to the eastern end of the house. The horse trailer that had been used to bring the racehorse had been put into one next to it. He assumed the stable for the horse was at the back of the property, but he would be easily spotted if he tried to get a better view. And he wasn't ready yet to be seen.

It was midsummer and pleasantly warm, even at twelve hundred feet above sea level. Curlews were piping in the reeds to the south of the house, and a rare skylark was singing above its nest in the moorland grasses behind him. But the occupant of the house showed little interest in such things. He had spent some time removing items from the Range Rover and carrying them into the property.

He surmised that the occupant was getting stocked up for a long wait. Two young guys had turned up in a Jeep at midday and taken bulky objects, which looked like bedding, into the house. He had wondered if Phil Yates was renting or if he actually owned the place.

An hour's research on his laptop the previous evening, at the end of his third day's surveillance, had put the matter beyond doubt. The farmhouse and two thousand acres of surrounding moorland was owned by a firm named Midas Holdings, which was itself owned by a succession of shell companies. The ultimate owner of these companies was impossible to trace. The legerdemain of Phil Yates' accountant had obviously been cunningly employed.

Malcolm settled down in the warm moorland grasses to wait. He had noted the times when the young men visited the house, and there were no other callers. It was fitting for his new identity of birdwatcher and conservationist to have the tools of his trade around him: the field glasses, the camera, a backpack full of maps and protein snacks.

True to his new trade, he had to make notes of his observations: the moortop habitat of blanket bog with its variety of plant life, the nesting birds with their numbers of fledglings. The comings and goings of people, if any. He was enjoying himself so much he was tempted to take the life up full time in his retirement. A nice change from shooting people —even recalcitrant farmers.

There was a downside. The moortop was formidably bleak when it rained, and the downpours were heavy. There were no trees to drink up the wet, and the water plummeted down the steep hillsides, a constant threat to the villages below. And who cut down the trees? Answer: the mediaeval landowners, including the Church. Why did they do it? Answer: to turn the hills into sheep runs when wool was a profitable export, evicting all their tenants but the shepherd. He prided himself on his thorough due diligence.

What had happened since those distant times? Shooting estates had taken over—and they required heather, not trees, as cover and food for grouse. And were things likely to change? Not without strenuous persuasion. Fines, financial incentives, lectures from men like himself on the terminal folly of greed.

A figure appeared from the front door of the farmhouse. A small lonely figure in a drab waxed jacket and corduroy cap that stood looking at the uninhabited expanse of the moortop. That man had caused a deal of suffering to others. Now it was going to be his turn to feel pain. Phase One of the levelling had been thoroughly rolled out.

* * *

On the afternoon of the fourth day of his moorland sojourn, Phil exercised, groomed and fed Good Times then closed the stable and went to the house. The horse was still oddly withdrawn, as if he was merely tolerating the presence of his rider. Their lively repartee had completely gone. He couldn't figure it out.

He entered the house by the back door and was unprepared for the figure that sat in the shadows of the small sitting room pointing a gun at him.

"How the hell did you get in?" Phil asked, wondering if he could work his way past the stranger to get his newly acquired revolver from the kitchen drawer.

"A trick o' the trade, Mr Yates," the stranger replied in a thick Scottish accent. "Will ye be seated now sae we can natter."

It wasn't a question but a command. Phil sat by the embers of his wood fire and waited.

"Ye'll need to put more wood on; we's going to be some wee while."

Phil obeyed. He was unable to make out the stranger's features, but an inner chill spread through him as the voice, though harsher, reminded him of Tam. The house had no electric power, only bottled gas, so he was unable to flick on a switch to reveal the man's identity.

"Ye'll recall a wee matter o' four T'ang horses, will ye no?" the stranger asked. "My question to ye is: Why did ye want them? Think carefully afore ye reply. I want ye to tell me the truth."

Phil reflected. He had wanted to acquire them because he hoped they would bring him good luck. But to say this to a stranger seemed shallow, even slightly pathetic. And the horses hadn't brought him luck at all but had turned themselves into a curse. How could he explain that they had been contaminated by the hands of a man he feared and detested?

The stranger's voice broke the silence. "Ye's a lang while answering. Mebbe ye didna want them for anything at all. Mebbe ye only wanted them because anither body had them. Am I right?"

"I've nothing to say to you on this subject," Phil managed at last. "My reasons don't concern you."

"Ye's wrang there," the stranger replied sternly. "But we'll leave that question for the moment and ask anither: Why did ye not wish to buy the T'ang horses? Ye's a wealthy man. I've done a wee bit o' homework, and I ken ye's worth at least twenty Bernies—that's the term my associates use for twenty million quid. Plus the insurance for the house fire if it ever arrives. So why did ye not want to buy them? I think their owner might have been pleased to sell for a decent figure. Ye'd have been the official owner then, rather than a thief."

Again Phil had no answer. That he had left the matter entirely to Tam seemed a lame reply. That he had not offered to pay their true value of 600K seemed undeniably mean and petty. And it had backfired horribly. Instead of him being their proud legal owner, they had turned into vengeful monsters to be hidden away. But then they had escaped from their tomb to haunt him. How could he explain all that?

"I've nothing to say on the subject," Phil replied doggedly.

"Ye's not a very forthcoming body, are ye, Mr Yates?" the stranger said. "I'll mebbe have to resort to more persuasive means."

Ever since his father had been given a beating by Ambrose Smith, Phil had developed a horror of physical hurt. He had felt Smith's final blows in his own body, as his father staggered, unable to defend himself. Now he would do anything to avoid physical pain. Causing hurt to others with firearms was, of course, not included.

"Why are you asking me these questions? I'll give the horses back to you, if you like."

"So ye still have them?"

There was a long silence. Then, eventually, the reluctant admission: "No. I do not."

"But ye ken where they are?"

Silence. Then: "I'm not sure."

"So ye's lost them?"

Silence.

"I'll sum up," the stranger declared. "Ye wanted an item that belonged someone else. Ye didna want to pay for it, though ye could easily afford it. Now ye's lost them. Truly, ye sounds to me like a selfish and irresponsible man, Mr Yates. I might even say reckless, but with ither folk's lives, not ye's own. Ye's a no-account body, Mr Yates. I've nae choice but to treat ye as sikelike." Phase Two of the levelling had reached its midpoint.

The next moment Phil found himself slammed against the wall, his hands manacled and his head hooded. He was pushed roughly through the room and out of the back door.

His interrogator had evidently hidden his vehicle in the tall green bracken to the north of the farmhouse. Phil found himself tossed as casually as a dead dog into the boot of the Scotsman's car.

30

Luke and Cath were eating a belated evening meal in the kitchen at Cuckoo Nest while Angie and Zanda were happily cooking for Sy and Kingsley in their cottage. Angie had walked out of the back door with the comment: "I'm not abandoning my feminist values; I'm getting to know some interesting folk." Kingsley in particular, her mother thought to herself.

As Luke and Cath continued their meal in the easy silence that had developed between them, his sharp hearing picked up the sound of an approaching motor before it had reached the stackyard. He was on his feet and out of the door before Cath realised what was happening. From the stackyard shadows he watched the vehicle pull up near the back door, as he phoned Sy to alert him to the uninvited arrival.

His astonishment left him speechless as Malcolm climbed from the Jag and helped Phil from the boot. The Scotsman unlocked the handcuffs and took the hood from Phil's head. Luke stepped from the shadows as Cath appeared in the doorway.

"This villain has come to visit ye," was Malcolm's opening remark. "He's been judged and found wanting. Let's see if ye gude folk can apprize his future."

By the light from the kitchen doorway Phil stared in dismay at his captor. It was the first time he had seen the man clearly.

"Tam!" he exclaimed.

Malcolm laughed. "It seems my bro' is a well-known guy. Every wee body I meet thinks I'm him. Yet this dummy canna even gi'e him a fair day's wages! He's a millionaire who wants the world for naught." He propelled Phil forward with a shove in the back. "I've judged him to be truly unworthy of the surname he bears. I've brought him to ye gude folk to pass sentence."

Memories flowed like spectres through Phil's mind. The last time he had stood in this yard, he had been in almost complete control of events. The farm had been only a few days from becoming his property. Now he was here with nothing, surrounded by enemies.

They went into the kitchen, where Malcolm dumped his subdued prisoner on a milking stool while his accusers sat at the table. They were joined a moment later by Angie and Sy, responding to Luke's summons.

"Here's a body who has made owwer mony folk feel wretched and afeared," Malcolm began. "He's stolen T'ang horses and paid not a bean. He's caused a weel respected chappie to lose his life, not to mention a deal o' ithers. He's sorely injured my dear bro', as well as making a death threat agin him. I want each o' ye's to give a reason for his punishment." He looked first at Luke.

"I risked my life for him," Luke stated, "and he offered me not a penny. He killed my mother and sister in a trailer fire fifteen years ago and feels no regret."

"Ye's comments are duly noted," Malcolm stated with gravitas. He looked next at Cath and Angie.

Cath put her arm around Angie's shoulder. "He wanted our farm cheap. He pressured us and beat us up. He even abducted us and threatened to kill us."

"I hear ye's accusations," Malcolm said solemnly. "Are there any ither comments?"

Sy revealed the jagged scar on his arm. "He wants everything his way. He don't like losing. He uses violence whenever it suits him."

"Have ye onything to say to these gude folk, Mr Yates?" Malcolm asked.

Phil sat on the milking stool, mute. He shook his head. He did not look up.

"Ye made a comment to my bro' a while back, so he tells me, that ye thought it might ha'e been his *Lang Gude Friday*. I can say to ye, Phil Yates, that day has now come, and it's all ye's own. I'm asking ye gude folk if ye'll allow me to provide just closure?"

There were no voices of disagreement.

"Apprizal has been made, Mr Yates. I can tell ye that the value o' your future is naught."

Malcolm dragged Phil to his feet and propelled him to the door. Phil offered no resistance. He seemed hardly more than a stuffed effigy of himself—a man whose name had already been forgotten.

Malcolm turned to the accusers sitting around the table. "It's been my pleasure to meet wi' ye gude folk."

With that he was gone into the brief darkness of the midsummer night.

* * *

A little before midnight, Luke and Sy arrived at the moorland farm in the Toyota pickup, following the directions Malcolm had given them in a brief phone call. They never heard from Tam's brother again.

There was no evidence of life in the darkened house and no sign of Malcolm's vehicle. Harry's Range Rover and a horse trailer had been left in open-fronted outbuildings.

The gypsy travellers quietly ushered Good Times into Sy's horse trailer and drove back to Cuckoo Nest. Luke took the Range Rover, which he planned to sell with help from his reluctant brother. Construction work on the loose boxes and tack room was finished and Good Times was placed in the loose box next to Prince of Thieves. The two horses nickered softly to each other in affectionate greeting. Good Times had returned to stand guard over the T'ang horse figurines.

The next morning Good Times' distinctive blaze was dyed by Sy, until the animal became a beautiful overall glossy chestnut and much harder to recognise. Then Sy and Luke took the two horses out for an hour's pleasant exercise on the local bridleways.

Sy laughed. "Never thought I'd be riding a grye that belonged to Phil Yates. He's ours now. I'll ask Davey what he thinks we should do to make the best of him. Mebbe we'll have that stud here after all!"

"We should give him a new name," Luke thought. "One that has nothing to do with that criminal!"

"Any ideas?"

"How 'bout Travellers Bounty?"

"Mush, I like it!"

Sy, Zanda and Kingsley were joining Davey Wood for the day to attend a sale of gypsy vanners on travellers' land further south. While Cath and Angie were tethering the goats, Luke busied himself applying wood preserver to the exterior woodwork of the loose boxes and tack room.

As he was finishing Cath waved to him from the kitchen doorway. He washed his hands under the outside tap and joined her.

"There was an item on the news just now," she announced as he stepped through the door. "Phil Yates' naked body has been discovered at the gallops sitting in a deckchair in the car park. He'd been shot twice, once in the heart and once in the head. The police are calling it a professional job."

Malcolm had got justice for them all, Luke thought, for Ambrose and his family, for Cath and Angie, for Tam and finally for the London mob. And, most importantly, the tit for tat killings would stop. "It's over," he said. "We can start a new life."

But Charlie Gibb wasn't listening. High up in the sawmill loft, the albino was watching Luke in his telescope as he walked across the farm stackyard. Charlie talked on his mobile. "That the police?... Well, I ain't saying who this is, but I got some information I reckon you people should know..."

Half a minute later he rang off and clapped his telescope to his good eye. "Come on! He's there! He ain't looking!" He lowered the telescope and emitted his eerie, high-pitched laugh as he swung himself through the spider's web of timbers in the sawmill's roof space.

"Ain't no one gets one up on Charlie! Oh no, not on *Mister* Gibb!"

* * *

An hour later Cath and Angie crossed the yard from the deep litter houses with full baskets of eggs. Luke had just finished grooming the horses and was letting them into the orchard to graze. A long goods train could be heard in the distance slowly approaching on the down line.

Two police cars swooped into the stackyard and half a dozen uniformed officers leaped out. PC Bailey and PC Pearson were among them, their faces retaining signs of fire damage from the crash of six weeks earlier. They stepped forward aggressively and addressed Cath and Angie.

"Are you the owner of this farm?" Bailey demanded to know.

"I am," Cath replied. "What of it?"

"We have reason to believe an escaped felon by the name of Luke Smith is currently living at this address," Pearson announced.

Angie laughed. "You can believe what you like!"

"We have a warrant to search the premises," Bailey declared, brandishing a document in Cath's face.

Cath shrugged. "Be my guest."

The women deposited their eggs on the kitchen table. Led by Angie, the police officers trooped through the house. Cath returned to the stackyard and looked for Luke. There was no sign of him. She glanced towards the railway bridge.

She smiled. The goods train on the down line trundled slowly under the bridge. Luke stood for a moment on the parapet. Then he was gone.

She knew, as the true dromengro he aspired to be, he would go to his uncle Taiso's and clear his name. And she also knew she and Angie would go there too, one day. Because there had to be a gypsy wedding. Perhaps there would even be two.

POSTSCRIPT

Cath was the only other person Luke had told about the T'ang horses hidden under the loose box floor. He thought she should know, as he felt if he said nothing he was taking her for granted.

"Did you steal them?" she asked.

"I'm not going to lie," he replied. "So it's best I say nothing."

The day after Luke's escape from the police raid, Cath received a call from him letting her know he was at Taiso's and had begun the legal process of clearing his name. He could be away for a few months, he said, but he had been told to expect a successful outcome. The wedding—or weddings— would be at Easter. Cath was delighted. And Angie and Kingsley, too, of course.

But the presence of the T'ang horses troubled her. She was alone with them and didn't know what she should do if, unlikely though it might be, they were discovered. What action should she take? Should she bury them in the willow wood? Sink them in the farm pond? In the end she resolved to take expert advice.

She took Travellers Bounty—or simply Bounty—as Good Times was now called, out of his loose box and put him to graze with the Prince. She found the T'ang horses in a box under the floor and took one of them only, as all four were of the same size and a similar style. Then she drove into the town and called at the valuers' office, saying she'd had the horse for years and wondered what she would re-alise if she sold it.

The senior partner of the firm put on his spectacles, took a magnifying glass and looked carefully at the horse, turning it over several times and examining the detail of its caparison. After a few minutes he surprised Cath by handing the horse back to her.

"We won't be able to sell this for you, I'm afraid, but one just like it was auctioned in London last month, if I remember." He took a sales catalogue from a shelf behind his desk and riffled through it. "Ah, yes, it's a pretty close likeness to yours." He read from the catalogue: "*Tang-style Caparisoned Horse.*" He glanced at her over the top of his spectacles. "It sold for three hundred pounds."

She must have looked surprised because the valuer laughed.

"Were you hoping it was an original?" he asked. "You'd certainly be in the money if it was."

She was embarrassed. Did she look *that* mercenary? "I've really no idea how old it is. I'm clueless as to what its value might be."

"The key words in the catalogue description are *Tang-style.*" The valuer smiled, she thought, in sympathy. "That one and yours are modern copies. They're actually quite common. You'd do well to get more than a three-figure sum, unless it was much bigger or more spectacular. Try Sotheby's. They're probably the best auction house for these."

She returned to Cuckoo Nest and put the horse back with the others. She decided not to break the news to Luke until after Easter.

* * *

"You're very quiet tonight, Mam." Angie looked quizzically at Cath as they ate their evening meal in the farm kitchen. "Has something happened I should know about?"

Cath shook her head. "I'm just a bit tired. We've had a lot of excitement lately."

"Bit of an understatement, ain't it?"

Cath was still stunned by the valuer's revelation. So much that had happened in the past couple of months had been caused by the existence of the T'ang horses. So many new relationships and unexpected twists of fate. So many deaths. One question beat at her brain: Who had been conning whom? Her suspicions fell on Tam McBride.

* * *

Tam and Malcolm sat on the terrace of Tam's Mediterranean villa. The building commanded a view of olive groves and the sea.

Malcolm studied the prospect in his field glasses.

"Is it pirates ye's expecting, bro?" Tam asked with a smile.

Malcolm lowered his glasses. "Ye's a lucky body. The shore's too rocky for a safe landfall. Who kens wha' micht get washed up, though?"

"I dinna fash mysel wi' sic thoughts, now the de'il hissel's dead in his deckchair!"

The brothers laughed. Tam stood and fetched more wine. He was walking normally now.

"I'll be meeting a body in the trattoria in an hour. Ye's welcome to join us. He's after selling me more o' those Chinese figures, but I've a mind they'll be fakes. He's an eejit, though. He thinks I willna ken. I'll make mysel a wee profit if I find the right buyer."

Malcolm studied his brother over his wineglass. "D'ye think the universe needs us, bro? Ye ken, do ye not, that wherever ye go I'll be there, too?"

Tam looked blank. "Ye's lost me. I thought ye was away back to Lunnon in a week."

Malcolm smiled inscrutably. "Think about it."

There had to be justice, of course. At every level.

ABOUT THE AUTHORS

.

The authors have been active in the creative sector for more than twenty years. Ian is a widely-published award-winning poet. Rosi is a professional actress and voice artiste.

The Price of Horses is our first jointly-written novel, a revenge thriller set in the colourful world of gypsy travellers and larger-than-life villains.

The Price Of Horses
ISBN: 978-4-86750-590-8
Large Print

Published by
Next Chapter
1-60-20 Minami-Otsuka
170-0005 Toshima-Ku, Tokyo
+818035793528

7th June 2021

CPSIA information can be obtained
at www.ICGtesting.com
Printed in the USA
LVHW090129220621
690829LV00008B/660

9 784867 505908